A Touch of Irish

A Touch of Irish

A Touch Series Novel

Wendy A. Wilson

Copyright © 2012 by Wendy A. Wilson.

Library of Congress Control Number:		2012907245
ISBN:	Hardcover	978-1-4771-0095-0
	Softcover	978-1-4771-0094-3
	Ebook	978-1-4771-0096-7

All rights reserved. No part of this book may be reproduced or transmitted in any form or by any means, electronic or mechanical, including photocopying, recording, or by any information storage and retrieval system, without permission in writing from the copyright owner.

This is a work of fiction. Names, characters, places and incidents either are the product of the author's imagination or are used fictitiously, and any resemblance to any actual persons, living or dead, events, or locales is entirely coincidental.

This book was printed in the United States of America.

To order additional copies of this book, contact:
Xlibris Corporation
1-888-795-4274
www.Xlibris.com
Orders@Xlibris.com

This book is for my husband William.
He always supported me in everything I wanted to do.

1

Edwin de Ballard walked quickly down the hall, the hard soles of his boots clapping against the ancient stone floor.

William of Normandy was not even crowned king yet, and already the man was making demands. All he wanted to do was stand through the ceremony in the morning, then sail back to the land he was promised for aiding William. He was a sailor who cared nothing for the pomp and intrigue of the court.

His mind solely on getting the meeting finished, he did not feel the cold of the night. Nor did he hear the scream the first time it sounded.

The second scream made him stop in his tracks, the hairs on the back of his neck standing on end. Someone was in trouble. It sounded like a woman. The third time it came, Edwin started running.

Stopping before a door at the end of the hall, he knocked and asked, "Do you have need of my help?"

"No, I scream just because it makes me feel better!" The voice was delicate, even when shouting. Her accent showed that French was not her first language. Her wit tugged a smile at the corners of his full mouth.

"I am a gentleman. I never enter a lady's chambers unless invited." If she were in a mood for a little fun, it was fine by him. "Do you require my assistance?"

Inside the chamber, Morghan could not stop her frustration at the man's ignorance. Gentlemanly ways were one thing; this was ridiculous. It was getting ever closer to the stool she stood on. Soon, it would be climbing near her feet.

"Oh, just get in here!"

Her father warned her not to allow anyone but a maid into the chamber, but in this instance, he could take his orders and put them where… She was not about to simply stand here allowing that… thing to get any closer, waiting for his return.

She did not care who was at the door; she wanted him in here now. Right now!

The door slowly cracked open, and Morghan lost the last hold she had on her dwindling patience. "What are you waiting for? Someone to guide you by the hand?"

Again, Edwin tried to hold back a smile. She did not sound as if she were outright danger . Still, he should go in armed. Sliding out the knife he always kept in his right boot, Edwin flung open the door and rushed in.

Edwin saw no danger. Looking right and left, he searched the shadows for anyone posing a risk to the woman's life.

He found only a maid standing on a stool in the center of the chamber. Her bright green eyes were the size of small dishes.

She was tall for a maid. Standing on the floor, she would come to his nose, not the typical chest-high woman he was accustomed to. She was clothed from head to toe in a simple white tunic tied tightly about her tiny waist. Her head and neck were covered with an opaque veil, allowing only her perfectly round face to show.

Edwin's heart immediately began to pound. She had to be the most beautiful woman he ever laid eyes on. Deep in his gut, he wanted to shout "mine" but knew she was not for the likes of him. He was nothing but a simple sailor who offered his vessel to William in exchange for land and a small title.

"Do not just stand there, you dolt. Get *it* out of here." Once more, it took Edwin a moment to figure out what she was saying. Shaking his head, the spell of her beauty was broken.

Looking about the chamber, he saw nothing. There was no man or woman lurking about to threaten her. No large beast ready to devour her. Relaxing his stance, he quietly asked, "Exactly what am I saving you from?"

Morghan wanted to scream all over again. "Are you blind? Look. The snake is getting ever closer." Her hand shook slightly when she pointed toward her right. Lord, how she hated snakes.

"A snake? All this fuss is over a mere snake?" Reaching down, Edwin replaced his knife. In two strides, he was at her side, reaching out and grabbing the small garden snake by the back of its head. "The poor thing is simply trying to keep warm. It is cold outside, you know."

"I do not care why it came in here or how cold it is outside. I simply want it gone."

"You have a fear of snakes?" The small laugh in his voice made Morghan want to slap him.

"Yes, I do." Each word was enunciated between gritted teeth. It made Edwin want to laugh all the more.

"What say you, little beast?" Edwin spoke to the snake as if it were a friend, turning the head to face him. The snake's tongue flicked out, coming within inches of his mouth. He heard the woman groan and knew it was time to end this game. He was having fun, but obviously, she was not.

"Come along now. I will see you safely to ground."

Morghan waited until both man and snake were out of the chamber before she stepped down from the stool. She did not know who he was or where he was taking the snake, and frankly, she did not care—just as long as it was away from her.

Before Morghan could do more than run her hands over her tunic, Edwin returned, brushing his hands back and forth together as if to rid them of the snake's slime.

"Gone and well taken care of, my lady... ?"

"Morghan. Morghan O'Ceallachain."

The name was Irish, so she came with one of the many supporters of William. "I am Edwin de Ballard." Taking her fingers, he raised them to his lips and pressed a small kiss to her soft knuckles. A tingle ran up his arm, settling in the vicinity of his heart. How strange. Never before had he experienced such an odd reaction.

"My men and I brought some of the king's men and supplies from Normandy. As reward, I now carry the title Baron of Ironwood."

It was impossible to miss the small gasp Morghan made, looking into his eyes. They were the color of the deepest sea, tossed during a storm. His shoulders were broad, and his chest was muscular, stretching tight the tunic he wore. His waist was trim, encircled by a wide leather belt.

He *was* a sailor. If she could feel his arms, she was certain they would be hard from hauling rigging and binding ropes. He was built very much like her brothers.

"Such a beautiful name. Ironwood." Her brilliant green eyes reminded Edwin of emeralds he once saw at a Spanish market. Her face was flawless and round, nose small and pert. He could not tell what color her hair was. Every last strand of it was tucked neatly inside her head covering.

"Wherever did the name Ironwood come from?"

Edwin needed to stop staring at her eyes and focus on something else. His eyes drifted down slowly. Her lips. They were full and lush, just begging to be kissed.

She was speaking again, but for the life of him, he heard nothing but the pounding of his heart. Lord, he needed to get out of here before he made a complete fool of himself.

"I wanted a strong name for my land." The words came out in such a rush, he knew she heard only half of them. "You are safe now, my lady. I have need to be…" Morghan smiled at his stumbling words. "With the king. Yes, that is it. I was summoned by the king when I heard your cry for help."

"It was like a scream for help." The way Edwin was acting reminded her of her brother Sean. He tended to stumble over himself when he got nervous.

"Yes. Well, I must be going." Edwin rushed out of the door so quickly it banged shut and bounced back open.

Morghan sat on the stool and allowed the laughter to take her. By the time she was done, tears streamed down her face. God help the woman who wedded him.

"You cannot ask that of me."

Edwin stared at his king. This was not what he expected when he was called to the private chamber. Aiding the crossing was one thing; this was quite another.

"Arrangements have already been made. The contract needs only her father's signature, and it will be binding." William of Normandy sat there, a goblet in one hand, a piece of meat in the other.

"What about my consent? Do I have no say in the woman I would take to wife? Before I left, I made arrangements to return to Normandy and wed as soon as my land is secure and a fortress is built. I plan on leaving immediately following the coronation on the morrow."

Fury rolled in Edwin's gut. This was not fair. His life was his own, not there for another to offer it to the highest bidder. "You said nothing of this before leaving Normandy."

"I had not finished all the details then. Now they are complete. *It is done.*"

Edwin's hands clenched and unclenched at his sides. All his own plans, gone. "Why sacrifice me? Is there no one possessing a higher title you could give her to?" The woman must either be long in the tooth or have some deformation to be bartered so. Frankly, he wanted neither for a wife.

"All others are taken. I have need of you and think the two of you perfect for each other." The king was not listening to a word he said.

"When am I expected to wed this lady?" The king gave no clue as to the status of the woman, only that she was the daughter of a noble and was being given in exchange for men and essential supplies.

"After you secure your land and build a proper keep." William smiled, a drop of wine spilling out of the side of his mouth. "See. I did consider the young woman."

Young woman. The king was nearly old enough to be his grandfather. What exactly did he consider "young"?

Fine, if the man wanted him to wed in this way, he would take his time securing his land and building his keep. Perhaps after a year, William would give up on this insane idea and allow him to wed a woman of his own choosing.

After all, the king could not be everywhere at once. While the king was occupied elsewhere, he would sail back to Normandy and take Rowena to wife. Once he was wed, William would be forced to find another to fulfill the contract.

"If it pleases Your Grace, it is getting late. Your coronation is early in the morn, and I must see that my ship is ready to leave thereafter."

"You have my permission to leave." William of Normandy waved the cup toward the door.

Edwin couldn't get out of there fast enough. No man, king or not, was going to plan his life. No, he would see he had what he wanted no matter what.

That night, Edwin dreamed of smiling green eyes and lush lips.

2

Christmas Day 1066

Morghan resisted the shiver that ran up her spine and the near-overwhelming urge to look around and see whose eyes were on her.

Actually, she knew who watched her. Even though their touch was brief last evening, a bond was already beginning to form between them. Edwin was behind them somewhere, and the urge to turn around and find him was near overpowering.

Despite the dreadful weather, Morghan and her father, Connor O'Ceallachain, braved a winter's icy storm-tossed sea to journey from Eire and witness William of Normandy being crowned king of England.

A biting cold wind whipped about the thick stone facade of Westminster Abbey, the chill penetrating through Morghan's fur-lined cloak. Pulling it more securely about her slender shoulders, she glanced to her left to see if her father noticed her breach of etiquette. Connor's disapproving scowl indicated he had not missed one of her movements.

Morghan's gaze roamed to the small glass windows lining the high sanctuary walls. Clouds of falling snow swirled outside, blocking any warmth the weak winter sun may have provided. Another shiver ran up her spine.

Thoughts of family and the holiness of this day when they all spent time on bended knees in church flooded her mind. No matter what, her father always made a point to be home during the winter months to celebrate the winter solstice of the ancients and the Christian day set aside to celebrate Christ's birth.

There were not many in Eire that openly acknowledged the Christian religion. Most clung to the old Druid ways. Her father heard of the new religion while traveling and brought it home to his family. To save further trouble between his wife's family and his own, his children were taught both religions and celebrated the holy days each observed.

Morghan grew up knowing the ways of a warrior as well as that of a sailor. Her father was forever looking for a way to advance his influence in the world and to better his position at home in Eire. He never once turned out any of William's emissaries. He listened to their offers and made up his mind that William was powerful enough to take charge of England and rule the land well.

Odo—bishop of Bayeax, William's own brother—conducted the coronation mass. He droned on and on. Was this never going to end? Latin was a language she never aspired to learn, and at this moment, she knew why. It was dry, dull, and boring. Just the sound of it could put a person to sleep in minutes. She wanted desperately to look about her and find the man who captured her attention last evening. He was here somewhere. Edwin made her feel easy and safe. His banter gave her a hope they would suit.

She knew Edwin would be the principal means of transport between the king and his men. It would take him away from home often. Her life would not be a simple one, yet still she looked forward to seeing Edwin again.

Lined up by rank, William's dukes stood proudly in the first row beside him. De Montgomery stood straight and tall, first in line. She knew from talk at the feast last evening that at dawn, the duke and his men would head out toward the Welsh border. It would be his job to secure the entire length for William.

De Montgomery was actually looking forward to the task assigned by the king. The man thrived on a challenge, and there was no one better suited for the job than him.

Though Morghan knew it was important for the growth of England, she could not help being a bit selfish. A wife should want her husband at home to protect and love her. Each of her older brothers faced the strain of long separation early in their marriages. It took hard work and dedication on both parts to keep the bond strong.

Their small encounter last eve gave her hope. She would hold on to each of Edwin's words until they had the chance to exchange more.

The voice of the bishop droned on still, threatening to lull everyone into a stupor. Even her father looked to be fighting slumber.

The sun suddenly broke through the clouds and beamed through the high clear windows. Idly following the narrow ray, Edwin de Ballard saw it ended at a most interesting sight. The sight was one of the few women who were attending the ceremony.

She was tall for a woman. Though he stood a few rows back, he knew she would come at least to his chin. Most women of noble birth barely made it to his chest, and this woman was definitely of noble birth. Her stance was regal, reminding him of William's royal wife.

Only her mantle and veil could be seen from where he stood. The outer garment was of a bright lush green that reminded him of the rolling hills of Ireland on a bright spring day. Some sort of white fur trimmed the edge and no doubt the inside as well. Her veil was of the sheerest ivory material he ever saw. Small seed pearls lined the edge and formed a circlet about her head.

There was something about her that seemed oddly familiar. His interest was instantly piqued the moment the men before him parted and his view became unobstructed. When she turned to speak to the gentlemen beside her, a lock of hair escaped the fine mesh of her veil. Edwin's breath caught in his throat. It had to be the most vibrant shade of red he could ever remember seeing.

The loose lock cascaded over her shoulder to curl at her tiny waist. His fingers itched to touch those silken tresses. Yes, they actually itched. Never in all his two and twenty years of life could he remember such an overwhelming desire to touch another's hair. Not even Rowena's golden locks brought this odd sensation to his fingers.

What would it be like to feel the strands slipping through his splayed fingers while he made love to her?

A sudden bolt of desire shot through him, settling low in his body. Church was not the place to indulge in such thoughts and feelings. God would surely strike him down for this transgression. Standing right here in this holy place, he would end his days gazing at a woman he knew he had no right to even dream about. She was noble; he was a common sailor who supported the right man and in return was granted a title and land.

A thought occurred to him. He could use his encounter with Morghan last night to show the king just how unsuitable he was for the woman William chose. Morghan he would not mind wedding. In fact, the thought of her in his bed was at the moment doing things to his body.

Shifting, Edwin tried to minimize the evidence of his attraction.

"What is it you stare at?" Henry D' Arrington asked, leaning close. Personally, he found the pomp of the service utterly boring. Being Edwin's closest friend since they were seven, they were often found inseparable. People often mistook them for brothers; their looks were so similar. Six foot tall, blond, and muscular, Henry more closely resembled Edwin than Edwin's own brother Louis did.

"Her." Edwin whispered, raising his chin toward the woman. Henry's eyes followed.

A moment later, Henry turned on his friend with a "Have you become witless?" look. The look of pure lust on Edwin's face stunned him. Did his lord and friend have any idea his feelings were so plain for all to witness? "I caution you to school your features, my friend. You allow too much to show. This is the house of the Lord, not some brothel."

Henry's words acted like a cold bucket of ice water poured over his heated body. A simple touch last night, and now this. What in heaven's name was wrong with him? How had he allowed a simple lock of hair to bring on such thoughts? "She has a fine form." What he could see through her dark green mantle only managed to tantalize his imagination.

"That color hair is often accompanied by a fiery temper. You had best stay away from her." Henry's voice held a note of humor, though Edwin did not feel much like laughing at the moment.

"You sound as if I look to her for a lady wife. Have you forgotten I have a woman waiting in Normandy to wed? By the end of summer next, Rowena will be my wife—sooner, if I can secure my land and complete the keep."

Henry nearly choked, trying to hold back his groan. He and the king spent many an hour discussing the woman Edwin insisted on wedding. They both could see exactly what she was. Why was it that his friend could not see her as the whore everyone else did?

Edwin now held a title and a necessary position under the crown. He deserved a loyal wife, not one who lifted her skirts for any man who paid her a passing look. Rowena would not only break his friend's heart when the truth came out but also destroy it for any other.

Perhaps William was right. A few well-placed nudges and Edwin would find himself turned away from the one he thought he wanted and into the arms of a deserving and loyal woman. "You speak of a time too far-off. It would not harm you to keep an open mind and eye."

Kneeling for the benediction, Edwin lost sight of the woman who had so effectively captured his attention. With the service completed, horns sounded, their notes echoing off the stone walls. There was no stopping Edwin's attention from drifting to the woman's companion.

He was old. Actually, he was nearly old enough to be her grandfather.

His tunic and mantle were of the finest quality. His stance and bearing denoted a lofty title. On his left hip hung a ceremonial sword, the scabbard encrusted with more jewels than Edwin had ever seen. Personally, he never thought one so garish totally necessary, but the golden scabbard was enough to denote the type of wealth this man possessed.

A feeling Edwin never experienced before seized his chest. It could not be jealousy, as he had one woman in Normandy and another from the king. All he needed was a woman to make him happy and warm his bed on cold winter nights. Who this man chose for wife was none of his concern.

But she deserved better.

She deserved him!

For the love of God, where did that thought come from? What gave him the right to be thinking of a woman he did not know as if she belonged to him?

First that maid last night, and now this woman.

Rowena.

Rowena.

He repeated her name like a litany until he banished all thoughts of the redheaded woman three rows before him.

Try as he might, Rowena's face would not appear in his mind. All he could conjure was an endless sea of bright red tresses, cascading down lush curves. His body instantly reacted. How could the image of one woman's back and hair cause him so much pain? Again, he had to remind himself church was not the proper place to encourage such thoughts.

But oh, how his fingers itched to reach out and touch that single loose tress. It called to him like the sirens of old that caused sailors to crash their boats against the face of Gibraltar. If he was not careful, he would end up as they did—broken and dead upon the rocks.

He needed to think of her as having the most hideous face he could imagine on a woman. A beaked nose, thin lips, weathered skin. There, that helped some.

"It is time." Henry's nudge burst the image. At least he had himself under control again.

"What?"

"Have you not been paying attention? It is time to kneel before William and vow our fealty."

Already, the dukes of Wessex, Essex, Ashford, and De Montgomery were kneeling before the king. Their vows of loyalty rang clear through the throng, their words resounding off the stone walls.

Stepping into the end of the steadily moving line, Edwin and Henry fell in step. Later, in the privacy of his own chambers, Henry would give his oath to Edwin as lord. Once his service to William was completed, Henry would serve Ironwood as master-at-arms for as long as God gave him life.

"She stands in the first row." Henry leaned close and whispered in his ear. "It should be easy to see if she is the same woman." Was the man a mind reader now? The thought was just forming in his own mind when Henry put it to voice.

Edwin's heart leaped into his throat. Could she be the very woman from last eve? The one so frightened by a snake she allowed a stranger into her chamber to remove the creature? Could she possibly be Lady Morghan?

To see her face would do… what?

Put an end to the wonder of who caught his attention? Telling himself he was not so bored and lonely, he tried to turn every woman he saw into the one whose smile captured his mind.

Stepping before the king, Edwin went down on one knee and spoke the formal words necessary to bind himself to the king of England.

He would only take a quick peek at her, just to satisfy his curiosity. After all, the possibility it was Lady Morghan was a thousand to one.

Her head was bowed when he turned to leave, and if he had any sense at all, he would want it to stay that way as he passed by.

Look up at me! his mind screamed.

Something deep inside him wanted desperately for her to look at him, just once.

Look up! Please!

Ever so slowly her eyes rose, as if in response to his silent pleas. Edwin's mouth dropped open at the sight of the last woman he thought to see. An instant later, the beauty of her made his heart stopped beating.

Behind Morghan's back, her father looked to William and nodded.

3

The clash of steel.

The cries and shouts of the combatants filled the abbey, reverberating off the cold stone walls.

Seconds after the trumpets sounded, heralding William as king, a roar went up. Saxon rebels among the crowd mistook the cheers of victory for their king as a call to attack. A battle broke out among the crowd, not able to enter the abbey. No one actually knew who took the first swing.

Men from all around Edwin drew swords and headed out into the street to defend their king.

When Edwin tried to join the melee, he found himself grabbed and placed in a position to protect a single person: Lady Morghan.

"I know you would rather join the others in their fight." Though Edwin's back was to her, she could see and feel every muscle in his body, taut and poised at the ready.

"Not really." Edwin allowed a smile to tug at his lips. He wondered if he would get a chance to see Lady Morghan one last time before he left. Here was his chance.

The simple kiss on her hand last eve started strange feelings in him he could not quite identify. It wasn't exactly lust, though he would never refuse an advance from the lady. Even now, he could feel the heat from her lush form along the length of his back and legs.

The urge to turn and kiss her was near overwhelming. All last night, he dreamed of what it would be like to hold her close, his mouth on hers. Would she taste as sweet as she smelled?

"No?" Morghan's single word brought his mind back to his duty. Odd how being around this one woman set his mind to wondering into places it should not go.

"I am a sailor. My fighting skills are limited, I fear. That is why I was set to protect you, not join the masses beyond." Edwin's words were spoken over his shoulder, turning only far enough to catch a glimpse of Morghan's soft features. A row of barely visible freckles ran across one cheek, the bridge of her nose, and then across the other cheek. How had he missed them last eve.

Would the warm sun of summer bring them out brighter, adding even more to their numbers? Oh, how he wished he could be with her to find out the answer. They gave her a young fresh look, endearing.

"All my brothers are sailors." Again Morghan's soft tones brought his mind back to his duty and where it belonged. "Still, our father made certain each knew how to wield a sword."

Her feet were beginning to ache. First she stood during the long and boring coronation. Now backed into a corner, the only thing she had to take her mind off her pain was a conversation with her guardian. And getting Edwin to talk was like pulling a rotted tooth. She knew he needed to keep his mind on the skirmish outside, but really. He could spare some time to give her more than short answers. God only knew how long they were going to be standing here before her father returned for her, releasing Edwin from his duty.

Somewhere deep in her heart, Morghan prayed it would be a long time before her father's return. True, she did not want to contemplate the number of men perishing at another's sword, but it was so easy to speak to this man.

"Exactly how many brothers do you have?" There was a small warble in Edwin's voice that brought a smile to her lips.

"Six." Morghan couldn't stop the laugh when she saw Edwin's cringe. His reaction was identical to so many others. "And you?"

"Thankfully only one."

Morghan stopped deluding herself. Talking to Edwin was not simply a way to occupy her mind. No, it was more than that. It was easy to carry on a conversation with the man. She was here to meet her intended husband, and before her father presented her yet another old wrinkled man, she wanted the illusion that Edwin could be the one.

"It must be nice to have a brother who shares your views and who joined you in the new land."

Two men, their swords clashing, drew near the open doors of the abbey. Seeing them, Edwin backed his charge even farther into the darkness of the sanctuary. "My brother Louis did not share my view of the future. He remains in Normandy. Besides, he is worthless with a sword. What little skills I have were learned at the hands of my best friend Henry."

"But I thought… the man who stood beside you before King William… He looks so much like you, I thought him to be your brother."

The longer they spoke, and the closer Edwin came to touching her, the harder it was to ignore the feelings running rampant through his body. Every nerve in his body screamed out to be touched by her. Surely, his thoughts alone in this most holy place would send him to hell.

Still, his fingers craved the feel of her skin beneath them. They itched to thread through her hair. That stray lock still dangled from beneath her veil, tormenting him. What would it look like spread across the white of his pillow? Would it blaze in the light of a thousand candles? It was wrong that fashion demanded a woman keep such a treasure hidden from the world.

An instant of some emotion Edwin had never experienced before assaulted him. Lady Morghan was not his. He had no right to think of her in any way but as someone he was assigned to guard. Still, telling his mind and body such was impossible. It was as if his body had a mind of its own and no longer cared where they stood.

"Henry D' Arrington is closer to me than my own brother. When his service to the king is finished, he will join me at Ironwood and become my master-at-arms." Edwin swayed slightly back and forth. Anything to distract what Morghan's nearness was doing to him. His heart pounded so hard, he swore it struck his ribs with each beat.

"You do not need to guard me, you know. I doubt anyone would find me hidden in these shadows." The longer she spoke to Edwin, the stronger the bond between them grew. She could feel it reaching out and joining her. How would she survive a severing of this bond when she was given to the real man her father chose for her.

Damn her curse and that of her heritage. It was to only happen with the man she would wed. But surely her father would never allow his only daughter to wed such a simple man with a small title. No, he bartered her for as much as he could achieve. To say her father did not care about her was wrong. He simply needed to use her to gain the most for himself.

Edwin finally turned about, a smile tugging at his full lips. "I see. Last eve you were so frightened of a snake, you stood on a stool and screamed loud enough for me to hear you all the way into the hall. You forget, my lady, I was the one who removed it. What is it about sword-wielding knights that make you so brave?"

"I never said I did not fear them." If Morghan thought her nerves on edge while Edwin stood with his back to her, it was worse when he faced her directly. Her hands twisted together before her, trying desperately not to reach out and touch him. Finally giving up, she folded her arms about her waist and held them tight. She would not give into the building desire to touch him. "I have some skill with a bow."

It rankled Morghan to think she needed to defend herself. Never before had anyone challenged her skill or courage. Then again, she was rarely away from home and among strangers.

"Exactly where would you plan to shoot your arrows? You would need to be on the roof of this abbey to be effective. If you think I would help you to such heights, think again. Not only are you not dressed for such an action, but all would consider you a bit daft."

"I am not delusional." Morghan's Irish accent smoothed out the hurt Edwin was certain would be in her voice.

"Fine." Edwin admitted, still trying to hold back a smile. "Your attire would preclude your ascending to such heights."

Oh, he wanted to play this game, did he? She could play at this as well as any man. Grasping the edges of her cloak, Morghan pulled them apart, exposing her garments beneath. "I see what you mean."

Holy mother of God!

Before Edwin could only guess at her figure. Now it stood out in full view. He swallowed hard. Her figure was nothing less than perfection.

A creamy smooth neck, broadened onto delicate shoulders. The neckline of her tunic showed enough creamy skin to allow his imagination to determine just how large her breasts would be. They would fit perfectly into his hands.

The emerald green fabric hugged tightly to her tiny waist before flaring out to hips, made for barring children. The golden interlocking rings of her belt sat low on those hips, accentuating every curve. Knowing her manner of dress would be rich did nothing to prepare him for what he saw.

The overtunic looked to be made of silk from the eastern lands. Metallic golden threads were sewn into some sort of knot design about the neckline, cuffs, and hem. They were unusual and tended to draw the eye to their glittering twists.

A pale green undertunic showed through the sides where the bindings were drawn tight. The points of soft leather boots peaked out from beneath her hem. For a simple sailor who had limited interaction with the gentry, Morghan looked like the most beautiful woman in the world.

And oh how his body was letting him know that. It was becoming harder and harder to control his growing lust for this woman. Not even reminding himself he was in the house of the Lord could prevent the physical reaction. Shifting slightly, Edwin prayed he could minimize the evidence.

"My lord." Edwin jumped at the touch on his shoulder. Morghan snatched her cape closed so quickly, it was as if it was never opened to reveal her lush form.

"What is it, Henry?" The slight warble in Edwin's voice brought a brilliant smile to Morghan's full rosy lips and a sparkle to those deep emerald eyes. She was enjoying his discomfort far too much. Then again, having six brothers, she was not new to his feelings and actions. Most likely she'd seen it six times before.

"The lady's father requests us to escort her back to the keep." Henry winked at Morghan, knowing what must have transpired between the two of them. After his friend spent an hour last night going on and on about the woman he saved from a snake, and then watching Edwin stare open mouthed at Lady Morghan earlier, Henry could imagine what sort of conversation they shared.

Curiously, he stood a moment watching the two interact. It was not like Edwin to spend so much attention on a single woman. Her figure wasn't hard to look at, and her intelligence shown in the sparkle of her eyes.

"I feel, however, the lady's delicate footwear will not survive the distance." The street beyond the abbey was not only covered with snow and mud, but plenty of blood now mingled to cause a gruesome mess.

Brushing down the front of his blood-stained tunic, Henry turned to face his friend. "I am not fit to carry the lady. You must do the honors."

Edwin groaned. Henry laughed. Morghan blushed.

It was one thing to stand here and want to touch the woman, and quite another to actually hold her in his arms. "Come now. We must hurry."

Edwin threw a glare at his smiling friend. Henry was enjoying his discomfort just a wee bit too much. Sheathing his sword, Edwin reached around Morghan's back, pulling her tightly to his chest. His right arm bent beneath her knees.

The instant her arms wound about his neck, Morghan laid her cheek against his shoulder. Lightning ran along every nerve ending in his body. Forget about what was happening in his groin, his entire body wanted her with such a need, he could barely breath.

Lungs strained to draw in a breath. Each lift of his chest pressed against her full breasts. The hardening of her nipples stabbed his hard muscles.

"Come," he said, before turning and moving quickly toward the doors.

Every exhale of Morghan's breath sent shivers over Edwin's oversensitive throat. The walk back to Turney Keep felt miles longer than the actual distance. Once safely inside, Edwin slowly lowered her feet to the cold stone floor, sliding her front all along the length of his.

Fire flared between them. There was no way she could miss the evidence of his arousal lying against his leg. "I bid you, adieu." Edwin bowed slightly before hurrying away.

Any more time in her presence and he would disgrace himself as he had not done since he was a young man of fourteen.

Morghan and Henry exchanged knowing smiles before they each turned toward their own chambers.

4

"I WILL *NOT* DO it."

Together, Henry and Edwin walked the deserted halls of Turney Keep. The clap of Edwin's hard leather soles sounded out just how angry the king's edict made him.

"He knew I wanted to leave immediately after the coronation. Now I am forced to dally here, attending a feast and eventually wedding some dried-up old spinster the king is forcing on me. I did not want this when I offered my ship for his use. I asked only a small title and land to call my own."

"You could always defy the king and leave."

"Not hardly. William made it clear that if I do not do as he commands, I can take myself back to Normandy and stay there. All the contracts I have concerning the shipment of his men and arms will be null and void. I would have done all this for naught."

Henry matched his friend step for step. "He would see that no one in France would have dealings with you either." Henry sighed. "Have you considered that the maid may be young and of some beauty? He could give you Lady Morghan."

Edwin stopped dead in his tracks and turned on the one man he thought of as a brother. "Morghan is not an issue. As for the woman he would give me, if she were of any quality, she would have been wed long before now.

"To be used as barter. I feel like a hog being led to slaughter, not a titled man. I fought beside the king. That alone should count for something. I only ask to be allowed to make my own choices." Edwin's hand slapped at his sword hilt.

"It sounds as if you have already found one you could love. The woman from last night? Or Lady Morghan?"

"They are one and the same, and you know that. Besides, there is no such thing as love. What one might call true love does not exist." Edwin drew a deep breath, letting it out slowly.

"Your parents have been wed for a very long time. Surely, they love each other."

"Do you think so? My father wed my mother six months before Louis was born. I came nine months after one drunken night. I never once saw my parents holding hands, let alone kiss." Edwin began stalking down the hall again. "They tolerate one another's company. Nothing more, nothing less."

"Say we forget about love for now. Is there a woman you could tolerate as a wife?"

Morghan's face popped instantly into his mind. "There may be one, but she is beyond my meager grasp." There was only one woman he could see in the rest of his life, and that was Morghan. She was one dream that could never come true.

"Come, the king will be angry that I have procrastinated so long. I am certain he is quite excited about introducing me to my intended bride." Henry had to hide his laugh. Edwin sounded like a man headed for the gallows, not a feast.

She made an utter fool of herself.

Imagine, standing the house of the Christian god, staring at a man.

One would think her a tender maid, out for the first time, instead of a woman fully grown. At one score, she was far beyond such antics.

But oh, how simply looking at his shoulder-length golden hair and sea-green eyes quickened the pace of her heart. That was once it started beating again.

Edwin de Ballard. Her father admitted that was his name. Her father admitted he was the one. It sounded perfect on her lips.

As far back as she remember, Morghan was told her marriage would be used to seal some sort of deal her father endeavored in twice before her father pledged her. Both were old men who died before the vows could be said. Right now, she wanted to thank whatever fate took those men and gave her Edwin.

Now that she actually laid eyes on her husband-to-be, all she could say was, "Thank heavens he is young and vibrant."

"Did you say something?"

Morghan whipped around, her hand flying to her chest. Heat rose in her cheeks. Had she really said her thoughts out loud?

Edwin's smile was seductive, sending heat spiraling through every inch of her body. A dimple appeared in his left cheek, making him even more handsome. Her fingers wanted to reach out and touch it.

"Forgive me, my lady. I stood at the end of the hall for several moments watching you pace back and forth. One as beautiful as you should not be out here alone. Any rogue could come along and take advantage of you." There was a laugh to his voice and when Edwin winked at her, she laughed.

"Need I remind you it is not polite to spy on someone that way?" Morghan tried desperately to make her voice sound outraged, but it only came out breathless.

"Again, I beg pardon, my lady." His words may sound sincere, but there was not an inch of anything but sensuality in his lean form. From his broad shoulders to his firm chest and flat abs, he was male perfection.

Edwin was dressed much as he had been earlier in the day. The belt about his narrow waist was hammered leather, not the gold or silver links so many lords preferred. What would it be like to reach out and run her touch over the hard plans of his tightly sculptured body?

His physique told her that Edwin was a man who worked alongside his men, not one to simply sit about ordering others. She was certain if she was to feel his hands, they would contain calluses, giving affirmation to her suspicions.

"Have you changed your mind?"

"I thought you came this way to escort me to the feast. Surely, you would not leave a woman standing in such a drafty hall waiting another to come along."

"No, we could never allow such a thing. But where are your guards? Your father would never allow such a treasure to remain alone for any passing rogue."

"I fear they were needed elsewhere." Actually, several of them stood behind the door, making certain only Lord Edwin approached her. That was her father's idea, and she had no qualms about it.

"Then come." Edwin held out his arm to her. Instantly, Morghan laid her delicate hand atop his forearm. No matter what he was, he was enough of a gentleman enough to know his manners.

The instant her fingers closed about his forearm, Edwin could have sworn he was struck by lightning. A charge ran up his arm, settling in his chest and gut.

Silently, he groaned. If her touch burned him like this, what would it be like if he were naked? Lord help him, he actually wanted to keep this woman for himself.

Unlike in the abbey, she wore no mantle. Her body is shown through the thin rose color of her tunic and darker overtunic. Every curve, mound, and valley of her enticing shape was perfection.

"Good even to you, Sir Henry." The way she smiled at his friend made Edwin want to curse.

Jealousy was an emotion Edwin had never experienced before. He knew from the first moment Rowena stroked his arm and smiled at him, she was no innocent. Even when he witnessed her speaking to other men, there was not even a twinge of jealousy.

What was it about this woman that made him want things he could never have? Face feelings he never experienced before? She was a nothing but a casual meeting. When he sailed away, he would leave her and thoughts of her behind. Or would he?

Still, the thought of another touching her baby soft creamy skin, looking longingly into her deep emerald eyes, kissing her red lips, soured his stomach and boiled his blood.

He needed to stop thinking of her and leave this place. She was not his. Someone else waited to be his wife, one the king insisted on. If he were free to choose… but unfortunately, he wasn't.

If his attendance was not demanded at the feast, he would go now and jump into the filthy cold water of the Thames. Feasts were not something he was ever asked to attend. Thank goodness, his low rank would put him far away from this woman and those piercing, all-seeing eyes.

Could he survive the evening, watching Morghan smile, laugh, and lean close to another man when he wanted so badly for that man to be him? Would there be any scrap of his dignity left after sitting for hours watching her play court to another?

When the trio arrived at the hall, a thousand male voices mingled in a hundred conversations. A rather large group of finely dressed men stood before the hearth at one end of the hall. Edwin knew few of them, but in a year's time he would know all of them. Each would pay his price for transportation of goods and men between here and Normandy.

Here and Spain. Here and the eastern lands.

Henry bowed to them before making his way to the lower tables where the household knights sat.

"It has been my pleasure to be allowed this chance to escort you, my lady." Oh, could he sound any more odd? What he truly wanted to say was inappropriate and would not be welcome coming from him.

"I assure you, Lord de Ballard, the pleasure was all mine." Oh, how that sweet voice was going to haunt all his days to come.

Edwin paid no attention to where the page escorted Lady Morghan. If he did not know where to look for her, perhaps he could survive this meal. Surely, she would be seated beside the king and her father. He would be placed below the salt, on one of the lower tabled reserved for the lesser barons.

When the page stopped before his assigned place, Edwin realized he hadn't been taken as far from the head table as he thought. Looking down his partner for the evening surprised him speechless.

"Good eve, my lord Edwin." The Duke of Wessex stood and extended his arm. Edwin grasped it and shook it in greeting.

Surely, there was some sort of mistake. He would never be set near a duke, unless...

Looking down, Edwin saw a face looking up at him. Pale blue eyes sat in an oval face. The woman must possess blonde hair, as her brows and lashes were so light, one could barely see them. Where Lady Morghan had a healthy glow to her skin, this woman was almost translucent.

What he could see of her figure was thin and flat. Goodness, she was barely more than a child.

His heart sank. Here was the woman the king would have him wed. All thoughts of fleeing the marriage fled. To turn down the daughter of a duke would be humiliating and detrimental to his fledgling shipping business.

"May I present my daughter, Lady Olivia."

Taking her offered hand in his, Edwin bent a light kiss to the back. "It is my pleasure, lady." If anyone heard the flatness of his tone, it was not commented on.

Sitting, Edwin knew he would be spending the evening in silence. If this was the woman the king wanted him to wed, she would do nothing for him.

"It seems we are to be dining partners, my lord Edwin." Edwin stared down at the last person in the world he thought he would see.

5

"I do not like this."

Connor paced back and forth before the man who favored his own plan. "It would be better if you told the boy he was to wed my Morghan and have the ceremony performed right now." Stopping, Connor turned his full attention on William. "I have seen the way they look at each other. The marriage will be a good one. Hell, they nearly undress each other every time they see one another. I tell you, all in the great hall have begun noticing it."

Connor drew his black cape about his legs and sunk into a cushioned chair before the hearth, accepting a goblet of rich French wine from his host.

"Aye, the two of them offer more entertainment than the jugglers and harp players." There was a laugh in William's voice that made Connor growl. "I feared they would not have enough time to become well acquainted before Edwin sailed."

"God provided you with that help." Connor stretched out his long legs before the fire, taking another sip of wine. Eyes so like his daughter's turned to silently question the other king. "Their displays make me wish the vows were already set. Still, I have the feeling you have not yet told the young man of his upcoming good fortune."

William sobered. "The boy thinks he is not worthy of your daughter. He plans on returning for a whore in Normandy. Even now, the woman takes Lord Edwin's own brother to her bed." No one questioned just how William got such information. Every king worth his rule had spies that kept him informed on all manner of information.

"If the delay distresses you so, I could give him to Wessex's daughter. Twice the man has come to me and offered his daughter for the marriage."

"You know I can provide far more men and arms than Wessex. You need my aid. All of England is not under your rule yet. Need I remind you of the blood bath just days ago after your coronation."

"Nay. There are still so many opposed to my rule. More than I would like were loyal to Harold."

"Then why wait? Tell him the truth and let us get the contracts signed. Tomorrow the sky could clear, and Edwin would be on his way home."

From his curt words, William knew his friend was getting impatient. Still, he could not see a gently bred lady like Morghan living under the very primitive conditions that awaited at Ironwood. "I promised Lord Edwin time to prepare his home before he could even bring Rowena from Normandy. Would you have me place Lady Morghan in such a position?"

"The time will come soon enough when Edwin will discover exactly what is happening in Normandy."

"It cannot come quick enough for me."

Edwin smiled at the way Morghan tried to look in all directions at once.

As a child, he could remember the excitement of visiting a market in Spain. Right now, he saw the same look in Morghan's eyes.

Lady Olivia was just the opposite. She rarely looked at anything the vendors offered, turning her nose up at food, drink, and cloth. Nothing was to her liking. Why he needed to bring her along was a question he asked himself every five minutes.

It was obvious she was not enjoying herself. More than once, she informed him she wished to return to the keep and ready herself for the evening's festivities. Yet Edwin ignored her whiny voice. It grated on his nerves. He only put up with her to be in Morghan's company.

He could not point to the exact moment, but the prefix of "Lord and Lady" was dropped from their conversations.

"Oh, look." Morghan was off and moving again. Edwin could only smile and follow in her wake. What he thought would be just a few hours in her company turned into days and more memories to hold close during cold winter nights.

"Not again." Lady Olivia whined, drawing attention. "When are we going to return? It looks as if the weather is going to turn once more."

"There is not a cloud in the sky, Olivia," Morghan said, lifting her face to the weak winter sun. Come along." Threading her arm through the other woman's, Morghan smiled brightly. "Do you not like the bazaars?"

"Not particularly. Whenever we needed something for Mother or the household, Father had merchants bring their wares to our hall. We never needed to go out in the weather. Then it was always Father who made the decisions."

"One day, you will have your own household. You will need to make decisions such as these for yourself. Your mother and father may be a great distance away, unable to choose." Morghan practically pulled the younger woman along. "Who do you expect to make those choices?"

"My husband, of course." As Olivia spoke the words, she looked straight at Edwin. His cringe was almost imperceptible. Almost.

So this woman would make him choose every item for their home, even down to the cloth she would use for her clothing? Not if he had anything to say about it. What would she do while he was gone transporting men and goods for the king? Wait until his return?

No, if she was the woman the king had in mind for him, he would simply need to change the man's mind. Perhaps in another five years she might, *might* be old and mature enough to be a wife. Right now, she was only a spoiled little girl.

At one point, last eve, Edwin found himself standing outside the king's privy chambers, wanting desperately to ask for Morghan's hand. His promise to return to Normandy for Rowena no longer held substance for him. Morghan was all he wanted for a wife, and he would perform any transformation necessary to attain her.

His good sense kicked in, and Edwin went back to the small quarters assigned to him. He had nothing yet to offer for the protection of a wife. It would be late spring or early summer before he could even ask for her hand. By then, his ignoring her might lead her father to look elsewhere for her hand.

Then again, would her father allow the dissolution of the contract? A piece of him wanted to try.

"Are they not the most beautiful colors you have ever seen?" Morghan's happy voice sliced through his thoughts. Delicate fingers brushed over each cloth on the table, ending at a royal blue.

"I must admit," Edwin said, "I never thought much of the colors a woman prized. My mother stitched from simple browns." The more Edwin thought he knew about this woman, the more he found he needed to learn. "Are there any you prize, Lady Olivia?"

"If I did, I would have my father pay for them. You need not spend your coin on me." Olivia gave Morghan a disapproving look. The woman was making a spectacle of herself, and Olivia wanted only to leave this place.

"As you wish." Pulling out his purse, Edwin paid the merchant for the eels of cloth and passed them off to a waiting page, who ran back toward Turney Keep as fast as his long legs could carry him.

"You need not pay for everything I like. What if I only admired the cloth but had no use for it?" Placing her hand on Edwin's outstretched arm, they began wandering to the next stall. The sun dipped behind a cloud, and Edwin was glad he wore his fur-lined cloak. The day began bright and sunny, but now that midday approached, clouds threatened.

"Do you have a use for it?"

"Actually, I do. In fact, I need to begin sewing my trousseau when I return home."

Edwin's heart skipped a beat. Could a woman act so happy and content in the company of one man and return home to wed another?

Why not? Men often took one last lover before committing to a wife and marriage. All this time he was gaining feelings for the woman who would soon be another man's wife.

Just the thought caused bile to rise in his throat. He had procrastinated too long, and now the woman he wanted was lost to him. There was no returning to Normandy and claiming Rowena. Just the thought of touching her after knowing Morghan made him ill. Perhaps if he went to William this night, he could claim Morghan for his own. Until the vows were actually spoken, a woman was free to choose her life. Was she not?

Whom was he trying to fool? A woman wedded where her father could get the best connection for his own purposes. He had little to nothing to offer. His heart was good, and he could work hard to provide Morghan with each and every little thing her life required. They were in a new land where anything was possible.

Still, he needed to try. His mind set, Edwin led the two ladies toward a pub for the midday meal.

"I will not enter there." If possible, Olivia's snooty attitude sounded even worse. "Do you know what kind of men reside here? Why, filthy, uncouth ones." Folding her arms across her chest, Olivia refused to budge. "You should not enter either, Lady Morghan. 'Tis not fit for a real lady."

At the turn of so many heads, Edwin knew every person within hearing distance heard Olivia's words. All heads turned to look at her. A marriage to that woman was not going to happen, no matter what the king did to him.

"Now, Olivia," Morghan patiently said, "it is not that bad. I have been in one or two such places with my father and his men."

"Surely not." If possible, Lady Olivia sounded even more outraged.

"If you dislike it so," Edwin offered, "I will have the guards escort you back to the keep."

"That would please me well." Head raised, Lady Olivia surrounded by six of her father's guards, turned about and walked away.

The place smelled of a cooking fire, stale ale, and unwashed bodies.

The knight she now knew as Sir Henry, Edwin's closest friend, sat just inside the door at a spot where he could easily watch them. Sir Henry was always near when she was in Edwin's company. The man made her feel safe and well chaperoned.

Finding a seat near the fire, Edwin ordered two tankards of ale and stew. A short portly man, a white cloth rapped about his large girth, gave them an odd look before walking away. A quick glance about told Morghan she was the only woman in the establishment. There was an uncomfortable feeling here. If they were closer to the keep, she might have suggested they return there for the meal.

Perhaps Olivia was right. There was an uncomfortable feeling here.

A young lad, about six or seven, gently placed two tankards before them.

He was young, his clothes little more than dirty rags. His dark hair was filthy, his bone-thin form made her wonder when his last decent meal had been. She could feel a deep sadness in him that nearly choked her.

What an inopportune time for her curse to kick in. There was something about the lad that prevented her from erecting a barrier again his emotions. The only thing she could think of was the boy held an amount of Celtic blood.

Morghan watched as the boy slowly walked back toward them, two wooden bowls in his small sturdy hands. Since all his concentration was on what he was doing, he never saw the foot a man stuck out in his path.

The boy fell before Morghan could shout a warning. All the men about one table laughed. Morghan could only feel the fear in the boy. Silent tears formed in his eyes. How cruel could these men be?

She was about to find out.

"Damn Saxon spawn." The huge man who took their order grabbed the child by his thin arm and yanked him into the air. The boy dangled at an odd angle, his feet at least a foot off the floor. "That was my finest stew, meant for nobles, not the rats that run the floors at night." A flick of his wrist, and the boy was tossed aside. Morghan heard the snapping sound of a bone. As a healer and woman, she could not stand by and do nothing.

"It was not the child's fault." Morghan stood, hands on hips, facing the fat man. His breath held the smell of sour ale, and his unwashed body far outdid any in the room. "That man tripped him on purpose." Pointing to the laughing man, she caught movement of the child trying to crawl away. Too late. Every man in the place was about to see her temper.

"Now, Harek, would ye do such a thing?" Though the owner asked the question, he never turned toward the man, nor did he take his eyes off her.

"Nay, I did nothing." The stupid man, ale dripping from his scraggly beard, replied. No one could miss the laughter filling his voice.

"How can ye say that?" Edwin knew just how angry Morghan was, when her words turned from the very proper French she spoke, to one filled with a thick Irish accent. He needed to defuse the situation before she got herself into something even he could not get her out of.

Edwin heard the pull of a sword and knew Henry stood on Morghan's other side, weapon at the ready. "I believe you owe the lady an apology." Edwin's voice was even and smooth, though he felt neither.

"My apologies that the little bastard ruined your meal. He shall be disciplined, and another can bring your food."

Edwin never saw Morghan move. One minute she was standing between him and Henry, and the next she was shielding the child with her own body.

"Touch him, and I will kill you myself. And believe me, I will take great pleasure in it." Where Morghan got a dagger, he had no idea, but she held it as if she knew exactly how to use it. The look in her eyes told him she would not think twice about using it. Morghan looked like a mother bear protecting her only cub.

"Try it, and I will have the king's own men on ye."

"Since I am one of King William's men, I doubt you could call any of them to harm the *princess* Morghan." The word princess caused only a momentary change in the man's expression.

"I want you all out of here and away from my property. I have the right to refuse any I deem unfit."

"If I go, the boy goes with me." Morghan countered.

"Fine, pay for him, and he is yours to do with as you wish." From beneath her cloak, Morghan pulled out a bag of coins and threw it at the man. It struck him square in the face. The sound of his nose breaking made her smile.

"Lady Morghan." Five of her father's men pushed past the patrons, coming to stand between the crowd and their mistress kneeling on the floor. "Your father sent us for you. An urgent message just arrived from home, and he requires you attend him immediately." One of the men announced.

"I cannot simply leave the boy behind. He is injured and needs tending." By now, Morghan cradled the boy in her arms. Tears streaked his dirty face, but no sound came from him.

"I will see him taken care of." Edwin offered. A nod in Henry's direction, and the knight sheathed his sword. In two steps, he was beside Morghan, reaching for the child.

"He needs a healer. This bully broke his tiny ankle. His arm needs to be checked also." Edwin knew Morghan would not give up the boy easily. When she had her own children, she would make a very protective mother.

"I have a healer on my ship. I will see the boy taken care of." Edwin offered.

"Do you promise?"

"Trust me, Morghan. The child will get the care he needs and find a safe place in my household. I may even teach him to love the sea."

"Please, mistress, your father was adamant that we escort you to the keep immediately." There was a touch of panic in the guard's voice now.

"Fine." Morghan spat at the annoying guard. "You will tell me later how the boy fares?"

"When I see you at the evening meal." As Morghan rose to leave, she pressed her lips against his.

When Edwin entered the hall for the evening meal, he found Morghan and every member of her father's household gone.

He turned about and left.

When he left his assigned chambers, Edwin received the king's latest gift.

6

It was worse than he was led to believe.

William reined in his horse and stared at the keep before him. Both the seaward and land gates to Ironwood stood wide open. No guard could be seen walking sentry. All was inhumanly quiet.

No sentinels stood upon the battlements. Not a man, woman, child, or animal could be seen or heard in the bailey.

Turning in his saddle, William stared at the ship moored at the long pier beyond the sea gate. It was as quiet as the keep. There was no smell of death to indicate Ironwood had been overrun by the rebel Saxons. There was simply nothing. It was almost as if every living soul packed up and deserted the land.

Anger boiled in his gut. Reports had reached him of the careless way Edwin was acting. A sennight ago, when the man failed to arrive for a movement of some troops, William had gotten so angered, he'd ridden off. When he found Lord Edwin, the man had better have a reasonable explanation, or he would feel a king's wrath. In his opinion, no woman was worth this.

Though he had rarely been home to Normandy, he received near weekly reports from his son, Robert. A particular one confirmed what he tried to tell Edwin just last fall. Surely, he could not still be suffering the humiliation he had been dealt nearly a month ago.

"Do you see even one man about, Henry?" William turned to the man sitting a horse to his right. Since Henry's service to Ironwood would begin now, he may as well start earning the position.

"Nay, sire." Henry continued toward the open gate, determined to find

someone, anyone, to tell them what had happened here. Ironwood's defense was his responsibility now, and it looked as if he was just in time.

As the master-at-arms, the final blame for this lack of security fell square on his shoulders. He could have requested a release from William's service the moment the first report came from Normandy, yet he had hesitated. The last major battle had been a month ago. At the moment, peace had settled on the lower half of England. It was so peaceful, William thought to go home for a visit. Man could not live by battles alone.

Dismounting, William looked for any sign of life. A gray cat trotted by, a fat rat dangling from its mouth. This was not a good sign. Ironwood was too new a keep for such vermin.

A round of male laughter sounded from a long building to their right. There was nothing to denote that building from any other. They ran like fingers along the curtain wall. The concentration of male voices indicated it must be a barracks of some sort.

"Excuse me, sire." The small voice of a boy drifted up to them. He stood beside the horses, a hand extended toward Henry. He could not be over seven, his thin body covered in well-worn but clean clothes.

Was this boy the only person about? Dismounting, Henry handed him the reins. William and the other knights followed. "I remember you, sire. Ye held me down while Lord Edwin reset my shoulder and my leg."

Kneeling down, Henry met the boy face-to-face. "I am pleased to see you are well healed." It was difficult to forget those days when the boy raged with fever, and none of them were certain he would live. He and Edwin took turns holding the tiny fevered body, forcing cool water down his parched throat.

"I remember you, Tommy." The lad's small chest puffed up slightly. "It is good to see you have recovered so well."

"Lad, I have come to be master-at-arms for Ironwood. Tell me, where are all the men, and why are there none on the walls?"

"It is their resting time." Leaning close, Tommy took on a stance of one divulging a secret. "When Lord Edwin drinks, the men wait and watch. When he falls asleep, they wander off and begin their own drinking. Who is that?"

"That, Tommy, is your king," Henry answered.

The boy's face drained of all color. "Lord Edwin is in the great hall," he shouted before pulling the horses off toward the stable.

"Shall we find my wayward vassal?" William took one last look about and headed for the hall.

"Marcus," Henry stopped one of William's guard. "See if you can locate anyone sober enough and get them on these walls. Pull them out of their bottles if need be. A good dip in the cold water of the sea should help bring them to their senses."

"Aye, Sir Henry." Signaling to several others, Marcus headed the men toward the stable.

It took a moment for their eyes to adjust to the dim light of the great hall. Few candles were lit and only one lamp. The high narrow windows let in almost no light. Even on the sunniest days, this place would still look dark and gloomy.

Two huge hearths lay on opposite ends of the hall. Neither was lit.

Before one sat a long trestle table. Several men lay sprawled across the surface. The one in the center held the blond hair of the lord of Ironwood.

"Fetch me a bucket of seawater." William ordered, his arms folded over his broad mail-encased chest. The stench of unwashed bodies and stale ale permeated the entire place. It was enough to turn even the strongest of stomachs. "Leave the doors ajar when you go. This place could use an airing."

Henry looked about but saw nothing that could even be remotely used for a bucket. "The kitchen looks to be that way." William pointed toward the back of the hall. "Do you see Robert about?" Edwin's squire. Henry had nearly forgotten about de Montgomery's son.

"I will look into the matter. If I see Tommy again, I will ask after the boy." One last shake of his head, and Henry left.

Unconscious bodies littered the floor. Picking his way between them, William headed toward the object of his anger. The walls were bare, the rushes on the floor stank of vomit. How anyone could live under these conditions was beyond his understanding. Even his siege accommodations smelled better.

Edwin sat in an enormous chair behind the head table. The arms, back, and legs had been elegantly carved to represent a forest scene. Animals sat staring out at the occupant. The craftsmanship was phenomenal. Each strand of fur shone in every face. They must have cost a small fortune.

Beside it was a smaller version. Obviously made as a matched set for the lord and lady of the keep, he admired them greatly. His wife would love such a set. When this was all done, he would speak to Lord Edwin as to who carved them.

Head leaning back, his arms draped over the arms of the chair and legs spread out before him, Edwin looked ill. His skin was so pale, no one would have known the healthy glow hours in the sun once produced. His eyes were sunken in his head, and lack of proper sleep created dark circles beneath. The bag of his clothing told of his lost weight.

All the hard muscles the years of working his ship had given him would soon turn to fat if this problem was not stopped right here and now. Edwin allowed what happened to him in Normandy to affect his judgment. William was here to see that error corrected, and soon.

There was a simple cure for what ailed the man, and she was at this moment on her way to Ironwood. It was long past time William confronted this particular lord and set him back on the right path.

"Have you come to take charge, my lord?" A timid voice asked from behind him. William snapped around. He had been so deep in thought concerning Edwin's behavior, he completely missed hearing the woman's approach.

"Aye." It was not until the woman moved toward Edwin that William paid any attention to her. In her midtwenties, she possessed hair as black as night. In fact, she reminded him very much of Tommy. "Are you the cook?"

"Aye, when there is food to prepare." The venom in her tone said much for the few people still loyal in Ironwood.

"How long has there been difficulty in procuring food for the men?"

"Robert, my lord's squire, has done his best, but he is only a lad. My husband is the smithy." That was good to know. "He tried to get some of the guards to help the boy. Besides, Lord Edwin has not eaten enough in the last sennight to keep a babe alive."

William watched the way the woman's expression softened when she looked at Edwin. "I think he tries to kill himself, though I know not why and he will not tell any of us. Do you know what happened to turn him from the generous, kind lord that gave me the position of cook?"

"I, good woman, do know the why of it. I also came baring the solution. Tell me, mistress, have you set the evening meal to cook?"

"There is naught but a handful of vegetables. I have already set them to boil. If young Robert is successful, it will mean meat for the stew."

"Boiled vegetables should do nicely. I doubt Lord Edwin's stomach could handle anything more robust at this point. My men have plenty of provisions. See Sir Marcus for anything you need."

After a couple steps, the woman stopped and turned. "I am Oleta, Your Grace."

"You know who I am?" So far, this woman was the only one living in this keep to acknowledge his identity or his arrival.

"My adopted son, Tommy, ran in to tell me you were here. I am thankful you came to help us." Silently, she turned back toward Edwin. "Whatever happened to him, it must have been horrid. I feel as if something inside the lad died." Her piece said, Oleta left.

Sitting into the "ladies" chair, William sighed, pinching the bridge of his nose. He was so tired. When the first reports came from Ironwood, he hurriedly finished his business, sent a messenger to Ireland, and then handpicked his guard. They'd ridden straight through stopping only long enough to eat a sparse meal and rest the horses.

Three days of travel left him tired and angry. He had important things to attend to in the north. There was still opposition to his rule in York and many of the northern cities. This matter needed to get cleared quickly so he could get back to the running of his kingdom. No matter how competent Northumberland was, he needed to oversee his own campaign.

"The water, sire." Henry's voice cut through the haze of thoughts. Far too much required the attention of a king. This one small problem would be handled now before it grew beyond his control.

"Thank you, Sir Henry." Grasping the bucket, William advanced on his vassal. "Have the men resumed their posts?"

"Aye, I saw them there personally. Most are in no better shape than their lord, but at least they will stand the watch."

In one smooth motion, William emptied the contents of the bucket onto his target. "Trim the sails!" Though the words were slurred, they were loud enough to be heard over the most brutal of winds. "Prepare to bring her about!" The second order was only slightly more legible.

"Easy, son." A gentle hand restrained the young man from his flight. Edwin only made it one step from his chair before stopping.

Through swollen bloodshot eyes, Edwin squinted at the figure before him. How dare one of his men disturb…

The familiar darkness of drunken oblivion crept against the outer reaches of his vision. He was on his ship, was he not? Or was this another of the nightmares that haunted him? Surely, he had drunk enough last eve to banish the memory of her.

Squinting at the tall figure, Edwin tried to remember the last time the king had invaded his dreams. Not for months. There was something nagging at the back of his mind, but try as he might, no clear thoughts would solidify.

He needed to do something for William, but the ale he had consumed kept all coherent thoughts from coming forward.

Perhaps if he sat back down, it would come to him. Dropping back to his chair, he reached for the wooden tankard.

William watched a myriad of emotions cross the young lord's features.

Anger gave way to bewilderment, which in turn gave way to a look William knew all too well. Too many days of drink and no food created a riotous stomach. "Lord Edwin needs air." Grabbing the man by the arm, William propelled him toward the door.

Edwin's mind reeled, his stomach protesting. Why was he being forcibly removed from his own home? The afternoon sunlight in the bailey near blinded him. It took every ounce of effort, but he managed to stumble forward, keeping his wobbly legs beneath him. The hand at his back persistently pushed him forward.

Twenty yards out, Edwin lost the battle.

Dropping to his knees near a fresh pile of dirt, he vomited all the stale ale. After that, dry heaves gripped his guts. Would it never end? This was one of the reasons he hadn't allowed himself to become sober. Granted, it was a poor excuse, but the other was far too painful to contemplate.

After what seemed an eternity, it stopped. Sitting back on his heels, Edwin tried desperately to focus on the instrument of his torture. His men knew better than to disturb him. The last one to try to sober him found himself off his crew and thrown out of Ironwood. He liked the numbness the drink provided. He needed to forget their faces. How they smiled at his misery and pain. Even his parents sided with them, not him.

A stab of pain these memories always brought clutched at his chest, robbing him of breath. The wound was too new, too devastating. They had betrayed him and only drink dulled the pain of what his family had done to him.

William watched his friend struggle against himself. He was not ignorant of what had transpired in Normandy. He had known what would happen when this young man returned and had even tried to warn him. Edwin had always been a very stubborn man. Until now, William did not realize just how stubborn.

A quick glance at the wall walk told him Henry had things well in hand. Though half the men looked no better than their lord, it was good to see them set to protecting their land.

"Here, drink this." William held out a small skin he brought just for this reason.

"Why can you not simply leave me alone in my grief?" Edwin wanted nothing but to drag himself back into the hall and drown his pounding head in more ale.

"Take a drink." William's voice was firm. Removing the stopper, he held the skin beneath the young lord's nose. He knew it smelled much like sweet ale. He had used some the morning after his coronation and knew well its healing properties. "Essex swears by it."

Still, Edwin resisted. He sat in the dirt, skin in hand, staring at it as if it were poison. Heaving a deep sigh, William knelt beside him in the dirt. Being careful to keep his voice low, the king leaned close and whispered, "Drink the damn stuff, or I shall forcefully pour it down your throat. Is that the impression you would give your men? Many now walk their posts and watch you."

Edwin knew the man commanding him would not give up until he did as he was told. The first tentative swallow soothed his burning throat. The second deeper one settled his stomach nicely. Perhaps this stuff was not so bad after all.

A warmth began to spread through Edwin, radiating out from his stomach. Tight muscles loosened. Whatever was in here made his head and body feel better than they had in a month. When the last swallow was consumed, he turned and handed the skin back to…

No, he could not be seeing the man he thought. The king was in Dover. As each moment passed, his head cleared more. "Forgive me, sire." He awkwardly scrambled to his feet. "I had not been aware you were coming to visit. Have I missed a rendezvous?"

"Aye, though not an important one." William rose and looked about at all the activity. This was what a keep the size of Ironwood should be like. "Come, we must talk."

No offer of assistance came. Struggling to move, Edwin looked about. He hadn't seen this much activity since the curtain wall was completed. Cursing, he hurried to catch up to his king.

Edwin knew without being told what was coming. And he deserved it. For over a fortnight, he'd been trying to drown his shattered heart in ale. He was ten kinds a fool to believe the lies of a whore. He had given up the pleasure of a woman who made his heart race, his palms sweat, his body harden, for a promise made by a naive boy going off to war.

There were no feelings but bitterness and hate left for Rowena. Every dream he could remember showed the face of Morghan, her red hair falling softly about her beautiful face and lush body. In keeping his promise to one woman, he'd lost forever the other. His heart and soul belonged to a woman he would never have.

"I find I am sorely disappointed in you, Edwin." Each of the king's words struck like a fist to his gut. "I had thought you better than this." William's waved in a circular motion, encompassing the entire keep. Watching it made Edwin dizzy, so he closed his eyes and waited for the nausea to pass. "You have begun a strong home here, yet at the first sign of trouble, you allow it to crumble at your feet."

Edwin made no reply. What could he say? William was right. He allowed himself to wallow in his hurt and pain like a boy disappointed in his first love.

Turning on his vassal, the king chose his words very carefully. "You know my plans for England." It was not a question but a statement. "On the day the crown was placed on my head, you swore allegiance to me and those plans. Though I try to avoid them, battles still rage and will for some time to come. It is most important I keep my allies intact if I am to finish what I started.

"I set a contract just before my coronation that has been kept in only one part. In exchange for supplies, food, and men, I need to give one of my loyal barons in marriage."

Edwin stopped dead in his tracks. "Surely, you do not mean for me to keep that promise now. It has been so many months, I thought you would have found another husband for the lady." Even before the words were out of his mouth, Edwin knew the answer.

"Aye. You will serve the contract well."

"I am honored you believe me worthy, but I must decline, sire. I want no wife. The only one I would have chosen is lost to me now." Again, the image of Morghan's laughing expression as they danced about Thorney Island's hall flooded back to his mind. A stabbing pain ripped through his chest. "No woman will ever sit beside me as wife."

"You have no concept of how important this contract is to me. I need those supplies and men." What a fool he'd been to think distance and time would change the king's mind.

If only he could go back and change things. If only he could take what that wonderful woman had so openly offered. If only he listened to his heart, not his mind. But "if only" was for fools and dreamers.

He was neither.

William's next words struck him like a blow. "I wish I could give you a choice, but I cannot. It is too late. I have already sent for your bride. She will arrive on the morrow. I have also sent for the priest. I will witness your vows before sunset."

Anger flared raw in Edwin's gut. How dare he? King or not, the man had no right to treat his life like a puppet. A wife demanded love and loyalty, two things he would never again be able to give a woman. A life as his wife could only mean one thing: a lonely and loveless existence. How could his king expect him to foster such on any woman?

From the look in his friend's eyes, William knew a protest was forthcoming. Whether Edwin knew it or not, he needed this woman as much as he himself needed to fulfill the contract. "Do not think to gainsay me in this matter. If I must, I shall call upon your vow of loyalty to accept the woman as wife."

"Would it help if I told you, you already know the woman. You met her and spent time in her company last Christmastime." Silently, Edwin groaned. He would be saddled with Lady Olivia.

"It would make no difference, sire." Taking a long look around,

Edwin knew he would give in to what was demanded of him. "Would you take everything from me if I refuse this offer? Again, I tell you, I want no wife."

"Because of what happened to you?" Edwin spoke not a word. "You must not allow their perfidy to affect you. They are your past. Ironwood and your wife are your future."

"You know nothing of what happened in Normandy."

"I know everything of what happened. I make it my business to know what happens on my land, be it here or back in France."

Edwin knew he would do as he was commanded. The king would give him no choice. It was time he stopped feeling sorry for himself and got on with his life.

Men again walked the sentry posts. Men-at-arms practiced on the tiltyard, the clash of swords ringing through the air. This was what life should be. Something deep inside knew he needed to do what was best for Ironwood and the men and women who depended on him.

Pushing his selfishness aside, Edwin capitulated.

"I will take the woman to wife." What happened between the two of them after the vows were spoken would remain between them. Once the woman was his wife, he could treat her any way he pleased.

"Do not expect me to take her to my bed, and never will she hold my heart." Cold eyes turned on the king. "The woman shall have my name and the protection of my keep. Neither you nor anyone else in this world can ever force me to give her my body or my heart."

Only time would tell if it would be true. If given a wager, William would put his gold on the one woman who could change this man's world.

7

William stood on the battlements above Ironwood, watching the small group of horsemen approach.

Plainly riding in front beside her father was the bride. His heart felt for her. She had no idea what waited for her, but he knew this was best for all of them.

Nature had cooperated on this day. No rain loomed just over the horizon as was the case for the last two days. The bright sunshine would make things seem happier, even if it were anything but. Too bad the groom was not as accommodating as Mother Nature.

The cockcrow has been two hours past, and Edwin was yet to appear. After capitulating last eve, the man had effectively disappeared. At this very minute, twenty men were out searching the grounds for their lord.

Normally he detested taking such drastic measures, especially against one who had shown only loyalty in the past, but if he allowed Edwin's disobedience to continue, he would be in danger of losing control over some not so set to his rule. Those who opposed him could see this as a weakness and begin circling like vultures, waiting for him to falter.

"Father Matthew just arrived, sire," Henry announced.

"Any sight of Lord Edwin?" William never turned about but watched the ship draw ever closer. A deep breath ended with a sigh. A missing vassal and a swiftly approaching bride were far from his idea of the perfect wedding day. He would much rather be fighting an enemy than trying to find the words of a diplomat.

"Nay, sire. It is as if he disappeared from the face of the earth."

Sighing, William pinched the bridge of his nose. He was getting too old for all of this.

Edwin sat back against a rock and stared at the group of horses and men riding directly for Ironwood. He knew without a doubt that his future wife rode in the front line covered from head to toe.

Long into the night, he attempted to persuade William he wanted no wife, though a tiny piece of his heart desperately wanted to believe he could trust a woman. He knew he could not.

His own family had turned on him. It was not just his expected bride, but his brother and parents as well. They claimed they all believed him dead, killed in William's battle to gain England.

Why could they not wait longer to make certain of his fate? After all, he was only gone seven months. His own father was often gone longer when he took a position on certain trade routes. No, what he had witnessed could only have transpired days after his leaving.

Lifting a skin to his lips, Edwin drank deep of the honey mead. Tucked securely in his tunic pocket was the only thing he had to remember Morghan. He found it lying on the floor at the inn when he lifted Tommy to take him away. It was little more than a square of linen, but it held her scent.

Placing it against his nose, he breathed in the soft lavender scent. Barely any remained, yet it was just enough to bring memories of a woman who had fired his body and filled his dreams.

Until the arrival of the king, he still held out some small hope he would find the one woman he desired above life itself. It would be certain torture, but when he next visited Ireland, he would take his battered heart in hand and ask about her and her new husband.

Morghan.

Simply thinking her name brought back images of red flowing hair against a most lush body. Her brilliant green eyes and smiling face appeared in his mind, just as they did every night when he closed his eyes.

Drinking himself unconscious each night had been the only way to keep her image at bay.

Just as steel bands encased the wooden planks of Ironwood's doors, a barrier was built about his bruised and dying heart. He was being forced to wed this day to prove his loyalty, but no man alive could force him to take her to his bed or his heart. If the woman was a virgin, which he figured Lady Olivia to be, she would forever remain that way.

Again, the skin of mead pressed against his lips. The cool liquid slid down his throat. By the time he spoke his vows, he planned to be so drunk he would not even remember speaking them.

Edwin's mind drifted to the chamber he had prepared. Portioned off at one end of the great hall, he'd spent countless hours filling it with everything he had thought a bride might like. After returning from Normandy, he took an ax to most of the exquisite Spanish furnishings. Only the hand-carved bed remained.

Gone were any treasures he thought to present to a bride. This wife would enjoy none of them, not even the bed since he never intended to lay beside her in it. He hoped she liked being alone because that was all she would get from him.

Carefully folding the cloth, Edwin tucked it lovingly back into his pocket. One last look at the horses headed toward the stable, he was ready to face his future.

"Lord Edwin?" Ah, his squire finally found where he was hiding. So be it. He knew he could not hide from his future forever. It was simply a matter of time before someone stumbled across him and reminded him of his duty to king and country.

"Is all in readiness for my bride?" He actually did not care if it was or not. Personally, it would please him if the king, his choice of bride, and the rest of the world just let him be. William could go back to his war, and his wife-to-be could ride right back to where she came from.

But since that was not about to happen, he may as well face them all. Another long drink bolstered his courage enough to face his fate.

"Aye, my lord. Father Matthew has arrived. The king seeks a word with you before the ceremony begins."

"Tell the king..." Edwin had to stop himself from saying what he truly meant. He needed to get the ceremony over, his king sent on his way, and all would be back to the way he wanted it.

All except he would have a wife hanging about his keep. Still, his sodden brain could see a benefit to having a wife about. He would be gone often. It would seem the king had done him a service despite everything. His bride would be so busy handling everything, she would not have much time to wonder why he never went near her.

Yes, now he could see how this would work to his advantage. "Robert, tell the king I will be along in plenty of time to attend the ceremony."

Robert stood silently watching his lord drink. Besides the near-empty skin in his hand, two full ones lay on the ground at his side. If Edwin consumed them all, it would be a wonder he could even stand at his own wedding, let alone clearly speak his vows.

When the boy was first given to Lord Edwin as squire, he thought the king was mistaken. This was not a fighting man but a man of the sea. Though he never minded a good sea voyage, Robert knew his life lay in another direction.

He was the son of Duke de Montgomery, a duke who now secured the Welsh border for William. In France, his father had been one of the major forces behind the invasion plans. Even now at fourteen, he wanted very much to follow in his father's footsteps.

Tall for his age, he nearly looked Lord Edwin in the eye. His midnight hair and blue eyes bespoke his mother's Roman heritage.

So far, his only experience in battle came in the fight against Harold.

Truth be told, he was limited to preparing for the battle and to tending his wounded lords and a few others after the engagement.

If only it was as easy to tend the wound Edwin now suffered. He stood back and watched a proud, honorable man reduced to a drunken sod in a single course of the moon. And for what? A woman?

There was plenty of talk behind Lord Edwin's back. Many speculated on the reasoning, but he knew the truth. One night, deep into his cups, Edwin spilled the entire sordid story.

Though his heart ached, his mind could not believe any of them worthy of such sacrifice.

Robert met the lady who would be his mistress. She seemed just what his lord needed to bring him back to life. If only Edwin would give the woman a chance.

"Are you still here, Robert?" Edwin's words were beginning to slur, indication he was well on his way to being drunk. "I would have thought you'd be gone by now."

"My orders from the king are to bring you back. I cannot leave until you are ready to accompany me." That was not exactly the wording William used, but close enough.

"If that is what you must do, then fine. Have a seat and wait until I am ready." Tossing the empty skin aside, Edwin reached for the next. He had until dusk to get as drunk as he could.

At first, Morghan thought her betrothed would be waiting to greet her. Yet it was Sir Henry that stood just inside the gates, anxiously waiting.

Ironwood looked so very different from last winter. Pestering her father had gotten her a pass by this land on their way home. Not much besides rough wooden walls and a small cottage stood testament to the dedication of the owner.

Now a two-story stone keep dominated a large bailey and outer wall. Several smaller buildings lined the perimeter wooden wall on all sides. This was typical for a Norman keep, and she most heartily approved.

Twenty yards about the wall, she could see newly cleared woodlands. Grass was just beginning to grow over the low stumps.

Morghan knew then something was wrong. There was a cloud of subdued emotions hanging over this land, like the heavy cloud of a spring thunderstorm rolling in from the sea.

Edwin's essence did not come from Ironwood, but a distance up the shore. The feelings from last December were still there but buried deep beneath something else, something that nearly choked her.

It was part anger, part hurt, and part hatred. All the dark emotions were hiding the softer, gentler ones she had felt in the days they spent time together. Closing her eyes, Morghan tried very hard to find his exact hiding place. Opening them, her gaze settled on one specific spot. Though she could not physically see him, she knew he was there. He was watching her approach, not with excitement or anticipation but hatred and dread.

She turned to her father, but Conner quickly looked away.

Whatever happened here changed the man she came to know last Christmastime. She intended to find out what, and God help the man, woman, or king who got in her way.

"Morghan?" Connor's voice sounded far away, though the hand on her arm was warm and comforting.

Focusing on that touch, Morghan struggled against the darkness that threatened to engulf her.

Connor studied his daughter, not liking what he saw. When the messenger arrived conveying William's summons, he'd been thankful. It was long overdue, in coming.

He remembered well the look that came over his late wife when something weighed heavy on her soul. The last time he saw it was the night she died. He prayed never to see it in his only daughter. Those prayers were not answered. He saw it now, and it frightened him.

"Listen to me, daughter." Prying her fingers apart, he examined the damage. Her nails dug crescents in her palm. No blood. That was a good sign. "Listen to me, Morghan," Connor started softly. "It is not too late. I can turn about and head for home. Just say the word, and I will make it so."

"If I do that, your contract cannot be fulfilled." Morghan spoke staring down at the grass beneath her feet. "A pledge was made and accepted. Besides, I want to be his wife."

"You have no idea what you want, child. How can you think that way after sitting beside the man for the length of a few meals, some meetings in a garden, and a simple walk through the stalls of a bazaar? Why, you have no idea what the man is truly like."

"I know he is honorable, kind, and caring. Something happened to change him, and I intend to find out what that was and solve the problem for him."

A hand laid alongside her cheek turned her face to him. Unshed tears glistened in her eyes. "Lord Edwin does you no honor when he failed to appear when we arrived. If I suspect he is reluctant in taking his vows, I will stop the ceremony and demand another husband. I will not see you hurt. I had such high expectations for that man, but this!"

Connor's hand swept around at the sparse bailey.

"You mean more to me than any contract for goods." It was getting harder to hold back her tears. Morghan knew her father loved her, but as the daughter of a powerful man, she had been raised to know her place in life. Her birth had made her a bargaining tool, yet she knew his love for her was as strong as what he held for his sons.

"No matter what happened to Edwin, I know in my heart that he is my soul mate. If I cannot have him, I shall have no man." Morghan looked past her father toward the men approaching them. "Please, Father, let me try."

Connor's heart lurched in his chest. He was old, nearing fifty. Morghan was his last child, the one of his heart. At this very moment, her heart showing in her eyes, Morghan looked exactly like her mother. Just like Lady Maddlyn, his only daughter could turn his heart with just one look.

A deep sigh showed his resignation. "I will give you one month, daughter. When your brother Kerwin brings the remainder of your belongings, my orders will be to bring you home if young de Ballard has not accepted you."

One month. She had only one short cycle of the moon to find out what went wrong and enact a solution. "I will not let you down, Father."

"I never thought you would. It is Lord Edwin I am more concerned about failing me. I know well the determination you possess once your mind is set to a task."

"You need not concern yourself about Edwin either, Father. He just needs time to trust me." Time to trust.

Perhaps he should demand a week or more before allowing the wedding to proceed. Morghan was so very precious to him. To see her hurt would near kill him.

"Thank you, Father." Reaching up on her toes, Morghan kissed him on the cheek. "I know I can bring Edwin back to me long before Kerwin arrives."

"We shall see."

8

Morghan was not sure what she was expecting, but this certainly was not it.

The hall was large, though quite devoid of much furnishings. Three long trestle tables had been arranged in the center to form a large *U*. At the center of the head table sat two elaborately carved chairs. All three tables and the benches beside each were brand new and unscarred.

Besides that, no other chairs or furnishings littered the massive hall. No tapestries hung on the cold stone walls, and the rushes beneath her feet were weeks old and desperately needed to be changed.

Though the ceremony was planned for sunset, there was time for a few modifications before speaking her vows. This was going to be her home after all, and the sooner she changed it to her standards, the better.

"Welcome to Ironwood, Lady Morghan." Sir Henry bowed to her. "Do you remember me, my lady?"

"How could I forget you?" Morghan turned a beaming smile on the knight.

"I now hold the position of master-at-arms for Lord Edwin. I am at your service, so if there is anything you need, do not hesitate to ask."

"Your welcome is most gracious, Sir Henry."

"You make it easy to be." Henry bowed slightly.

The king rose from behind the head table, coming to stand before Morghan. "I bid you welcome, Lady Morghan." Lifting her hand to his lips, William placed a small kiss on the back.

"I do not see Lord Edwin about. Is there a problem that has taken his attention?" Looking in all directions, Morghan attempted to appear as if she expected to see him. "I expected him to be in the bailey for my arrival."

Morghan watched an odd look pass between the master-at-arms and the king. There was definitely an odd atmosphere in the hall. It hung about every person like a thick storm cloud.

The strained atmosphere only served to heighten her sense that something was wrong. "There was a problem at one of the cottages and Lord Edwin felt he needed to handle it personally. He should be back in plenty of time for the ceremony."

He was lying to her. A moment ago, Henry was all smiles and had an ease to his manor. Now he stood ridged, his smile forced, eyes looking anywhere but at her. The truth was something altogether different. There was a problem all right, and she would not stop until she found out what it was.

Morghan had patience. She already waited six long months for Edwin to send for her. A few more hours would not be overtaxing. "I pray the trouble will not keep my lord from attending his own wedding." Again, that odd look passed between the two men. "My father needs to ride at morning's first light. To delay even one day could cause him untold trouble at home."

Home. No, Ireland was no longer her home, England and Ironwood were.

"I assure you, Lord Edwin will be here in plenty of time to speak his vows. Now I am sure you have much to do to ready yourself. If you follow me, I will show you to your chamber." Turning, Henry headed toward the portioned-off spot at the far end of the hall.

After a few steps, Morghan turned back. "Are you coming, Father?"

"No, you run along. King William and I have a few things to discuss first." From the sour look on her father's face, Morghan knew exactly what type of questions her father would ask. Her heart was heavy knowing Edwin had purposely avoided being at her arrival.

No matter what either of them said, Morghan knew the truth. Edwin had planned on being gone when she arrived. The why is what eluded her. The people about her were loyal to her husband-to-be, and she doubted she would get any answers from them.

Morghan continued through the hall toward the small portioned-off area. This had to be their chamber. Surely, Edwin did not expect them to sleep in the hall with the rest of the men.

There were barely two walls separating this tiny area from the remainder of the hall. There was no roof to the area, and she doubted anything said in this space would not carry out into the hall.

Her mind drifted to her wedding night. Pallets stacked against one chamber wall indicated many men slept in the hall each night. The image of her brother Kerwin and his wife making love in the dark of night drifted through her mind. Neither was very quiet in their passion.

Would she be able to awake tomorrow morning and face the men in her husband's service if they heard her cries of passion in the night? Would she have cries of passion? Though her dreams always made Edwin a very attentive lover, she actually knew nothing about his preferences. Men did not speak of their love conquests, especially before their sister.

Her five sisters-in-law had given her every piece of advice they could cram into her head before leaving Ireland. If even half of what they said was true, she had much to learn from her husband.

"Where should I put this, my lady?" A deep voice sounded from behind her, making Morghan jump slightly. The man who stood behind her made her brothers seem small. The muscles of his arms and chest bulged as he carried her coffer of personal items on his back.

A quick look about the chamber said there was only one place for it. "Beneath the window I should think." An elaborately carved bed sat immediately to the left of the door. It took up the majority of the nine-foot square chamber with a single small table beside it. Two rough metal candlesticks sat atop, holding the nub remains of tallow candles. Tonight, she would use the fine beeswax ones she brought.

A small stone fireplace sat against the outside wall, with a tiny window to the right of it. Against the fourth wall, she saw an old leather- and iron-bound coffer only minimally larger than hers. An old wooden chair sat beside it. The chamber was devoid of any other furnishings.

The floor was bare stone. Not even the thick rushes that covered the hall floor had been spread in here. Someone slapped a quick coat of whitewash on the walls, but no other covering had been spared. She sure had her work cut out for her. The place cried out for a woman's touch.

"Do you require anything else, Lady Morghan?" In her inspection of the chamber, Morghan forgot the man standing behind her.

"No, I believe the remainder of work needs doing by me." Turning, she again realized the huge bulk of the man.

"If you should need anything, simply send Tommy after me. I am Daniel, the smith. My wife is the cook, and you can find our adopted son running about the keep and bailey most times of the day."

"Thank you, Daniel, I shall remember that." A bright smile saw the smith on his way. A quick bow and Sir Henry followed the other out. Obviously, she was not going to be allowed to question the man further.

Removing her cloak, Morghan rolled up the long sleeves of her rose-colored overtunic and prepared to tackle the keep. She may not be mistress here yet, but by nightfall, her vows would be said, and her fate would be sealed. So what difference did a few hours make?

No matter what happened here before her coming, she would set things right.

The wedding feast preceded the ceremony.

That in itself was odd, and when the groom never showed, Morghan began to worry. Though William continued to say Edwin would be present to speak his vows, the looks that passed between the king and her father were not reassuring.

There was a quiet, somber mood to the entire keep. No one smiled or jested as in a normal evening gathering. The hall was utterly quiet. In fact, it was so quiet one could hear the crackle of the hearth fire.

The ornately carved lord's chair remained empty for the entire meal. Memories of Edwin's smiling face at the coronation banquet, the way he had offered her the most tender cuts of meat and avoided the fish, flooded back to her mind. Oh, how she wished their vows could have been said that night.

Dressed in her wedding finery of cream brocade tunic, girdle of intricate gold links, sheer veil and gold circlet, she felt very out of place among the men of Ironwood. Many were simple men-at-arms, others she learned were Edwin's crew.

Few women were about. The smith's wife was one, and there were two other serving women who helped pass out the mounds of food. If only there wasn't such a rush to leave. Not even one of her sisters-in-law was available to accompany them. Perhaps the lack of women would mean a foregoing of the bedding ritual. One could only hope.

"It is time, my lady." Father Matthew's voice broke through her very rattled thoughts. A quick look at her trencher showed she barely tasted any of the fine-looking food set before her.

"Has my husband... I mean, Lord Edwin arrived yet?" Holding her breath, Morghan was not sure if she was ready to hear he wouldn't make an appearance. Was she to be wed without a groom standing by her side? Would that be legal?

When she rose, her father was at her side. It was odd how he and William had remained as quiet as the rest in the hall. "He is here." Connor answered. A quick flick of his hand dismissed the priest. "I want a word with you before the vows are said, daughter."

"I will not change my mind, Father. My heart belongs to Lord Edwin, and I intend to go through with the contract you made. Please do not try to dissuade me again."

It was on the tip of Connor's tongue to tell his child everything. Once William divulged the reason behind Edwin's reluctance, there were lingering doubts in his mind that the king's plan would work. He did not agree in William's assessment. Personally, he wanted the young lord brought before him and a good thrashing to take place. He was not above giving a good beating to bring the young lord about.

Still, he promised William he would hold his tongue and give his daughter a chance to show Edwin real love. In his opinion, Morghan's love was the only thing that could change the young man's life.

Pulling the veil down to cover her face, Morghan heard her father sigh. Accepting his arm, she walked toward where someone had placed a small wooden table. A fine white cloth covered it, hanging nearly to the dirt floor. Earlier, Father Matthew placed a tall wooden cross in the center and a golden goblet to one side.

No sooner had she stopped before the short round priest than the hall door opened and in walked Edwin. A young man dressed as finely as his lord followed in his wake. That had to be Robert, his squire.

She met the boy's father at the coronation and knew immediately he was the duke's son. He looked very much like the brave and clever soul who kept the Welsh borders.

Silently, she watched her future husband's stiff movements. Looking in no other direction but straight ahead, Edwin joined her before the priest. He wore, she noted, the same tunic and boots he had at the coronation. They were slightly wrinkled, and Edwin looked as if he did not care.

Men. None of them gave much attention to their wardrobes. Well, starting tomorrow, she intended to see to expanding his wardrobe befitting a man of his station. She was good with a needle and had brought several eels of fabric to use. She would see he was outfitted well.

"Lady Morghan? Did you hear the question?" Father Matthew was frowning at her as was her father and King William. Her mind had wandered off, and she must have missed what was said.

A hasty "I shall" was uttered to the satisfaction of everyone present.

She had best keep her mind on what was happening about her before she missed her own wedding altogether.

Grabbing her hand, a touch too roughly, the priest placed it in Edwin's large calloused one. A jolt ran up her arm and lodged in her chest. A quick look out of the corner of her eye said Edwin felt it too. Surprise shown for an instant in his eyes before it faded away.

Edwin tried not to stare at their joined hands. Only once before did he feel a touch like this one. The instant he touched Morghan's hand after disposing of the snake, he experienced the same phenomenon. He thought it odd then, now it frightened him.

If he drew a deep breath, he could almost believe he smelled Morghan's sweet lavender perfume. If he squinted, he could envision his bride was the woman lost to him.

What an imagination drinking brought on.

Prompted by Father Matthew, Edwin slipped the simple band of gold on to his wife's finger. They were soft, delicate hands. Long slender fingers rested trustingly in his palm, such a contrast to his own calloused work-hardened ones. Surely, these never saw a day's hard word in all her life. If his wife was a pampered lady, she would get none here.

When it was time to kiss his bride, Edwin lifted the veil away from one cheek and placed a chased kiss there. In the next breath, he spun on his heel and left the hall. His honor was done, his loyalty proven. He had no intention of taking this woman to his bed, and no person alive could force him.

His little wife—hell, the woman was nearly as tall as he was—would simply have to adjust to the way things would be around here. He was lord, she was now his chattel. What he said was law. If she did not care for it, she could leave right now and go back to where she came from.

Hate-filled eyes watched the ceremony binding the wrong people. If it had not been for the slut not being able to keep her skirts in place, she would be standing here right now, and he would be safe.

Morghan was far too clever for her own good. He had seen that in the way she properly prepared the hall and everyone for the ceremony. If he did not tread softly, everything he'd spent the last two years building would be gone. Oh, why did things simply not go the way he planned them?

In disgust, he left the none-too-happy hall.

A single tear spilled from her eye and rolled slowly down her cheek. Whatever happened to Edwin hurt him deeper than she first imagined.

Her hand angrily brushed the offending tear away. She would not cry over something she could not control. There was enough love in her heart to sustain them both until Edwin remembered what they briefly shared in London that night. Hope was all she had left, and she would cling to it for both their sakes.

Turning, Morghan walked to the bedchamber and slammed the door.

9

It was well past midnight.

Morghan sat alone on the huge bed in what was now her marital chamber, knees pulled up to her chest, arms wrapped about her legs. Never in all her wildest dreams did she envision herself sitting alone on her wedding night.

It had been such a long day. First the journey here, and then the discovery that her husband was forced to attend his own wedding. Now she was left to spend what should have been the most memorable night of her life, alone. It all pressed in on her to drain any enthusiasm she might have felt.

Leaving her standing before the priest, just moments after being joined as man and wife, had been bad enough, but now it looked as if she would be spending the night alone. Sleep tugged at her senses, making her eyes droop, her head falling forward to rest on her knees.

It was the most beautiful day he could have imagined.

Edwin stood on the edge of the tiny pond, thinking of the odd direction his life had taken. The sun was bright and warm on his back. A stiff breeze stirred the scent of hundreds of wildflowers behind him.

He needed this. Every time he needed Morghan, he came here, his mind providing what his soul cried out for. Edwin knew the instant she appeared behind him. Her soft lavender scent blended gently with the flowers to tease his senses.

As Morghan stood graceful and tall among the pale blue blossoms, the soft yellow tunic she wore did little to hide the pleasures hidden beneath. The breeze ruffled the sheer fabric and blew a stray lock of bright red hair across one cheek.

Watching her, Edwin stood mesmerized by the simple act of her delicate hand brushing the strand back from her cheek. Slowly, sensually, she smiled at him, the promise it gave reaching all the way to her emerald green eyes. Edwin's hands itched to touch the flaming tresses, just as they had that day in the abbey when he first saw her.

Stepping away from the edge of the pond, Edwin stalked her like a tiger does his prey. Lust, pure and simple, coursed through every cell of his body. Of all the places Edwin dreamed of taking Morghan, this was the single most favorite place to make love to her. He thrilled listening to her cries of passion floating about them on the breeze, the heady scent of sex and the flowers mingling to heighten their passion.

Not a word was spoken between them. None was needed. They both knew what the other wanted and needed. Hands caressed flesh still hidden beneath too much clothing. In silent reply, Morghan reached up and undid the tie that held his soft wool cloak in place.

It fell to the ground behind them, creating a soft bed among the blossoms. Her eyes drifted closed as his open mouth met hers. It was all the encouragement he needed. Hungry hands grasped at the tunic, drawing it off her shoulders. It joined his cloak on the ground.

Kisses, featherlight, trailed down the long column of her neck and across one collarbone. Edwin's hands felt what his lips would soon confirm. Skin, soft as a rose petal, large firm breasts, a tiny waist, the triangle of soft curling hair at her most intimate place.

Hands kneaded one breast, while his mouth captured the other.

Drawing it deep into his mouth, Edwin listened to the soft mewling sounds from Morghan's throat. They encouraged him.

Moving to the second breast, he slowly lowered the woman in his arms to the bed of clothing among the flowers. "I want you so badly, I can hardly wait."

"So do not wait." Threading her fingers through his unbound golden hair, Morghan held his mouth in place.

The need to touch and kiss every inch of this woman was rapidly taking every ounce of resolve from him. He needed to go slow, make this time last forever, for it would most likely be the last such encounter they would share.

When he woke, it would be to a different life, one he had not chosen and did not want.

Would he still be able to dream of the woman he wanted above all else? Would his mind be able to see his wife and hold to Morghan's memory, or would she be gone from him forever? The need running through him made it near impossible to think. What he wanted was to bury himself so deeply in the woman he held whom he never had to let go.

"You are the most beautiful woman I have ever seen. Your skin begs for my touch. My lips crave yours above nourishment." His voice was harsh, giving evidence of his need.

Heart pounding, Edwin fought against the primal need to quickly join their bodies. Blood pumped wildly through his veins, settling in his groin. He was hard and ready to join them. The instant her wet tongue brushed against his skin, his resolve broke.

Edwin's lips took possession of hers in a brutal kiss, meant to brand her as his. She tasted as he always imagined she would, the way she did that day in the pub before her father's men ushered her away.

One hand threaded through her unbound hair, the other lightly tracing its way down her abdomen. Though he desperately wanted to sink himself deep in her warmth, he would take his time and love to Morghan properly.

It was when her hands reached around to stroke his back that he knew he would lose the fight. A need, raw and demanding, surged through him, robbing him of any coherent thought. "I want you so badly."

"Then take me. I am here for you to love." Morghan's voice was a husky whisper. "Why hesitate? I am ready." Her legs rose to clamp about his waist, and Edwin knew his need could be held back no longer.

Slowly, he joined them. If this was to be the last time for them, he would make sure they both received a measure of pleasure from the joining. His slow movements brought soft keening sounds from his partner. They only fueled him on more.

"How can I ever give you up?" Rapid breathing made it difficult to speak. "I want you beside me for the rest of my life."

"I have never been lost to you, my love. Open your heart and accept everything I would give to you." Morghan's heart was pounding as her husband's body moved against hers. She was building toward the release she so desperately needed.

Pounding.

Pounding.

Morghan's eyes flew open. Total darkness met her probing gaze, a warm body pressed against her back.

The pounding continued, in earnest now. Struggling to get a hold on her pounding heart, she realized the sound was coming from the chamber door. "My lady, please." The voice on the other side pleaded. She recognized it as Robert, her husband's squire.

Shaky hands reached for flint to light a candle. The fire was nothing but embers. It left a chill in the chamber. The pounding came again. "Lady Morghan, you are desperately needed." There was more panic to the young man's voice now.

"One moment, Robert!" she called, hoping that would stop the pounding. Her heart was racing from the dream she experienced, her thoughts still on what she'd imagined. A twinge in her thigh muscles gave her pause. When she sat up, a wetness coated her most intimate place.

What in God's holy name had happened to her? Looking back,

Morghan discovered her husband lying beside her. She had not heard nor felt him join her in the bed. There was a look on his face she had seen many times on her brothers after a night spent in the passion of their wives' arms. He looked to be a man well sated.

The dream had been his, not hers. This was something she never expected.

"My lady, do you require any assistance?" This question was accentuated by a soft knock.

Moving quickly, Morghan grabbed the tunic she laid out the night before and slipped it over her head. The material was soft but seemed to chafe against her skin. Bare feet padded across the cold stone floor.

"What has you waking me so early, Robert?" Morghan snapped, opening the door just a crack. She desperately wanted to return to the dream, but one look at the squire's worried expression told her that was not about to happen. Her mind jumped to the first possible problem. "Has something happened to my father?"

At fourteen, Robert matched her in height. His sandy-colored hair was cut short. A blush stained his cheeks, proving his being sent after her was not what he considered his duty.

"Nay, though your father was the one who sent me to wake you." A blush warmed the boy's cheeks when he realized his mistress was only half-dressed. Turning away, Robert struggled to fight his growing embarrassment. Morghan found the boy's awkwardness endearing. "He told us all of your healing skills. There is one in great need."

"Prepare the horses while I finish dressing." It was her natural response. Many a time, she'd been awakened to tend someone who had fallen ill or been injured in an accident.

"Horses are not necessary, my lady. The carpenter's wife has gone into labor. They live only a short walk from the keep." The candle Robert held was fat and boasted three wicks. The light from it illuminated a wide circle about him. In it, Morghan saw the number of men who slept in the hall. It would be a miracle if they made it past half them, not wake a considerable number.

"Give me two minutes to finish dressing and grab my medicines."

"Again, I offer my assistance. I could get the medicines for you while you dress." Robert quickly said before she could close the door.

"I thank you for the offer, but…" Oh my, how to put this delicately? She did not want to offend the boy, but she needed to think of a kind way to dismiss him. It would not do to offend him outright, when his heart was in the right place. "I realize you aid my husband in dressing, but I require none. I have never had a personal maid and can manage nicely on my own. Give me a moment please." Before Robert could say another word, Morghan quietly closed the door.

Edwin lay on his back when she turned, his features relaxed in sleep. Holding the candle high above him, she studied his soft expression. "Oh, how I wish you could trust me. I would do my best to help settle your troubled mind." Setting the candle aside, Morghan reached out and softly brushed a lock of hair back from his pale face.

There was no time to dwell on what could not be accomplished now. There was a woman who needed her skills. But perhaps she could help Edwin at the same time. Reaching beneath the bed, Morghan withdrew her sewing kit. Taking the sheers, she cut her hand across the palm.

Blood welled, not much, but it would be enough. Pulling back the sheet, she dropped blood on the pristine white surface in several places. Removing the sheet completely, she placed several more drops against her husband's lax member. Perhaps if he thought the deed already done, he would not fight her so hard.

Hungry eyes roamed the length of the sleeping man. He was by far the most beautiful man she had ever laid eyes on. A broad chest held only a light scattering of blond hair. Muscles bulged in his upper arms and chest, even in sleep. One arm lay above his head, the other across his flat abdomen. His long legs showed the muscles a sailor needed to stand a tossing deck. Such perfection belonged only to her now. All she needed to do was convince Edwin of that.

Morghan did not much care for the reaction her father would create if he thought Edwin neglected to give her the wedding night she deserved. Her father's angry words echoed through her mind. "If your husband dishonors you this night, I will take you back to Ireland and lock you in a convent for the rest of your life."

A shudder ran through her at the remembrance of her father's hard expression. Ironwood was where she belonged, not some convent where she would spend her days kneeling in prayer. How could she find a way to set things right, if her father took her back to Ireland? Edwin was more in need of her patience and caring than some dried-up old nuns.

Life could not proceed on the course it was presently taking. Too many people needed what Morghan knew only she could provide. Whether Edwin accepted her as wife immediately or not for months, she knew he eventually would. The Almighty, her father, and William would forgive her this deception.

Praying her husband was just drunk enough that the ruse might work, Morghan pulled the covers back over his naked form. A strip of cloth from the sewing kit was hurriedly wrapped about her hand. The cut had not been deep, and already the bleeding stopped.

Tonight she planned to find a way to break through Edwin's defenses and reach his heart. No man could look at her the way Edwin did last Christmas, and not hold a hidden longing deep inside. After the birthing, there would be plenty of time to formulate a plan.

Sir Henry and Robert were both waiting when she closed the chamber door. Henry looked at her bandaged hand, raising an eyebrow in a silent question but said nothing. He simply held up his lamp and began moving through the maze of men.

Once at the outer door, Henry pointed to the right. The sky was beginning to show the warm reds and golds of dawn. Such a beautiful sight to start a new day, a day that would see a change to the rest of her life.

Every window of the small two-room cottage was ablaze when they arrived. Even though it was just before dawn, nearly two dozen men stood about talking softly. Morghan recognized Daniel the smith, a sleeping Tommy held in his strong arms.

Several others were only slightly familiar to her. Many she had seen working about the bailey when they arrived yesterday. A scream pierced the air. Everyone turned toward her, a silent plea for help evident in every look. These men were united in a concern that touched Morghan's heart.

"Make way for Lady Morghan." Robert literally pushed men out of her way. "She is needed more than any of your gaping looks."

It was difficult to hide the smile that tugged at the corners of her mouth. For such a young man, Robert took his position seriously.

Inside the cottage, a lone man sat at a beautifully carved table, elbows propped on the polished surface, head resting in his hands. Terror was etched in every line of the man's features when he looked up at her. "Please, my lady," the carpenter begged, turning pleading, bloodshot blue eyes on her. "Twice my Anna has given birth to dead babies. Please, you must save this one."

"I will do my best, though my skill in delivery is limited." Wrong thing to say. Morghan knew it the moment the words left her mouth. The man needed hope no matter how slight it might be. "I need clean sheeting and plenty of hot water." Turning toward Henry, Morghan was pleased to find the man already taking charge.

Orders were shouted, and the authority in Henry's voice brought instant compliance.

Slipping into the other room, Morghan took one look at the woman on the bed and knew it was going to be a very long day.

10

Edwin stretched and reached for the other side of the bed.

He had been well into his cups by the time William and Henry poured him into bed. The instant his naked body slid between the cold sheets, his eyes focused on his wife. She was fast asleep, turned on her side, her elegant naked back to him.

The damn sight had appealed to him, much more than he cared to contemplate. It was the only explanation for how vivid his dream of Morghan had been. His body actually ached in places that had not felt a woman's touch in far too long. And it was all *her* fault. If that woman did not smell so much like his precious Morghan, he would never experience such an intense dream.

Drawing a deep breath, her scent assaulted his every sense. It clung to the sheets, blanket, and straw pillows like a fog. Last night, he allowed William to bind his life to this strange woman, and now he was paying a painful price for that interference.

Throwing back the covers his muscles protested. Moving would be painful at best today. Perhaps if he closed his eyes and laid back, he could gain control over his rioting senses.

No such mercy would be granted him this day.

His stomach heaved, and it was a close thing to make it to the chamber pot. Once his stomach was empty, Edwin sat back on his heels and hung his head. He could not begin each day like this. In a year, he would be dead.

A movement out of the corner of his eyes caught his attention. The figure sitting across the chamber gave him a start. He was the last person Edwin thought to see this morning. Had the man not done enough all ready?

"I see you took my advice and consummated the marriage." Edwin heard the words but could not quite believe them. What in heaven's name was the king talking about? When he followed the other's gaze toward the bed, Edwin thought he would be ill all over again.

Several spots of blood littered the center of his white sheets. *No!* his mind screamed. No, he could not have done what this suggested. There was no way he would have touched his wife, let alone taken her maidenhead. He was sure he was far too drunk to perform any act of husbandly duty. A quick look down his body confirmed his worst fear.

A soft moan actually escaped his tightly clamped lips. The dream. It had been so vivid, he must have actually taken his wife's innocence dreaming he was making love to Morghan. Now his fate was forever sealed to her. Morghan was lost. Any chance he ever had of ridding his life of the unwanted wife and seeking the only woman he desired was over.

Hanging his head, another soft groan escaped his dry throat. The ale was to blame for all this. It weakened his defenses and allowed William to talk him into speaking vows he could never honor, and now it had distorted his dreams and caused him to take his wife as any willing husband would.

William did not need to read minds to know what the other man was

thinking. When Edwin dropped back onto the bed, he knew what needed to be said. "At least her father should be pleased."

That makes one of us. "Dare I ask where my loving wife is?" Edwin asked, squinting through bloodshot eyes.

"The carpenter's wife decided last night was the best time to deliver her child. Since your wife is skilled in the healing arts, she naturally went to help." Edwin knew how important this child was to Derek and Anna. One night while deep in his cups, Derek had confessed his fear for his wife's life and for that of their unborn child.

He could not imagine having to live through the death of two children. Another more serious thought gripped him. What would he do if his wife already carried his child? Could a child already be growing in her? If there was, it would be the only child he would ever give her.

"By the way, she sent that for you." Pointing to a goblet sitting on the table beside the bed, William did not move an inch. He sat in a small chair before the hearth, watching his vassal.

Tentatively smelling the contents, Edwin groaned. The woman was trying to get out of the marriage by poisoning him. The dark brown liquid smelled far worse than it looked. "I would much prefer you gave me last rites."

"I fear that is no longer available." A secret smile touched the corners of the king's lips. Connor had explained what the goblet contained when he delivered it. It was exactly what Edwin needed right now. "Come now. You fought beside me, facing hostile Saxons. Do not tell me you fear a few herbs in a goblet of water."

The smell made his stomach cramp. "This stuff smells foul. I believe she is trying to kill me."

"Though your behavior warrants whatever the lady deems an appropriate punishment, I believe her heart is in the right place. She means only the best for you. She is trying to make some good out of this odd situation. It would please me if you met her halfway."

Scowling at his king's words, Edwin drew a deep breath and emptied the goblet in a single huge gulp. The stuff did not taste as bad as it smelled. In fact, it left a pleasing honey taste in his mouth. Amazingly, it instantly settled his stomach. If this was the measure of her skill, perhaps his little wife could be of some use to him after all.

The door to his chamber opened, and Robert entered, a monstrous beast lumbering behind him. Two steps inside the door, the thing sat on his haunches and stared at him. It was covered in a rough gray coat, from the end of his narrow snout to the tip of his long tail.

"What is that?" Edwin asked. Robert turned around, and William gave a laugh. Even the beast turned his head, looking for something odd behind him.

"You mean the dog, my lord?" Robert began pouring a ewer of hot water into a basin, readying the items needed for the morning routine. Clothing was chosen and laid out, the shaving knife readied.

"That is no dog. It's a small horse." William tried desperately to hide the laugh erupting deep inside. The only dogs he knew that were anything near the size of this one was his own mastiff. Size was the only thing the two animals had in common. His was bred for war, this one for hunting wolves.

Connor had assured him there would be no harm to come from the beast unless his mistress was threatened. Then he was quite capable of ripping the offender's throat out. So far, he had been the most pleasant of pets. In fact, the beast chose Robert to follow about. The only worry William had was how the dog would react if Edwin mistreated his wife.

"His name is Gunther. If you ask me, I find nothing frightening about him. Gentle as a pup he is." Robert handed his lord a cloth and silently commanded him to wash. Edwin never took his eye off the beast as he began to wash the evidence of his wife's virginity from his body.

"Lord Edwin, your father-by-marriage, is preparing to leave. He has requested that I... Well, that is, he wants..." The boy was turning so red William finally took pity on him and finished the sentence.

"You may take the sheet, Robert, and then leave us alone for a time. We have much to discuss."

The moment his lord rose, Robert ripped the sheet from the bed and rushed out. Gunther took one last look at his new master and trotted after the squire.

She was exhausted. It had been a long time since Morghan could remember being this tired. Not since that strange fever ran through her home in Ireland had she worked so hard to save a life.

It was by far the most difficult birth she ever tended. While Anna struggled to bring forth the life, nature worked against her. The cord had been wrapped twice about the infant's throat, and she had been forced to reach in and frantically pull him from his mother's body.

Oleta followed her instructions precisely, cutting the cord before the little boy was fully pulled from his mother's body. It was no wonder the other two babies died. If it were not for her hearing of such a thing and knowing the solution, Morghan doubted she would have been so successful this time.

Tears of joy filled her eyes when the tiny boy drew his first breath and screamed, easing her troubled heart. Would she ever know such happiness? How could she ever dream of feeling the life of her own child growing inside her if Edwin refused to touch her?

The dream last night had given her a plan, but right now she was too tired to contemplate the subtle nuances of it. Perhaps after a quick meal and a nap, her mind would begin to function again.

The cut on her palm had been deeper than she originally thought. Twice now it split open mixing her blood with Anna's. Oleta saw the wound but never said a word. For that, Morghan was grateful. The last thing she wanted was for everyone to know what she had done and that she was a virgin still. Edwin would certainly not take the news well.

A smile tugged at the corners of her mouth. By now, the king should have convinced her husband to drink the herbs she left. Perhaps a few days of being sober would help Edwin see the error of his thinking.

The only side effect of the tonic she prepared for him was the fact he would not be able to drink. Even the smallest amount of ale, mead, or even wine would cause such stomach pains; only emptying all contents would help.

It was a dirty trick to play on one so unsuspecting, but the only way she could get through to the man was using extremes, and then it was the way she would act. Above all, Edwin was lord here and many people depended on him to protect and care for them.

"My lady?" The carpenter's tentative request drew Morghan back from the view beyond the window. The bailey was alive and teeming with activity as the keep moved through its daily routine. "I would offer you a gift, my lady. Something special for the safe delivery of my son."

What she really wanted, this man could not give her. Only Edwin had the ability to fulfill what her soul cried out for. Only time and patience would bring her husband to her. "Whatever you ask of me, I shall see it done. Name your price. I owe you so much."

Turning, Morghan looked out the window again. There was so much Ironwood needed, so much only a woman's touch could provide. A hundred different answers filtered through her mind, though none felt right. This man was an artist with his hands. Her request needed to fit his talent. Finally, the answer came to her.

"I spoke my vows last eve in the great hall. Does Ironwood have a chapel?" Morghan knew the answer before she even asked the question.

Ironwood was too new a holding to have such a luxury as a chapel and resident priest.

"No, my lady. I have suggested such to your lord husband, but never received a reply. After what happened in Normandy, he was changed to the idea."

"Do you know what happened to Lord Edwin in Normandy?" If she could get this man to tell her what he knew, she would have a place to start in setting things right.

"Only part of the story. But forgive me please, I cannot tell you. None here will ever speak of it before Lord Edwin tells you the story himself. He vowed death to any who spoke the names of those involved."

"I see. I respect your honor and loyalty to my husband. I would expect nothing less from his people." Turning back to face the carpenter, Morghan smiled brightly. "My request is for you to find some small place where a chapel might be built.

"In it I would have you place an altar, the design can be all yours to decide. I would like two small benches in which I may sit, meditate, and pray, one for myself and the other for Lord Edwin. Also a kneeler for prayers. If you believe a window could be incorporated into the design, I can arrange for the payment of it. All I ask is that it be finished for the christening of my first child."

All right, that could be never at the rate she was going. Perhaps faking a night spent in loving by Edwin was not such a good idea. What if in doing so, she caused more harm in her relationship? Edwin could believe his duty already done and need never touch her again.

It was getting harder to remain optimistic. Somehow, she had to get through to Edwin and remind him she was still the same woman he stared at in Westminster and escorted to the market.

Her mind was wandering. That proved just how tired she was. Right now all she needed was a small nap, and her senses would return.

A cry from the other room drew both their attentions. "You have a family to tend, master carpenter, I have a keep to prepare and meals to plan." Yes, Morghan was sure a hundred things waited for her, but the euphoria of the new life she held a few moments ago was rapidly fading.

Stepping out into the late afternoon sun, Morghan stood a moment watching the activity about her. News of the successful birth spread through the keep like a wildfire. Many waved to her as they passed; all held bright smiles and kind looks.

Her father left that morning tide, not even bothering to say farewell. Maybe it was for the best. She had never been able to lie to him and if he asked, she just knew she would not lie to him.

A fluttering from her right caught Morghan's eyes. A moan escaped despite her desperate attempt to stifle it. There, hanging from the wall walk where all could see, was the bloody sheet from her wedding night. Why did her father allowed such a thing? Tradition be damned. She wanted the thing taken down and destroyed.

"Morghan!" Her feet froze in place at the sound of his voice. Surely, she had to be hearing things. Her father should be halfway to the Welsh coast by now. The prickling of the small hairs on the back of her neck confirmed what her ears told her.

He was still here.

"Morghan, I would know the truth of last night." Oh god, how she prayed the sheet would fool him.

Slowly turning, Morghan kept her eyes downcast on her folded hands. Her cut needed tending and if she did not see to it soon, infection could take a firm hold. "Father, I thought you gone on this morning."

"Yes, I know you did." Connor studied his daughter. He did not need to ask the question a second time. The fact that Morghan could not even look him in the eye confirmed the sheet was a ruse, a lie to settle his mind and send him on his way. "There is a look about a woman when she has been well loved. You do not have such a look.

"I held out the smallest hope Edwin had done his duty when I saw the sheet, despite the fact that I knew he was too deep into his cups when Robert stripped him and put him to bed. How could you do this to me?"

Anger flared, but Morghan tried desperately to hold it back. Her father did not deserve to be screamed at. Besides, it was her decision. "I did nothing *to* you, I did it *for* you. That's right. I did it for you and for Edwin. If he thinks the deed already done, he will no longer fight against me. I will have a decent chance to win his confidence and have him accept me as his wife."

When Morghan attempted to move past her father, Connor reached out and grabbed for her hand. Morghan winced. "My god, child, what have you done to yourself?" The cut across her palm was beginning to turn red along the edges. It also hurt badly.

"A good cleaning and my ointment and by tomorrow it will be fine." Slowly pulling her hand from her father's grip, Morghan winced again. The longer she stood here talking, the better chance the infection could turn serious.

"This is all my fault," he said, sighing. Connor turned toward the gate. His horse stood ready to leave, but he wanted to wait and speak to his daughter before heading home and the problems that awaited him there.

"When William came to me and offered de Ballard in exchange for what we have plenty of, I saw it as a chance to make amends. I am not fool enough to think you were happy in my first two choices. You would have never done for them what you did for Lord Edwin.

"In London, I saw the look on his face and knew he would make an attentive and caring husband. Even after what happened in Normandy, I thought he would turn to you, not the drink." Connor started walking across the bailey toward his horse.

"You know what happened in Normandy?" Morghan had to hurry to catch up to her father's longer strides. Hope blossomed in her chest. Surely, her father would tell her what she needed to know to bring Edwin back to her side.

"I do."

"Then tell me." Reaching out, Morghan grabbed her father's arm to slow him. All she succeeded doing was causing herself more pain. "If I understand what happened to him, I can easily find a way to help. Please, Father."

Connor drew a deep sigh and turned back on his child. He wanted desperately to tell her everything, but his promise to William stayed in his tongue. True, it was Edwin's place to tell his wife, but how long would it take the stubborn Norman to come to his senses and realize Morghan was the only cure for what happened? The pleading look in her eyes was nearly his undoing.

"If I had not threatened to take you home and lock you in a convent, you would never have done this." Gently, Connor caressed the wound as a parent trying to comfort his child.

"Give me the month you promised me. Give me the chance to make this marriage work." His instincts told him no matter how desperate Morghan was, she would not get through to her husband.

"You have your time." Thunder rumbled in the distance. A storm was brewing out to sea in the west. Her father and his men would be riding directly into it, but Morghan could not contemplate the dangers. Emotions stormed and burned deep inside her own chest.

"This is my home now. I belong here, and these people need me. I love you. Never doubt that. You have been a good father, but now it is time I made my own house and tend my own mistakes. You cannot protect me forever."

"A parent can try," he said. "One day, the good Lord willing, you shall have your own children. Then you will know what I feel at this moment."

Tears stung at the back of Morghan's eyes. She did not need children to know how her father felt. Every emotion was displayed on his face and in his expressive blue eyes. She would miss him terribly but knew she was needed here.

"Will you see me off?"

"I would not have it any other way. Give me a moment. I will be there before you ready all the men." A quick kiss on his cheek, and Morghan was running back toward the keep.

"My lady?" Morghan jumped at the now-familiar voice of her husband's master-at-arms. A hand was pressed to her chest, trying to slow the hard pounding.

"I did not see you, Sir Henry. Is there something I can do for you?" Her voice did not even sound normal to her. A quick look at Henry and she knew he had figured her ruse as well. Could she hide nothing from anyone?

"Forgive me, my lady, I did not mean to overhear the conversation between you and your father."

"My father is a large man, and his voice tends to be harsh and loud even when he tries for gentleness. I am surprised more have not heard his words and fear him." After a few steps, Morghan stopped and turned back. "Do you know what happened to change my husband?"

Yes. Henry's heart urged him to say. He too had promised William he would say nothing and allow Edwin the right to disclose everything to his wife. But perhaps a hint would not betray his promise. "Not everything, my lady. I do know it has something to do with a betrayal. I believe he needs to learn how to trust again."

Well, that was not anything she did not already know, yet it started her mind to working again. "Do you know where my husband is?"

"Lord Edwin and a hunting party rode out at midmorning. I do not expect them back until near the evening meal."

"And the king?"

"He plans to stay a few days. Right now, he accompanies the hunting party."

Good. When both kings were gone, life could settle into a routine that could only help her cause. "Thank you, Sir Henry." Morghan smiled brightly at the man. "I must see my father on his way then tend to the evening meal. I shall see you there."

Eyes were watching the lady smile at a man not her husband. He could not have planned this any better himself. He had failed to get Edwin to stop the wedding.

The bloody sheet hung like a banner from the wall walk, pleasing many of the people of Ironwood. To him, it was a symbol of how much work was still needed to achieve his goal.

One month, the old man had said. Plenty of time to be rid of Louis and the baby, set his sister back on the course he began for her, and secure what her selfishness had taken from him.

11

No matter how tired she was, Morghan vowed to begin the seduction of her husband tonight.

Out of necessity, she confided her plan to Henry. It was not so much she needed his advice; her mind was well set on the course. No one knew her husband better than this one man.

The first step was to force Edwin into their chamber to sleep. Not an easy task. There were far too many places her husband could choose to sleep beside their small chamber. The great hall was the first choice. Since her father's men were gone, there would be plenty of room. Henry said he could easily find a solution to that.

Morghan never asked what that solution would be.

Edwin was gone all day hunting. Once all her questions regarding daily routine were answered and orders were set among the Ironwood people, Morghan stole away to the chamber for a nap.

Dusk was just beginning to touch the western sky when Morghan opened her eyes, though she could have sworn only moments passed since closing her eyes; obviously hours passed.

Leaning her legs over the edge of the bed, Morghan looked out the tiny window. By fall, she would have heavy curtains made to cover the opening from the chilly days of winter. Would Edwin come willingly to their bed by then? A month was not much time. Though she sounded confident to her father, it was a struggle to keep doubts from her mind.

What would she do if her plans failed? How could Edwin return to liking her and one day love her, if he found excuses to stay away from her? How did one force her husband to pay attention to her? The questions were adding up faster than answers.

Fresh rushes crushed beneath her feet. The aroma of lavender and other herbs rose to greet her. One request fulfilled.

Walking into the great hall, Morghan was pleased to see all the changes taking place. One of the men had worked tirelessly to hang the few tapestries she brought as part of her dowry. On the morrow, following the evening meal, she would begin work on a special one whose design came to her months ago. By year's end, it would hang over their bed.

Edwin never appeared for dinner. Morghan was not surprised. The lord's chair was given to the king William, and the conversation was easy. Not once did he offer any information on her husband, past or present.

Lighting a single night candle, Morghan stoked the fire and prepared for bed. Her plan would begin as soon as Edwin slept. Praying Henry was able to keep his word, she checked to be certain everything was prepared.

Turning on her side away from the door, Morghan feigned sleep waiting for her husband's arrival.

"Where in the name of all that's holy did all these men come from?" The loud whisper was lost on no ears. Was every man living in Ironwood lying on his hall floor this night?

The hunting party rode out just after speaking to Henry this morn. The sight of the woman Henry said was his wife, as she walked the bailey, had driven him to distraction all day. The hunting had been good. They brought enough back to feed the entire keep for nearly a sennight.

The king was most pleased by the odd turn of events and did not fail to tell him.

Now he was stuck. He needed to find a way to avoid his wife until he could find somewhere else to send her. Perhaps he could tuck her away in a convent so he never had to lay eyes on her again. That would have to wait a few weeks.

Could a woman conceive after only one time? No other woman had ever carried his child. He made certain his seed was never left in any woman he took to his bed. Last night, could he would have been too drunk to pull away and give her no chance of conception?

The answer both thrilled and haunted him. If his wife already carried his heir, there would be no reason to ever touch her again. William would be satisfied, and that meant he would have no further need to come around and ask after her. Yes, perhaps his dream did him a service after all.

Would it be a son to carry on his name, or a daughter who looked just like her mother? A tiny spot near his heart began to ache. No matter his feelings for the mother, he very much wanted a child to hold and love.

Never, no matter what it did, would he turn his back on him or her like his parents had. The babe would have anything its little heart desired. He would take it on all his trips and show it the world. Yes, the thought of a child was becoming more and more appealing with each passing moment.

"Is something wrong, my friend?" Henry's loud whisper sounded right next to him. Edwin was so lost in thought, he had not heard anyone moving about.

"I am lord here and yet can find no room in my own hall to sleep. Where have all these men come from?"

"Is there something wrong with your own chamber? As I recall, you have a rather nice soft bed in there in which you may sleep."

"Oui, as I recall, the bed was rather soft. But it is already occupied. By my *wife*." The last word was nearly a curse.

Henry struggled to keep his mouth shut. At the moment, why Lady

Morghan wanted to save this man escaped him. She was far too good for the likes of such a stubborn man.

Several deep breaths brought calm to his temper. He gave his word to aid Lady Morghan, and that was exactly what he would do. "I believe the husband's bed is exactly where a wife should be."

"Henry, we have been friends since we were barely out of swaddling. You know I never wanted this wife, and you know why."

"I know you have allowed one woman to cloud your judgment. She was never loyal to you and if you search your memory, you know I speak the truth. But Lady Mo—"

"Stop right there." Edwin no longer tried to keep his voice soft. "I don't want her name passing your lips or any other in my presence. If you must refer to her, you many say 'your wife' or 'her,' but never speak her name to me."

Henry clenched his fists at his side, struggling not to reach out and give Edwin the sound thrashing he deserved. The man was acting just like a pompous ass.

Thunder rumbled overhead.

If only Edwin would open his eyes and take a good look at the woman the king had given him, he would be pleased. After all, the two spent days together last Christmastime. What happened to him in Normandy was a thing of the past. Morghan did not deserve to be painted by the same tainted brush as the other. "I have never known you to fear a woman."

"What are you talking about?"

"You have a perfectly good chamber waiting for you. Yet here you stand, allowing a woman to drive you from the comfort of your own room. Have you turned cowardly?" Henry nearly smiled at the anger that flared in Edwin's eyes. "If a coward is the image you wish your people to see, my lord, far be it from me to stop you."

"You know there are still many enemies to our ruler. Word would spread quickly of the cowards that he gives titles to. How long do you believe his reign could last if he allowed such to hold the position he gave you? You make yourself a weak link in his armor by your actions."

Not another word passed between the two men. Henry knew his point was made. Edwin knew it also. Clutching his pallet, blanket, and pillow, he slammed closed the chamber door behind him.

"I never thought Edwin a weak man." William stepped from a shadow behind Henry.

"You may not have, sire, but I think Edwin believes himself such. If he would just open his eyes to see the woman you gave him to wed, I know his heart would quickly follow."

"Henry, you have a faith in the man few can claim. I know Morghan is the best thing for him, whether he believes it or not. Never give up on them. She is exactly what Edwin deserves. She just needs to get past the wall he's built about his heart."

"Trust Lady Morghan to do that, sire."

The scent of lavender was the first thing to assault his senses when Edwin entered his chamber. It wafted at him from all directions. A memory of Morghan smiling at him flooded back so quickly, it nearly choked him in its intensity.

Why had he stuck so closely to a promise made when he was headed off to war? The woman he made the promise to obviously did not feel the need to hold her words close. In fact, she must have turned to his brother the moment his ship was out of sight.

In London, Morghan openly smiled at him, and in those smiles, offered everything he had ever wanted from a wife. She was young, vibrant, and made his body crave even the smallest touch. A quick pain stabbed his heart. She was most likely wed by now, a child of her own due before long.

His wife's back was turned toward him as she lay in the bed. The night candle did little to illuminate her features. A long slender back was shown through the thin sheet. Dark hair lay in a single braid against the pillow.

She was shapely, he would give her that. The covering left nothing to the imagination. Shoulders not too wide lay bare above the top edge of the sheet. A slightly arched back led to a very narrow waist and wide hips. She would have no trouble birthing his children.

Children? Where in heaven's name did that thought come from? If his child grew in her now, it would be the only child he intended to give her. Yet the sight of her long legs brought a vision to his mind he couldn't so easily dismiss. What would it be like to have them wrapped tightly about him, her tender young body open to his?

The stirring of his groin told Edwin he would have no trouble bedding his wife a second time. In the eyes of king, country, and god, this woman was his to do with as he pleased. Could he so easily forget what was done to him and turn to his wife?

His body said yes.

It was time he stopped trying to drown in drink. Where did that get him? His men followed him into the skin of ale and took advantage of his inebriation. So many people depended on him, and so far, he felt as if he let them down.

Anger flared at the memory of this afternoon. The instant he took a swallow, he found himself heaving his guts behind a bush. William sighed before explaining the herbs Morghan gave him would cause that reaction every time he tried to drink. His sweet wife was forcing him into sobriety.

Standing here now, head clear for the first time in months, he could envision a future filled by a tolerable peace between them. Perhaps in time, he could even come to call her by her name, though at the moment, he could not recall the word the priest spoke to bind them.

Removing only his belt, Edwin flung the pallet down before the cold hearth. Lying back, he made certain the thin blanket covered only his legs. Hands folded behind his head, he looked across the room, taking one last look at his sleeping wife. Deep in his heart, he knew there would be no dreams of Morghan this night.

It felt like hours waiting for Edwin's breathing to even out in sleep. All the while, Morghan never moved. At one point, she nearly revealed to Edwin she was still awake. There was such a long delay while he just stood there looking at her that she thought he might just change his mind and crawl beneath the sheet beside her.

Henry promised her to do all he could to encourage her husband to sleep in their chamber, even if it would not be in her bed. One step closer. Edwin was in their chamber where she wanted him.

On silent footfalls, Morghan walked across the room. The only sound in the room was Edwin's soft snores. It was a warm night. Silently opening the wooden shutters, she winced when a hinge squeaked. A quick glance over her shoulder told her Edwin had not stirred.

Slowly kneeling, Morghan's heart fell when she saw he was fully dressed. What did she expect? He barely accepted he had a wife, let alone lie naked for her hands to explore.

Baby steps. Edwin would not change overnight. Whatever happened to him she had no doubt it involved a woman. It would take time and patience to recover.

Would a month be enough time to break through his defenses before her brother arrived? Kerwin was the brother closest to her. He would not take her back if she refused to go, yet she hated having their father know she failed.

She could not allow herself to fail.

Edwin shifted in his sleep, a lock of hair falling across his forehead. Trembling fingers reached out to brush it aside. A tingling sensation started where her flesh met his. Snatching the hand back, Morghan waited for Edwin to wake. Surely, she was not the only one to feel it.

When he did not move, she got more brazen. Ever so slowly her fingers trailed a path down one temple across his cheek and around one ear.

Still nothing.

Edwin lay there limp while every nerve in her body felt on fire. A dull ache started deep in her belly, settling between her legs. It reminded her of the way she had felt in Edwin's dream the previous night.

Sitting back on her heals, a tear threatened. If only he would open up to her and tell her what happened to so change him, she knew there would be a way to help him. Trust was something one earned, and she began tonight trying to make him believe he could trust her.

She needed no one to tell her how sensitive Edwin was to others. Just look at the way he responded to her back in London. That smiling nervous man was buried deep inside this body, behind the wall he constructed to keep out any hurt, and she had no intention of stopping until she broke through every last barrier erected and she touched that man again.

The deep sorrow she sensed in Edwin yesterday was not so strong tonight. Could she hope things were already beginning to turn about? Time was what she needed, yet her father limited that time. She was caught between two stubborn men. Which one would win?

Loathing to leave his side so soon, Morghan felt she had done enough for one night. Hundreds of nights lay before them, and though she hoped it did not take that long to build his trust, she would be patient for now.

Rising, she took one last look at her sleeping husband. Tomorrow was another day, and she fully intended to utilize every advantage she could develop.

Lying back against the cool sheets, Morghan looked one last time at Edwin's still form. "Good night, Edwin," she whispered, blowing out the night candle. "May pleasant dreams carry you till the morn."

Edwin opened his eyes and stared at the retreating form of his wife. Had he actually lay still and allowed her to touch him?

Her touch was featherlight and more delicate than anything he could remember. At first he could not believe she was brazen enough to come near him, let alone caress him. There were men in his crew that showed a healthier fear of him than this woman did. How could so small and delicate a woman be so fearless? He showed her nothing but contempt, and still she dared to approach him in his own lair.

The soft gentle touch of her fingers felt pleasant, comforting. In fact, it soothed something deep inside. After the first couple minutes, it became rather difficult to show no sign he was awake and enjoying her attention.

His breath caught when he heard her voice bidding him a pleasant night. If he did not know better, he would swear he heard Morghan's voice whispering the words. Could he be so positive of how she sounded after so many months of not hearing her voice?

Was his wife just close enough in tone to play tricks on his mind?

No longer could he blame this innocent woman for what another perpetrated. It was unjust. Though his heart was still hard, there was something about her that brought a soothing to his wounds.

Closing his eyes, Edwin smiled. What would she do tomorrow night? Would she continue to touch him or perhaps try something new? Then again, he could always go to bed naked and see how she reacted to that.

This could get very interesting.

For the first time in many long hard months, he was actually looking forward to another day.

12

The salty sea breeze wafted in through the open window, caressing the slowly awakening figure.

Stretching, Morghan felt every one of her sore muscles. She was so tired last night, after beginning her plan, she fell into a dreamless sleep.

No one needed to tell her Edwin was gone. There was a quiet to the chamber that said she was very much alone. Still she looked toward the hearth, hoping she was wrong. The pallet was empty, the blanket he used folded neatly and placed atop her clothes coffer.

It was late. Judging by the height of the sun, it was midmorning. She must have forgotten to close the shutters last eve. Edwin left them open when he rose. A warm breeze filled the room.

It was nearly impossible to get her mind off what she did last night. Since when was she so bold?

Since her husband decided he did not want anything to do with her, that's when.

It was not as if she were a shrinking flower. No, there were moments in her life when she was bold and even adventuresome. Last Yuletide, she acted bold when she allowed Edwin into her life.

They formed a thin bond in those days, one that could not be broken no matter how much Edwin tried to avoid her. Yet it still left her wondering why he even wanted to. Somehow she needed to reach the feelings they sparked those days in London and rekindle them into a fire of passion.

Every time she saw Tommy, Morghan was reminded how nobly Edwin went to the boy's rescue. A man who did not care for others would have turned a deaf ear to the boy's pleas and walked away. Edwin not only saved both their lives, he sent the boy to his ship and took the orphan in, giving him a chance at life.

She needed to reach that person again, the one who took on the defense of the helpless, the one whose honor would not allow him to turn a deaf ear to the boy's cries. She admired that man's compassion as well as his body.

Thoughts of what she did last night flooded back to her mind. Not once in her life did she act so boldly. But this situation demanded it of her. She wanted Edwin. She wanted his body, his soul, his love. Already she felt the caring begun all those months ago was turning into love. If not completely full, it would be soon.

Was she wrong to want a husband to love her in return? So many marriages were based on contract and agreement, not love. Often, love never developed. That's why husbands strayed and wives became miserable. Morghan didn't want that for the remainder of her life. She wanted Edwin to stay by her side. If he strayed, it would kill her.

She simply needed to find a way so it would never happen.

Last night was the first step. There were many ways she could catch his attention. Sooner or later, he would take her bate and she would reel him in like a fish on a stout line.

Looking out through the wide open back gate, her gaze settled on the figure of her husband, standing the desk of his ship. This time of day, it was not unusual to find the captain and one other crew member checking sails, rigging, and tie roping. Unless she was mistaken, the second man was Tuce, a man in his midtwenties, wed to a woman named Alerie. In fact, the woman stood among a group beside the common keep well.

What would it hurt to ask a few chosen questions. It was not as if she was getting anywhere on her own. Women often gossiped, inadvertently revealing things without knowing its importance.

Dressing quickly, she put her plan in action.

"Good morning, ladies." Morghan hoped her voice sounded cheerful and not as desperate as she felt inside.

When all conversation stopped, and each woman stared at the other, Morghan felt a moment of fear. Had she gone too far too fast? Wanting to know what happened to change Edwin was an ever-growing need in her heart. She was not about to allow a few nervous women to dissuade her.

"Forgive their rudeness, my lady." Alerie seemed to be the spokeswoman for the group. She was a tiny woman, only coming to Morghan's chest. Her hair was the usual light blonde of the Normans, and her clear blue eyes sparkled with a secret laugh. "But we, none of us, have been addressed as ladies before. That is a title none of us possess. Only you may be called a lady, my lady."

Morghan looked from one woman to the next, and they actually believed what they were saying. She never meant it as a formal address, simply a casual way to address a group of women. Their shocked looks made her wonder if perhaps in her eagerness to gather some information on her husband's changes, she stepped out of her element and these women would not allow her to become one of their confidants.

A covert look around told Morghan the woman wed to Edwin's men-at-arms stood near one corner of the keep, buckets in hand, apparently waiting their turn at the well. So not only did the wives think they needed to distance themselves from the lady of the keep, but they isolated the sailor's spouses and guardsmen's wives. How odd. Back home, everyone worked together for the betterment of the whole. She needed to spend time thinking on how to get all these women together.

Morghan was not one to give up when there was something she wanted. Right now, she wanted information on her husband, and she would do just about anything to get it. "Tell me, how long have your husbands been in Lord Edwin's crew?"

"My Tuce has been there since the day the ship was delivered two years ago." Alerie's pride showed through every word. "He was not satisfied in simply delivering the ships. He wanted to join a crew and see more of the world. Most of the men joined right after. All were loyal to Lord Edwin before he ever decided to follow King William."

"There were very few who chose to stay in Normandy," an older woman said, attaching her bucket to the hook and lowering it into the well. Gray hair lay in a single braid to the woman's waist. Heavy wrinkles creased her tanned face. She looked several years her father's senior.

"Sarah is right." Another woman said. "My brother chose not to trust in King William's cause, and now he regrets it. By the way, my name is Tigon, and my husband is Aftar, the ship's navigator." Tigon went from woman to woman giving each name and the name of their husband.

"Do not worry about learning all our names so soon, my lady." Morghan blushed slightly. How could the woman have known what she was thinking?

"Is my worrying that obvious?"

"Only to one who has worn the exact same expression. Tuce and I have been wed just short of a year. In fact, except for Sarah and myself, most of us wed our husbands after Lord Edwin took possession of Ironwood."

"Then it is difficult to think of my husband as a lord, not just the captain of his ship. My brothers sail their own ships but hold no title."

"It is not difficult for us, my lady, but the wives of the men-at-arms think us beneath them." Alerie looked back over her shoulder. Morghan's gaze followed.

At the southwest corner of the keep, about a dozen women stood talking, buckets in hand, throwing curt glances at the group about her. "They think themselves above you?"

"Yea, they do," someone said. "They will not come near the well until every one of us is gone."

"That is ridiculous. This well is for every person living within the walls of Ironwood." Morghan looked from face to face. This was incredible. "Why would they wait for you to finish when there is a stream just a few minutes' walk beyond the east wall? The stream is not befouled or anything?"

"Not that we know of, my lady," Alerie answered, an odd smile on her face. "But what fun would there be in one of us using the stream instead of the well?"

The remaining women laughed.

Morghan found it impossible not to laugh along with them. She liked these plainspoken women.

A movement on the deck of the ship caught her eye. Edwin was removing his tunic, the early-morning sun glistening off his tanned muscular shoulders.

Heat washed through her, remembering her brazen act of last night. The tips of her fingers tingled, remembering the feel of Edwin's bronze skin stretched tight over his chest, shoulders, and back.

Though she could not see the exact expression on his face, her senses told her Edwin was watching her. A breeze ruffled her veil, allowing a stray lock of hair to break free. Quickly, she tried to tuck it back beneath the concealing fabric.

"I can see you learned much from your brothers, the sailors." Morghan's face heated. She thought the curse she uttered was silent. Obviously not.

"I never meant to say that out loud." The other women just laughed. "My hair is always trying to escape the confines of my veil. I wish I could wear a simple scarf as you do, but fashion demands I be presentable at all times."

Most of the women gave her a sympathetic look. "I always thought it would be so easy to be a real lady," Alerie said, resting her filled bucket on the ground beside her feet. "But I guess we all have our problems."

You have no idea, Morghan thought, looking back toward her husband's figure. Something happened to the man, and she was not about to let anything or anyone stop her from finding a way to break through to him.

"We women are slaves to what a man decides," Sarah said, looking

Morghan in the eye. "For once, I would like to see a man donning what they demand we wear."

"Exactly what man would you want to see wearing a woman's veil?" someone asked.

"Well, there is a part of my anatomy I would not mind seeing my husband removing a veil," Alerie said. "I guarantee you it is not my head, where I would put such a sheer thing."

"Alerie!" Sarah acted outraged, though she smiled like the others.

"Like you never thought of such a thing in your day and age."

"Certainly not. In my time, it was Viking and peasant girl. And since my Mellic actually has Viking blood in him, it made for more rocking than that ship over there. The man gave me six sons." A sad look swept over Sarah's face. "Only one lived to reach his twentieth year. He drowned on a French ship during a channel storm."

All the women instantly sobered. They knew each time their husbands sailed, someone might not be coming back. "Do not worry, Sarah, you have our little ones to bother you. Soon the lady herself will be increasing, and perhaps she would allow you to tend her children."

All eyes turned expectantly on Morghan. Oh, how she wished that could be true. Unless she found a way to break through the wall Edwin built about his heart, there would never be a chance of children.

The women began drifting away, and Morghan headed back into the keep. Before she was completely out of sight, Morghan turned to take one last look at her husband. Their time in London was so precious to her. She needed to find the perfect way to remind him of what they had.

A pain shot through her left hand. She needed to get the cut healed and her mind on reaching Edwin. She would never give up on him and their marriage.

No matter what it took, she would make it work.

13

"Careful, Captain."

Edwin startled at the voice behind him. Looking down at the mess of tangled line in his hands, Edwin saw the reason for Tuce's warning. Shaking his head and silently cursing, he began undoing the mess he made of the two lines he held.

His mind was not on the work he planned for today. Work that would keep him far enough away from his wife; he was not tempted to seek her out and take his first good look at what the king gave him.

They would not sail for two days, yet there were always small things to be done. Masts needed to be checked; sails could have tiny cracks in the canvas, spelling disaster when out on the open sea. Ropes constantly needed to be checked for fraying.

Even the nets used for catching fish while on long voyages needed periodical maintenance. In short, there was no end to small busy work needing attention.

Normally a simple crewman would be assigned such menial tasks, but today he was not yet ready to face the woman he was bound to. Thoughts of Morghan were still too fresh in his mind. He needed to come to terms with the fact she was lost to him and get on with the life King William forced on him.

But that was easier said than done. Rowena's betrayal still cut him deep, and losing Morghan made his heart sick, yet sitting here avoiding the reality that he had a wife and duty to her was making him miserable.

A movement through the back gates of Ironwood caught his attention, and for some reason, he was drawn to it like a fly to honey. It was just a group of women gathered around the common well. As far as he knew, they did every morning using jugs and pails to obtain their daily water.

Though from this distance their faces were obscured, he had a gut feeling the woman in a bright blue kirtle was his wife. It wasn't just the better quality of her clothing that differentiated her, but her stance and bearing. It reminded him of the way Morghan stood in the abbey, silently watching the coronation. So all women of high birth displayed such posture. That would not help him figure out who William gave him.

A laugh rang out, and the lightness of it sent tingles down his spine. It was somehow familiar, but try as he might, Edwin could not put a face to it. He met many of women while at Turney Keep. Obviously, the king decided he would be happy to be wed to one of them.

Did he want to be happily wed to one of them?

His hate-filled words to the king rang in his mind. He swore he would never be happy with the woman given to him. He wanted only one, and she was lost to him forever. Could he set aside the disappointment in his heart and accept this woman? Did one night of simple touches clear away all those nights of feeling betrayed?

One night.

Last night, she knelt beside the grossly thin pallet he chose to occupy in his own sleeping chamber. Only a few feet away stood a solid, soft, and inviting bed. Morghan chose well that day in the London markets.

How many nights did he spend lost in dreams of her in his arms, the feel of her soft breasts pressed against his warm naked chest? Even now, the thoughts of his dreams caused a reaction in his body. He was hard and aching for her, wanting her with all his body and soul.

That's why he chose to suffer on the cold hard ground, covered by only a thin blanket. He could not have what he wanted, so he needed to suffer to keep the dreams away.

Today it was not the memory of his dreams that haunted him, but the tiny woman who knelt beside his pallet in the dark of night, whispering words in a language he did not understand. Her touch was so delicate and light, it felt like butterfly caresses and tickled his taut skin.

Never in all his life had a woman touched him so. The woman he took to his bed tended to be selfish and demanding. Often, Rowena demanded complete control and his compliance.

Deep down inside, he knew this woman who so quietly spoke her vows and watched silently as he walked away would match him in passion. Her actions of last night proved she would not give up on their fledgling relationship. But most of all, her gentle explorations said she wanted very much to have him allow this marriage to work. It proved she was willing to do her part, if only he would do his.

Edwin felt the tiniest crack in the wall he built about his heart. He didn't want to feel soft emotions toward her. He wanted to keep the hate. He wanted to make it last until she gave up and… and what? Left him? Turned from him toward another?

Marriage vows were one thing, but constantly showing contempt toward another person would only cause her to hate him in return. It was not her fault the king chose him for her to wed. Royal marriages were arranged all the time. What he wanted was lost to him, and no amount of dreaming would make it otherwise.

God, what was wrong with him? His mind was filled by fanciful dribble and not the problems at hand. Months of his mind being soaked in wine and ale must be taking their toll on him. Always before, he attacked his problems with a single-mindedness few possessed.

So what would happen if he turned that single-mindedness on the woman he was now bound to? There was no longer a basis for annulling the marriage. Oh no, his wild dream of making love to Morghan ensured that option was stripped from him.

What would it hurt if he turned that single moment of madness into an excuse to learn about his wife? After all, in the darkness of night, he could imagine she was the woman whom he really wanted.

It would make dealing with the king easier. William was not a man he wanted to cross. Looking out at his property, he decided one woman was not worth losing all he gained and built here in this new country.

There was a fast trip coming up, and when he returned, he would have his mind set to at least speak to his wife. He would even learn his spouse's name and try very hard to use it.

"She is very beautiful, Captain." Tuce said, setting aside the now-untangled ropes.

"Who?" Edwin pretended to look at anything but the gathering of women about the well.

"I speak of your wife, of course." Tuce's voice held a hint of "dah" to it.

How could he respond to such a statement when he had no memory of her face and had done everything he could to stay away from her.

While she tenderly and boldly touched him last night, he was very careful to keep his eyes closed and feign sleep. The thought of her trying to touch him again tonight made his body react.

His pulse quickened; his groin hardened. It would be sheer torture to lie still and allow her to do what she wanted without allowing his body showing a reaction.

Just the thought of her featherlight touch stroking across his chest and arms set his body on fire. Never did such a simple touch affect him so. If he did not know better, Edwin would suspect his tiny wife possessed some sort of magic Morghan had over him. While she touched him, he thought of no one else but her and what she was doing.

He wanted desperately to ask which one of the smiling laughing women about the well was his own wife. But to do so would confirm the rumors that he did not know anything about her. Though it was no secret he was not exactly a willing participant in this marriage, the bloody sheets displayed the morning after his wedding gave his men-at-arms and crew hope that he actually accepted the king's gift.

"Tell me something, Tuce," Edwin asked, turning from the gaggle of laughing women. "I have heard from a man or two that she is… well, less than sympathetic toward the men in my command, be they sailor or soldier."

The look of anger quickly flashing across Tuce's face gave Edwin a moment of pause. He was trying to get some covert information without coming right out and showing his ignorance of his own spouse. In fact, Henry was so angry with him right now, the man would not speak a word containing more than one syllable.

"If you listen to James and actually believe his vile words, I feel nothing but sympathy for you. What was done to you was unforgivable." Tuce actually spat over the rail into the water. "The man has ice in his veins, not blood. Hell, I would not put it past him to have arranged the entire event to make you look bad.

"I have never trusted the man, and do not see why you do so willingly believe anything and everything he says."

"I have known James since we were young. Never before have I caught him in a lie to me."

Edwin began gathering the sails that needed minor repairs. There were more than usual. "Still, using the position you grant him, he should have warned you what waited in Normandy."

Edwin knew he should be angry at the liberties this man was taking, yet there was nothing but honesty and concern in Tuce's eyes. For so many months, he was angry at everyone and every situation. Perhaps Henry was right, and he needed to let go of some of his anger and allow the life he was offered to take its course.

"I am but a simple sailor, signed on to come to this new land and make a good life for my wife and me. How you choose to run your life, keep, and ship is not for me to say, yet I would ask you to take those sails to your lady wife. The last time you stitched a sail, it came apart in the first good wind."

Instead of being offended, Edwin laughed at the memory. "Perhaps you are right. Any woman would be better stitching than I am. When it comes to needle and thread, I am all thumbs."

Setting the bundle securely in his arms, Edwin stepped toward the pier.

Deep in his heart, he needed to admit his curiosity about his wife was beginning to get the better of him. He wanted to ask Tuce or any other man standing about the bailey if they could point her out to him, but pride held his tongue.

Asking his men to direct him to his own wife was to admit he was wrong. What would they think of him? Not that many could not think any less of him than they did over the past few months. They had gone by in an alcoholic haze.

A flash of red hair escaped the confines of one woman's veil. Edwin's mind snapped back to the lock of hair that escaped from Morghan's veil at the coronation. How brightly they showed in the single ray of sunshine on that cold winter day.

His body reacted just as it did all those months ago. His fingers itched to feel the silken soft tresses as they slowly slipped through his splayed fingers. Squeezing his eyes shut, he tried desperately to keep the memory of her bright green eyes from forming. Too late. They came to him with the force of a wave crashing over his barriers. His heart pounded against his chest as he held his breath.

Her smile assaulted him next. In silence, the full red lips turned up at the corners, a slight blush rising on her cheeks. He was choking now. His lungs could not take in enough air to keep him upright. Any moment now, he would fall over, making an utter fool of himself.

He knew the worst was yet to come. His body reacted as it always did when thinking of Morghan. His groin hardened, pressing against the tightness of his hose. Edwin savored the moment, not wanting it to end. Morghan lived only in his memories now, and try as he might, there was no extracting her from the deepest places of his mind.

But he needed to stop the torture. He could not allow the visions and sensation to overcome him every time he saw a slip of bright red hair. He would surely lose his sanity.

How was he going to allow the wife King William gave him a chance if he could not control his obvious lust for Morghan from showing. He just decided a few minutes ago that he was going to give the woman a chance to make a comfortable marriage between the two of them.

Easier said than done.

Turning back to Tuce, Edwin began to ask a question but found himself alone on the deck. Sitting against the rail, Edwin balanced himself against the slight sway of the ship on the incoming tide.

A quick look told him the women about the well had moved on. With them went the woman who sparked his tortured thoughts. Was he strong enough to survive the torture the king forced on him? Could he see that lock of red hair again and not allow images of Morghan to assault his mind and senses?

He needed to find a way.

He needed to find a way to make this marriage work. No matter what it took or the sacrifices it forced him to make.

14

It was not difficult to find the wounded man.

A crowd milled about one end of the tiltyard where sand had been laid out in an oblong pattern. Everyone parted when she drew near.

Sir Henry knelt over a figure lying on the ground. It was not a man, but a boy. It was Jacob, her husband's youngest squire. He could not be over nine or ten. Morghan recognized the look of a boy trying not to cry before his peers.

"See, Jacob, I told you Lady Morghan would come quickly," Robert said, patting the younger boy's shoulder. His encouraging smile eased her fear. It would not be difficult to win these men over to her side.

Kneeling, she unwrapped the blood-soaked cloth Henry used to bind the wounded arm. There was a six-inch cut along the outside of his left forearm. Very little blood seeped out now. "Oh my, you did manage to find a unique way out of sword practice, did you not?" Morghan tried to keep her tone light, but still the boy took offense.

"I did not do this on purpose, my lady. It was an accident. I want to be a knight when I am grown." The boy's words were hurried as if he did not say them fast, they would not get said.

"A very noble goal to set your sights on." Turning toward Henry, she said, "This will need stitching. Could someone fetch hot water from the kitchen?" Another boy ran off. She did not see who it was.

When Tommy arrived, she pulled a spool of silk thread and a needle from her kit. Washing the wound with the hot water, she dipped the thread in the water a moment before applying the first stitch. Jacob fainted just as she knew he would. "Good. I feared young Jacob would try to fight it. A squire's ego is so fragile."

Henry laughed. "You know the way of boys very well, my lady."

"And men." The silent look that passed between them told all. "Boys of course are a little easier to predict. They have not had the hardness of life to toughen them." Henry found he could no longer stand the knowing look his mistress was giving him.

Shouting orders, Henry got the remaining boys and men back to work. It took eight stitches to close the wound. Removing her crock of ointment, Morghan sighed. Why does everyone liked using her ointment, but none felt compelled to tell her when it was nearly gone? She would have to see that more was made. And soon.

"Back to work now." Henry shouted when nobody moved fast enough to please him. Morghan smiled before her eyes settled on Tommy. Why was he not allowed to take practice beside the rest of the boys?

"Because, my lady, his mother refused my offer to teach him." Oh my, she had not realized the thought was spoken out loud. A blush tinted her cheeks. Around this man, she would need to be very careful what she said.

The job done, Morghan packed up her sewing and medical items and stood. Strong hands reached out to catch her. "Are you ill, Lady Morghan?" Henry's voice held so much concern, she knew she must look very odd.

"Not at all." Several deep breaths eased the lightness in her head. "I must have stood up too quickly." He knew she was lying. "I do have a favor to ask of you."

"You have only to speak it, and I shall see it done." Seeing her more stable on her feet, Henry released her arm.

"I seem to have run out of my ointment. Perhaps you could lend me a man to accompany me into the woods, that I might gather the herbs needed for a new supply."

"I can accompany you first thing in the morn if you like. Three others should be enough to ensure your safety."

"Four men? You believe I need four men while I gather a few herbs? Surely, there is sufficient work needing to be done here."

"Word came before dawn, of a Saxon attack on a small village about a half day's ride north of here. The king rode out some time ago to run the bastards to ground."

"Very well, if you believe so many are needed, I will bow to your judgment."

It would be pointless to argue. Men needed to safeguard women. It was inbred into their very minds or something. Far be it for her to go against a man's natural instincts. Taking a few steps, Morghan turned back to the master-at-arms. "I will speak to Oleta on Tommy's behalf this eve. Do not be surprised if he shows up for training on the morrow."

"All are welcome, my lady. A keep such as Ironwood can use all the good men it can afford." A frown followed Morghan when she walked away. Morghan felt warm to his touch. If he did not know better, he would think she suffered from a fever.

He would have a word with Edwin before the evening meal. Something had to be done to ensure Lady Morghan's safety. It was past time Edwin acknowledged the woman and set a personal guard to be responsible for her safety.

Edwin reached his arms out against the sides of the door jam and leaned his head against the smooth surface of the wooden panel.

Preparing his ship had never been so frustrating. No matter how hard he tried, Edwin could not keep his mind from wandering back to last night and his wife's soft touch. Never had any woman touched him so tenderly, not even while he bedded her. This woman was unique and deep in his soul; he liked that.

It was the hardest choice he had ever made, but somewhere in the late afternoon, Edwin decided he would stand in his hall when he returned, look his bride straight in the eye, and try desperately to forget both Rowena and Morghan.

True, William did force this woman on him, but he was not the only one in this mess. His bride was innocent of any deception and deserved a chance to prove herself. William was right; he placed his wife in the same bad light he did Rowena.

All day he'd tried to remember the name the priest spoke for his bride, but nothing came to him. Drink so soddened his mind, he could barely remember standing beside her, let alone what was said. Hell, he couldn't even remember reciting his own vows.

He knew the basics of what he pledged before God and his king. He swore to cherish his wife, but how could he if there was no memory of her name or what she looked like?

He gave only a fleeting thought to ask Henry or Robert. Embarrassment stayed in his tongue. What would his people think of him if they found out he needed to ask his squire the name of his own wife?

Two days sober and already he could see how out of control his life was. Life could not continue on like this. Too many depended on him, both in the keep and aboard his ship.

No sooner did he hand the fish over to be prepared, than James descended upon him in a rage. As a first officer went, the man was good at his job. Everything ran smoothly under his watchful eye. Yet several times during the man's tirade, Edwin found himself wondering if it was at all wise to keep Rowena's brother in his service.

"I have heard enough. If you have an issue, speak to my wife. She now runs the household."

A good first officer was extremely difficult to find. It took years for two men to learn to work in harmony on the deck of a ship. James anticipated his every order and managed the men working smoothly as a team.

Drawing a deep sigh, Edwin ran his fingers through his hair.

His wife was trained in the running of the keep. So why not allow her to use the skills she already possessed? Yes, his wife would have her way in this.

He would be gone often, doing the king's service as well as his own trade routes, more often than he wanted to contemplate at the moment. It only made sense for his wife to be in charge of every aspect of the working of his holdings.

A smile tugged at the corners of his mouth. His wife would be very happy he decided to back her in this. Hell, he needed to find out the woman's name. He was tired of thinking of her as "my wife." He wanted a name to go along with the tantalizing body he beheld.

Would she possess a soft name that would roll easily off his tongue? Or perhaps one it might take him time to learn to pronounce correctly? Some of the names he heard in the past were difficult for his Norman tongue to pronounce.

On the morrow, all that would change. He would inform James of his decision, and either the man lived under his wife's decisions, or he could find himself another position. A first officer could be trained; his wife was forever.

The thought of his wife made Edwin smile. Would she try again tonight to touch him? If she did, would he be able to lie still and take her intimate caresses?

Stepping silently into the chamber, Edwin stripped down to his skin. He eyed the empty side of the bed. It would be so easy to slip between the sheets and press his body against hers.

Was he ready to accept this woman and everything that came with her?

The next few hours should answer that question. And oh, how he looked forward to it.

15

Morghan held her breath waiting for Edwin to either join her in bed or take his pallet and settle in for the night.

Damn, he chose the floor.

Well, what did she expect? One night of soft touching was not enough to endear him to her forever. It would take more time, something she had plenty of.

Edwin was making enough noise to wake the dead. If she was anywhere near being asleep, she would have been roused by whatever he was doing. Straining against her curiosity to look, Morghan held perfectly still. Eventually the noise stopped.

Determined to let nothing stop her, Morghan eased from the bed and looked toward the pallet Edwin still occupied before the hearth. The night was warm and pleasant, so why was there a roaring fire? The answer came to her a moment later. Light spilled over his... Oh my, Edwin was naked!

Surely, he could not have planned this. No one wasted time building a roaring fire on a warm night unless he possessed good reason or was totally insane. It was obvious that Edwin was not insane.

What a turn of events he handed her. She could not have asked for anything so helpful. Then again, Edwin did sleep naked on their wedding night. She thought that night was more the workings of Henry and the king. What if she was wrong, and this was actually the way he preferred to sleep?

A groom was stripped by the men in order for his bride to ascertain the condition of his body and his ability to perform the required husbandly duties.

Edwin was so drunk he could not have performed if he wanted to.

Last night, he slept fully clothed, barely stirring when she touched him. Her mind raced through all the possibilities. Had he thought of her and covered his body last night, or was he now exposing it for her touch? Was Edwin simply falling back into his normal habit or giving her what she wanted?

Either way, Morghan was not going to allow such a treasured opportunity to go unused.

A small part of her hoped Edwin would attend the evening meal. Wedded for two full days and not once did he make the effort to share a meal. Sleeping on a pallet across the chamber after she retired for the night did not count as spending time together.

If not for her plan, she would be by now. But this was too important to her to allow a single chance to slip through her fingers.

What could he possibly fear from her? Never in a thousand years would she hurt him. Her brothers provided good examples of how a husband and wife worked together to form a solid bond. That was what she wanted from Edwin, a bond that would withstand anything the world tossed at them.

The first morning of their marriage, she was called away early. Yester morn, Edwin left—not only from their chamber, but from Ironwood before she rose.

This game would end tomorrow. She planned on being up before him, and if she needed to sit on the floor beside that stupid pallet until he woke, she would force Edwin to look at her and see the real woman he wed. Having patience was one thing; waiting for a very stubborn man to make up his mind was maddening.

Kneeling beside the pallet, Morghan watched the steady rise and fall of his chest. Why was she hesitating? It's not as if she hadn't looked upon his naked body before. She stood studying his muscled form on their wedding night before putting the blood on his member.

Tonight, that was the only part covered by the blanket. Head, shoulders, chest, and even his legs lay exposed—begging for her touch.

Who was she to disappoint them?

Softly, Morghan ran the tip of her finger along one delicately arched brow. It was a sin for a man to possess such beautiful long thick lashes. They shone like newly polished gold in the fire's light. She knew plenty of women who longed for such perfection.

Smooth cheeks? Yes, there was not one hair on his cheeks or chin. If she did not know any better, she would swear Edwin shaved before coming to their chamber. Could that mean he actually looked forward to what she might do to him?

Hope blossomed. Perhaps she had a chance after all.

Could it be possible that on a subconscious level, Edwin knew what she was doing and approved? Did one remember what was done to them in their sleep? If so, she had no intention of disappointing him. The thought that he approved of her touches gave her courage.

Leaning close, she kissed his cheek right at the corner of his mouth. When Edwin did not stir, she grew braver. Light nipping kisses trailed across his cheek toward an ear. Shamus, her oldest brother, possessed very sensitive lobes. His wife found early on in their marriage, a few soft tugs did more to stimulate him than all the kissing and caressing she managed.

His lack of reaction when she tugged left Morghan wondering if her actions were doing anything to affect him at all. Either Edwin was not affected by this action or simply too sound asleep to give any reaction. There was no intention on her part of waking him, just let him know on some deep level that he was desired.

Kissing down the length of his throat, she headed along one

collarbone. A stray lock of hair fell from over her shoulder, brushing against Edwin's chest. His breathing changed, and Morghan held her own breath, wondering if she inadvertently awakened him.

When nothing happened, she drew a deep calming breath and continued.

Moist lips trailed kisses across the taut skin of his chest, stopping at one nipple. Swirling her tongue about the bud, she mimicked what Edwin did to her in the dream. An odd pulsing began deep in her belly; a moistening started in the intimate folds at the apex of her thighs.

As much as she enjoyed this, would she be as brave if her husband was awake and watching? Would she be able to kiss and touch him if his eyes followed her every move? Perhaps soon, she would be able to find out the answer.

Edwin's long muscular legs received a measure of attention next. Dragging her fingers ever so slightly up the outsides, across the top of his thighs, and then down the length of the inside produced a shivering of muscles. Repeating the motion, she spent several minutes on each leg.

Lying at his side against the thin pallet, his arms were next. Highly tanned, they were just as muscular as his chest and legs. In fact, she could find not one inch of fat on him anywhere. As her fingers trailed over one biceps, she felt a scar. It was not very old, perhaps four or five months.

No, it was closer to six months. She knew Edwin fought in the battle against King Harold, and this showed he was wounded in that battle. Robert most likely sewed the cut together. Though the boy did well enough, he left the wound rough and puckered.

Delicate kisses traced the length of the scar. There was nothing she could do for it now. If only she were there when it happened, she could have made sure the stitches were small and delicate, leaving only the slightest evidence of a scar.

This wound would forever be a physical reminder of his participation in securing William's throne.

Was it getting terribly warm in here or was it her? A trickle of perspiration rolled down her neck, soaking into her nightgown between her breasts. Unlacing the ties, Morghan spread the material wide. Staring at Edwin's calloused hands, she remembered all too well what they felt like on her skin in the dream.

Raising them to her lips, Morghan suckled each finger. "Oh, how I wish you were awake right now." The whispered words caught in her throat. Her body ached to be taken as it was in the dream. Being privy to that dream only served to torture her now.

Taking the hand, Morghan ran it down her neck and to the opening of her nightgown. Easing it beneath the material, she pressed the palm against her hardened nipple. A soft moan escaped as she rubbed it back and forth over her sensitive skin.

Eyes snapping open, Morghan feared she did too much. Surely, no man could sleep through the actions she was perpetrating against his body.

The ache in her intimate area was growing. She should stop this before she woke Edwin, but it felt so good, she was loathed to give it up. This was the way she wanted to be touched by her husband. How much better it would be if Edwin was awake and a willing participant.

"I can give you all the time needed to come to our bed," Morghan whispered laying his hand gently across his stomach. "Just do not expect me to keep my hands to myself until you make up your mind. I crave your touch as I have never done anything before in my life."

Pressing her lips against one ear, she softened her whisper. "I could wish you would hurry and make the decision to keep me. I have waited a very long time for you to wake and see who was given to you. I know something dreadful happened to you, and I could wait a lifetime if that is how long it takes for you to trust me.

"Please let my love and my heart heal the wounds *they* caused you. Together, we can be strong enough to face anyone or anything." Her heart spoken, Morghan kissed him lightly on the lips and rose.

Her head swam. Iron will and several deep breaths kept her from falling back down onto her husband's body. Though she would not mind being so close, they were at the beginning of this game to win his trust, and it would not do to move too quickly and frighten Edwin off.

Perhaps she was simply getting tired. Busy days and too little sleep while she tried to break through Edwin's defenses were playing havoc with her mind and body. If eventually she managed to breach the walls he built to keep her out, all the sacrifice would be worth it.

Lying back on their bed, Morghan allowed the exhaustion to claim her.

Edwin lay perfectly still until he heard his wife's breathing even out in sleep. He desperately wanted to open his eyes while his domineering, brave wife leaned over him.

He hoped leaving himself exposed to her touch might be enjoyable, but nothing could have prepared him for the gentleness of her touch or the tickle of her hair when it fell across his stomach.

Had there ever been a bigger fool born in the world? He made himself mind-numbing drunk for his own wedding, and since that time, done everything humanly possible to avoid the woman. Yet here in the dark of night, his wife knelt beside him and touched him as no one else ever had.

The fire he stoked showed every last curve of her sexy form. Barely slit eyes saw what he hoped the light would provide. It only made his decision easier to bear.

His fingers itched to caress the roundness of her breasts hidden beneath the nearly sheer virginal white nightgown. It was a good thing the blanket was bunched about his middle. Right now, he was so hard with need, he just might not wait until tomorrow to face his wife.

In the past, he was the one to stimulate the women he took to his bed. Even the one he thought to take to wife did little to please him between the sheets. It wasn't as if his bed was filled each night, but now and then it would have been nice if they spent time on pleasing him.

Would it hurt so much to give this woman a chance? True, his wife was not the one he dreamed of. Last night, his dreams were not filled with visions of Morghan but a shadowy figure that remained just beyond his reach. Could the delicate woman who just spent nearly an hour touching him allow him to forget about the one woman he wanted yet could not have?

Again he tried to remember the name the priest uttered during the marriage ceremony. If he had not been such a self-pitying fool, he would be lying in his own warm bed, his body buried deep in his own wife.

Shifting slightly, Edwin tried desperately to relieve the aching in his groin. It would not be difficult to bed his wife. After all, her maidenhead was taken the night they were wed. His body's reaction to her touch was not only encouraging, it hurt. In fact, it was downright painful.

A pain crawled across his chest, ending near his heart. In the moment she touched and kissed the wound on his arm, he felt a stirring there, deep inside. Could it be that she managed to reach some part of him he thought well buried?

This morning, he left a simple wildflower beside her meal. They grew in abundance outside the back gate. Oleta tracked him down and said his wife was pleased by his simple gift. If a mere flower could be appreciated by her, what would she think if he left an entire bouquet or other gifts?

Perhaps while she was touching him physically, he could touch her emotionally. There were a few items he brought back from Spain she might enjoy having. Though he originally purchased them for another, this woman deserved something for not running off on him, but staying to fight for what she obviously wanted.

For the first time in months, Edwin felt there was a good reason to rise on the morrow. Actually, he found he wanted to get to know what his wife's name was and what pleased her most.

Did she have a favorite color? What color were her eyes? If she so enjoyed his little flower, she would love what he planned for the morning. There was an entire coffer of fine fabrics and silks brought back from the Middle East and Egypt sitting in a storeroom gathering dust.

At one time, he planned to share them between his mother and the woman he took to wife. But since his mother chose to side with his father, not even looking at him while they tore his heart out, she lost the privilege of receiving anything he earned. On the morrow, he would begin his own form of temptation on his wife.

Turning on his side toward his bed, Edwin knew it would be a long time before sleep would claim him. His body ached in its need for a woman, though he found he wanted none but the one who touched and caressed him.

Yes, first thing in the morning he would begin getting to know the woman bound to him before man and God. Morghan was lost to him, but this woman was here and willing to share his lust. Love would never come, but perhaps there could be an amicable truce between them.

Could his wife live with the limited amount of himself he was willing to share?

It was time he stopped living on the heartaches of the past and look toward the future. Would it bring what he needed or fall short of his expectations?

Only time would tell.

16

Morghan awoke from a deep sleep to the sound of angry voices.

Last night, it took her forever to fall asleep. Visions of Edwin's naked body kept circulating through her mind, stimulating her body until she thought she would wake her husband and beg him to satisfy the demands. Finally in the wee hours of the morning, she slept.

She needed to stay her course and not move so fast she risked scaring Edwin off. And that was the last thing she wanted to do. Starting over was not an option at this point. Her body ached from the things she was doing now.

Touching Edwin last night felt wonderful. The morning following their wedding, she took only a few moments to study his body. Last night, she learned many sensitive places. Who would have guessed a man's knees could be an erotic place.

Perhaps tonight she could get brave enough to lift the blanket and explore the only part hidden to her. Would she be brave enough to actually touch the place that made him a man? Heat flamed her cheeks at the mere thought of being so brazen.

Or would it take her another few nights before she got that brave? The way she felt now, it just might be this night.

It was not like her to sleep so late. Last night, she resolved to sit beside Edwin's pallet and wait for him to open his eyes. Now she needed to find a time during the day to seek him out and force him to acknowledge her.

The voices grew louder. Though it was impossible to distinguish their every word, she could tell two men argued just outside the chamber window. What were they thinking to argue in such a public place?

It was not as if Ironwood provided an assortment of chambers in which to hold private discussions, but out in the open like that, they invited the entire keep to witness the heated exchange of words.

An instant later, Morghan recognized both voices. The first was of James, Edwin's scribe and first officer. He argued with her husband. Listening in on another's intimate conversation was rude and definitely not the actions of a proper lady. Still, something about their voices compelled her to draw near the window and listen.

Staying as silent as she could, Morghan heard, "I have given it all the thought needed, and my decision of yesterday stands." Though she had not spent much time in Edwin's company, she could hear the anger in his voice. What decision could have possibly caused such a disturbance?

The instant the thought came to her, the answer followed. They argued about what she declared to James yesterday. Yes, the scribe warned he would take his complaints to Edwin if she did not change her mind. Since she had not, James must have thought to follow through on his threat.

"I have every faith in my wife," he continued angrily. "I am certain her mother taught her how to efficiently handle all the household accounts. You have other duties to tend, and I have been thinking lately you took too much upon yourself. It was easy for me to have you tend the matters I never found very easy.

"In case it has slipped your mind, James, things have changed in the past few months. We have many more orders for my shipping services, and only this morn, I ordered a second ship to be built. I find only one cannot properly fulfill all that needs doing here in this new land."

That news brought a smile to her lips. Even though it meant Edwin would have more of his time taken up by the shipping side of his business, profits could be put to use to benefit everyone.

Was she ready to be a sea widow so soon after her marriage? Her sisters-in-law dealt well with having their husbands gone for weeks at a time. Still, most of them lived on her father's land, a short half-hour walk from each other. She was very far away from her father's land and knew very few here.

The pause in their conversation was so long, Morghan thought James might be done with his objections. No such luck in that. If he was nothing else, James was determined. "I know you never wanted the woman. You wed her only because William forced her down your throat. I heard all about his ultimatum: 'Wed the woman or relinquish your title and lands.'"

A hand quickly covered her gasp. It was not as if she should be surprised someone forced Edwin into the union. No willing groom walks into the ceremony deep in his cups a moment before the ceremony begins, and then leaves the moment the priest announced them man and wife.

If she knew this when they arrived, her vows would never have passed her lips. No man deserved to be threatened with losing all he fought to gain simply because he was reluctant to take a bride.

A sinking feeling began in the pit of her stomach, threatening to heave up the remains of last night's meal. Sitting on her coffer, Morghan struggled to keep from vomiting. How could Edwin ever accept her when such a marriage had been so brutally forced on him?

Looking back into the chamber, a single tear rolled down her cheek. This was not how she wanted a husband. One forced-through intimidation would never accept her. Maybe it would have been better if she had gone with her father.

No matter what she did, would Edwin ever accept her? She thought touching him at night was a safe way to gain his trust. Besides, she enjoyed the feel of his taut skin beneath her fingers. It gave her the illusion there was a connection between them.

Her heart in her throat, Morghan struggled to keep back more tears. Her mother once told her there was always a solution to a problem. She simply needed to find it.

She already knew Edwin held her heart, and no matter what, she would not give up on him. The next sentence made that resolve a bit hard to cling to.

"I dare you to tell me the name of your own wife." James's angry voice sliced through her thoughts like a sharp knife through fresh bread.

Yet another lengthy pause stretched between the two men. "You were so far into your drink that you cannot even remember what the priest said that night, can you? In truth, she is not your wife and never will be."

The next sound Morghan heard, she knew all too well. It was the sound of a fist connecting with flesh. Morghan held her breath wondering who was on the receiving end of the punishment.

"Do not ever speak to me like that again." It was Edwin's angry voice growling at the other man. "I made up my mind last night I was going to put my past behind me and accept what I was so generously given. Nothing you or anyone else says can stop me. The woman is my *wife* and as such, deserves your respect. Besides that, I have made her my wife in every way important."

A loud gasp was James's reaction. "That is right. She was a virgin the day we spoke our vows. She is not now."

Oh, how that ruse was coming back to haunt her. What would Edwin say if he found out she was a virgin still? Would he understand why she did what she did, or would he use the deception as motive to seek an annulment? He certainly had the right to use the knowledge against her.

Yet Edwin just said he intended to keep her. Hope flared in her breast. Did her middle-of-the-night activities do as she hoped and somehow reached him on a deeper level? Through her simple touch, was she able to break through some of his well-armed defenses?

His next words started the tears in earnest. "I do not love her and never will. The only woman I could ever give my heart to is lost to me forever. No other can ever take her place."

Tears ran unchecked down Morghan's cheeks, dripping onto her folded hands, lying across her lap. It was getting harder to breath. It felt as if a weight was pressing down on her chest.

What happened in Normandy? It was obvious even to a blind man, Edwin lost the woman he loved. She must be a poor substitute for his perfect woman. Would he ever be able to accept her love? Or would the other woman forever come between them?

The voices faded as the two men moved away. She did not need to hear any more. She knew it would take time to get through to her husband, but now she was beginning to wonder if anything she did could break through the wall he erected about his heart.

Given time, he would… what?

Edwin could not spend every day avoiding her.

Was she only deluding herself into believing she had a home here?

Several deep breaths took the sting out of their words. After dressing, she would seek out Sir Henry and try to find the herbs she needed for the ointment. Her wound needed tending before the infection became so bad she could not easily cure it. Looking down at the red irritated skin of her palm, Morghan knew it might already be too late.

It was hot and stuffy in the chamber. Morghan knew she was beginning to run a fever. It was imperative she mix a batch of ointment this morning. By tomorrow, she would be feeling more like herself and would have the courage to confront her husband.

There had to be something she could do to get Edwin to see who she really was, and that they had a chance of making a comfortable home together. Even if he did not believe he could ever give her his heart, they could find a way to be civil to each other.

When she was feeling better, she would have enough energy to combat Edwin's painful words. When she felt better, it would be a good time to discuss her marriage. She would give him one more chance to come about before she asked to be taken back to Ireland and whatever fate her father planned for her.

Heart heavy, Morghan chose her oldest tunic to wear. It would not do to traipse about the woods, digging in the dirt in one of the beautiful new kirtles her father ordered made.

Choosing a long-sleeved undertunic of soft brown, Morghan made certain the sleeves covered her swollen hand. No one could realize what she'd done before she had a chance to rectify the problem.

A darker overtunic covered the undergarment, and a matching veil covered her long braid; a simple silver circlet and girdle held it all in place.

The hall was nearly deserted when she arrived, just as it had been the previous morning. Her meal of cheese, bread, and watered wine were set at her place. But unlike yesterday, not one small wildflower sat waiting for her.

A small jug filled to overflowing with nearly three dozen of the small pink blossoms sat beside her trencher. Morghan's brow creased as her finger ran over the soft blossoms.

How could Edwin do something so beautiful and loving, and then turn about and tell another he would never love her?

The fever was confusing her mind. Surely, a man who did not have any feelings for her would not defend her or leave a bouquet of flowers for her.

It was when Morghan rounded the table to sit that she received the greatest shock of all.

There, folded neatly upon her chair, was a piece of dark green material. Only once was she privy to anything so sheer. Three years past, her brother Shamus visited Egypt and brought back several shimmering veils for his wife. This one was as fine, if not finer, than those.

Picking up the bundle, Morghan frowned. I was much too heavy to be a simple piece of sheer material. Trembling fingers slowly unfolded the sheer cloth. Tucked inside was an object guaranteed to bring tears back to her eyes.

Three intricate knots made of silver intertwined to form a broach the size of her palm. Yet that wasn't the most beautiful aspect of this piece of jewelry.

Three emeralds the size of her thumbnail were mounted, one in the center of each knot. They sparkled and shone in the light from the high hall windows like nothing she could ever remember seeing. Where did Edwin find such a magnificent piece?

"Lord Edwin brought that back from Spain nearly three months past, my lady." As if in answer to her unasked question, Oleta provided the information. "He said it reminded him of a pair of green eyes he saw in London at the king's coronation."

The only green eyes at the king's coronation were hers. What a contradictory man Edwin was. First he purchases this broach with stones that remind him of her eyes, and then turned about and denied he could ever love her.

Morghan's mind spun. Exactly which husband was she to believe was hers? The one who saw a stunning piece of jewelry and purchased it because it reminded him of her eyes, or the one he'd shown the world the past few days?

"You have not touched your meal, mistress. Is there something wrong? Would you prefer I prepare something fresh?" The concern in the other woman's voice broke through the shock of Edwin's gifts.

"You must not worry for me. I am simply not very hungry." Though she was not certain her stomach would hold anything, Morghan broke off a piece of bread, added a small bit of cheese, and ate it.

"You are looking very flushed, my lady. Should I send Tommy after your husband?" The very thought made Morghan panic.

"No!" The force behind the word was stronger than she intended. Taking a deep breath, Morghan continued in a subdued tone. "Thank you for the offer, but I am certain Lord Edwin has many things to prepare before leaving."

Biting another small piece of bread, Morghan chewed slowly, washing it down with the watered wine. "I know the king searches renegade Saxons and may need Lord Edwin's aid at any moment. I have found that when men prepare for war, women need to stay out of their way."

Oleta watched a moment then turned to leave. Two steps later, she turned back. "May I ask you something, my lady?"

Oh no, here it came. Oleta was wiser than she looked. Could she have figured everything out on her own? "Certainly. What is it you wish to know?"

"Why Tommy?"

Her question startled her for a moment. "Why Tommy what?" Her mind was moving slowly this morning.

"Why would you want Tommy to train alongside the other boys? Why would you fill his head with a want to be a knight? He was Saxon born. People of our class can never reach such places."

"I do not see why his being born Saxon should matter. My lord husband has many men in service to him. Not all are of noble birth. In fact, I remember Sir Henry telling me very few are. Most came from common stock such as sailors or farmers. Do you believe one should be relegated only to the social class they were born into?"

"No, my lady. I believe one should be allowed to follow whatever course the Almighty sets for them. I am of the minority though. Many believe Tommy should follow his adopted father and think himself lucky to be offered that profession."

"Well, perhaps your next one can be given that option."

Oleta's gasp proved her guess was right on the mark. Until now, it was only a guess. "How did you know? I have not even told Daniel yet."

"I have five sisters-in-law, six nephews, and eight nieces. I learned early on to recognize the signs. If I were you, I would tell your husband very soon, or he just might guess the news on his own. From personal experience, I have found a man would rather be told, not left to guess." Oleta blushed at her words.

"Is there anything else you require before I return to the kitchens?"

"Do you know where I might locate Sir Henry?"

"He said that he and the men would be waiting out by the back gate whenever you are ready." One last bite of bread was all Morghan could manage to choke down. The sooner she got out and collected her herbs, the sooner she could make the ointment and heal her hand.

Downing the last of her wine, Morghan wrapped the material about her shoulders fastening it by using the broach, and then headed out to find Henry.

Edwin's ship was under full sail when she stepped out into the bailey. Nothing was said to her about his sailing today. Then again, Edwin had not said much to her on any subject.

A questioning look at Henry and he informed her it was a quick trip to Rye to pick up some supplies, and they would be back before the evening meal. Sailing the distance used a fraction of the time a horse and wagon would.

There was no doubt Edwin was happiest when he sailed. He stood the bow, legs spread wide to balance himself against the waves, shouting orders to his crew. Often, there was such a look on her brothers' faces when they took to the water. The sea was part of him.

Henry, Robert, and three men-at-arms accompanied her into the woods. Though she personally thought it a bit much, Morghan remembered Henry's warning about the renegade Saxons. Gunther, now attached to Robert, ran along just ahead of them. The dog was well accustomed to his mistress's gathering walks and fell into the old routine.

Morghan gathered a virtual treasure of herbs. Besides the three bags of herbs, Morghan found some edible mushrooms and even some wild onions. The stew would be nicely seasoned this evening.

Barking at something he thought he needed to chase, Morghan laughed and watched him run. He never went very far, returning long before she needed to head back.

The midday meal, provided by Oleta and carried by one of the men, was plenty to feed them all. Sitting beneath a huge oak, Morghan made certain no one could see her wounded hand while she ate. Like breakfast, she ate slowly and very little. Too much too quickly and she just might become ill before the men.

Squatting down beside Morghan, Henry fought the urge to reach out and grab her hand. "Tell me about my husband, Henry."

Morghan asked the question to delay him. The woman knew what he was thinking. "What is it you wish to know, my lady?"

"I wish to know the kind of man I am wed to."

"Lord Edwin is honest and caring. I realize the two of you have not gotten much time together, but I have a feeling things will change soon."

"For the better, you hope?" Morghan's eyes bore into him.

Henry squirmed slightly under her gaze. "One always hopes a situation can be made better in time. I speak often to Edwin about you. It would not surprise me if he seeks you out this night." It was a wish Morghan shared. "If you will excuse me, mistress, I will see the men readied for the return to Ironwood." Henry left, pausing beside Robert.

"Sir Henry, have you noticed the way Lady Morghan keeps protecting her left arm? I think something is wrong with her," Robert said between mouthfuls. Half his next bit went into Günter's mouth.

As squire to Lord Edwin, part of his job was to protect his lady wife. At thirteen, he was tall and gangly, his dusty brown hair cropped close to his head. His pale blue eyes never seemed to miss a thing.

"Aye, I noticed lad. I also noticed her flushed and sweaty skin." Henry feared he knew exactly what ailed his mistress. But confronting her in front of the other men would undermine her authority. As soon as the meal was finished, he was going to suggest they head back to Ironwood.

"Hurry and finish, lads. The mistress needs to get back to Ironwood before it grows late."

It was unbearably hot in the kitchens. An hour ago, Morghan dismissed Oleta to take a short rest and sent the maids out to weed the kitchen garden. She did not need an audience while she worked on her ointment. Besides, the fewer who knew her hand was infected, the better.

Only a few more minutes and it would be ready. A quick wash of her hand and clean bindings would see her on the road to recovery. All would be fine before Edwin returned.

If only she could cool down a bit, the process would go easier. Wiping the sweat from her face, Morghan forced her mind back to her task.

Henry was standing on the pier when the tie lines were thrown from the ship. Judging from the look on his master-at-arms' face, something was horribly wrong.

The last time Henry looked like this, the kitchens caught fire and Oleta had sustained minor burns.

About an hour ago, Edwin got the feeling something was wrong at home. Though he had not a clue what could have gone wrong in the short time he was gone, Henry's look confirmed something serious happened in his absence.

"I would speak to you of your wife, Edwin."

Jumping down to the wooden pier beside his friend, Edwin began walking toward his keep. "I have not been gone long enough for the lady to get into much trouble. Tell me, what has you so concerned you felt the need to meet me out here?"

"I believe Lady Morghan is ill." There, he finally said it. It no longer mattered if Edwin wanted the name of his wife spoken or not, it was time the man learned to accept the life given into his keeping.

Edwin stopped dead in his tracks. Henry stood his ground. After all, he just violated a rule Edwin laid down about not speaking his wife's name. "I cannot believe William would do this to me."

"Do what?"

"Give me a wife bearing the same name as the woman who... No, he could not be so cruel."

"I dare not ask what you are referring to. The woman you stood beside in your own hall and spoke your vows to is the very woman you stood gaping at in Westminster and protected from the fighting. The king did not give you a woman like Morghan, he gave you Morghan."

Edwin could not breathe. A band tightened about his chest making it near impossible to draw a breath. Morghan was here? She had been here all this time? No wonder he smelled her scent everywhere he went. How much of a fool was he to ignore the one woman that occupied his dreams for months?

When he first realized he wanted to care for his own wife, Edwin thought he might have lost his mind. First Rowena, and then Morghan. Now his wife. He was confused, thinking his soul fickle.

"Wait." Henry reached out to stop him before Edwin took a step. He did not want to wait. Edwin wanted to shout his joy and race into Ironwood to find the one woman who held his dreams.

Henry's grip only tightened on his arm. Looking down at it, Edwin then looked up into his friend's clear blue eyes. "I did not lie when I said she was ill. I took her into the woods to gather some herbs just after you sailed this morning. By the time we returned, she was flushed with fever and barely able to stand."

Again, Edwin found himself unable to breath. What a fool he'd been. If Morghan was ill, it was his fault.

He could have opened his eyes and looked at her last night and seen who was given to him. If he had, would Morghan be ill right now?

He needed to go to her. His arms ached to hold her. All this time wasted through his stubbornness.

Well, it ended here and now. Whatever he needed to do to make it up to her, he would. He would go so far as to crawl on his knees before her and beg her forgiveness. "Where is she?" The desperation in his voice was there for all to hear.

"Last I saw, Lady Morghan was in the kitchens making some sort of ointment." Edwin took off running. Nothing mattered right now but getting to his wife and praying his friend was exaggerating.

Stopping at the kitchen door, Edwin stood breathlessly staring at the woman he thought never to see again. She was every dream he had coming to life before his eyes.

Henry was right. Morghan was ill. Her left arm was cradled against her body, her movements stiff, her gait a small shuffle.

She moved slightly hunched over, and even from this distance he could tell she was in pain. Oh god. This was all his fault. What kind of fool allowed his wife to become this ill and not even notice?

The piece of green material he left for her this morning was neatly folded and laid on the table. Morghan's veil was also gone. It lay across a bench half slid beneath the worktable. Unbound bright red hair was soaked in sweat.

"Morghan?"

Turning, Morghan's breath caught at the sound of her name on Edwin's lips. How she longed to hear that single word from him. Now she did, and it could be too late.

Their eyes met and held. There was recognition in Edwin's sea-green gaze. He finally acknowledged the woman he was wed to.

Standing still was costing her dearly. Oh, how she longed to see that look on his face.

Finally, Edwin knew who she was.

An instant later, Edwin was moving toward her.

As if in slow motion, Morghan watched him enter the kitchen and draw near. There was so much she wanted to say to him, but no sound would come out. A darkness was pulling at her.

Desperately trying to focus on her husband, the dark became relentless.

The instant his hand touched her, the darkness won.

17

Edwin could do nothing but stare at the woman in his arms.

For six months, he had dreamed and prayed for this moment. Well, not quite this moment. He did not want Morghan unconscious, the heat of her fever burning through his tunic, scorching his skin. Surely, God was not cruel enough to give Morghan back to him one moment, and then take her in the next.

Sorrow-filled eyes looked up at his friend. How could he have allowed this to happen? Why had he refused to open his eyes and see the gift given him? The king tried that first day, but being the drunken sod he was, self-pity would not allow him to listen.

Still, Morghan knew. She came to him two nights in a row and knelt beside his stubborn pigheaded self and tried to reach through the wall he built about his heart.

All this because one woman, who never deserved his trust, betrayed him. What a fool he was.

Each night he was warming to his wife, not even knowing it was Morghan. Somewhere deep in his subconscious, he must have known it was the woman he desired. Why else would he begin to soften to her so quickly?

The broach he purchased in Spain reminding him so much of her eyes now lay neatly atop the green mantle he laid at her eating place this morn.

Lifting his wife in his arms, Edwin eased down on the bench, gently moving them aside and settling Morghan on his lap. Her head lolled against his shoulder, the heat of her body burned through to his thighs and chest.

Fever radiated from every place on her body. A slightly shaking hand brushed damp hair back from her face.

"Good heavens!" Oleta's voice gasped from the back door. The basket she was carrying dropped to the stone floor, and several vegetables rolled out. "What happened to her?" In the next moment, the cook was kneeling beside her mistress. "Her fever burns hot. We must get it down quickly."

Henry watched while Edwin continued to sit there, cradling his unconscious wife, staring into her blank features. Guilt was written in every aspect of his face. Edwin was no longer thinking, just feeling. If someone did not take action soon, Morghan could very well lose her life.

"We need Robert," Henry announced. A squire developed many talents, medicine being only one. "He will know the best course to take." Oleta nodded but didn't move. Tear-filled eyes turned on the master-at-arms.

How had she missed just how ill her mistress was becoming? No, lately she thought more about herself than anyone else. Just this morning, she thought something was wrong but said nothing. Guilt settled firmly in her heart. She liked this mistress and would do nothing to ever harm her.

"Hurry, before it is too late." Henry's impatience was shown in his shout. "Do you want your mistress to die?" His commanding tone broached no argument. Oleta ran off.

"Edwin." Henry tried to soften his tone but got no response.

Time was of the essence, and he was surrounded by idiots. "Lord Edwin, listen to me. I have sent the cook for Robert. The lad will know what to do for you." Still no reaction. Guilt had a very firm hold on the man, but there was no time to indulge it. "Edwin!" he shouted in his best "I am master-at-arms, you had better listen to me" voice. That got a response.

"Do you need help getting your wife to your chambers, or can you manage on your own?"

"I never meant for her to die. You must believe me, Henry."

"I do. But now is not the time for self-pity. Morghan is very ill, and we must see to her needs."

"This is all my fault."

"Yes, it is." There was no reason to lie to the man. "If you had not been so stubborn, Morghan would not have done what she thought necessary." Henry softened his tone slightly. "Listen to me, no one can change the actions of the past. They are done and over. It is what we do from here on out that counts. Get Morghan to your chamber so Robert can see to her."

Lifting his wife, Edwin seemed to snap out of whatever pitiful hole he had crawled into. In their chamber, he paused to glance at the pallet rolled and set against the far wall. Could he have been a bigger fool? From now on, they would share the same bed as a true husband and wife.

Gently laying Morghan down, he inspected her swollen hand. It was a good thing her wedding ring was slightly big the night he slipped it onto her finger. It now pressed into the swollen flesh. Drawing his knife, Edwin cut away the tight-fitting material of her undertunic. The sight beneath made his stomach turn.

On one or two occasions when a wound on board a ship had not been tended properly, the simplest of cuts festered. But there was nothing in his memory to compare this to.

Angry red flesh surrounded a deep wound across the palm of her left hand. "How could this happen?" Edwin whispered.

"How much of your wedding night do you remember?" Henry's voice still held a note of anger.

"Not much. After speaking my vows, I went to the wall walk and drank myself nearly unconscious. I believe you and Robert stripped me and put me to bed. The rest is a blank." Though he remembered the dream, he was not about to tell Henry about it or the cost to him.

"Father Matthew said he wanted to wait until you were sober before performing the ceremony. Neither William or Morghan's father would allow any delays." Opening one coffer lid, Henry shut it immediately. Moving to the next, he found Morghan's belongings. He should have known they would be in the one that boasted inlaid bone in a rose design.

"At one point, you seemed to recognize Morghan. The king and I both held out the hope you would raise the veil completely and take a good look at your bride." Moving aside her clothes, Henry finally found the object he sought. "Strip her," he said, handing over a nightgown.

Fumbling hands unlaced the ties and eased the overtunic and undertunic from the limp body. Next came a very thin chemise. "What does my drunken mess of a wedding night have to do with a cut hand? You told me Morghan was out on the practice field yesterday. Could this have been done by one of those bumbling fools I hired for you to train?"

"Do you honestly believe I would allow anyone to hurt your wife like that? Use your mind, Edwin. Would a cut from yesterday fester that quickly? The ointment she used on young Jacob has his wound nicely sealed today. I saw the look in her face when she realized there was only enough ointment for one application. She sacrificed her own health to heal the boy."

If Morghan has not been cut on the practice field, then exactly when? The answer fell like pieces into a puzzle. The blood on his sheets and member was not virginal blood, it was from her hand. "That's right." Henry stated. "Morghan cut herself and bled on the sheets to save your honor. Do you think Rowena would have done the same for you? Why, the whore could not even wait for your return to spread her thighs for your brother."

Edwin pulled back the punch an instant before it smashed into Henry's jaw. Anger blazed in his face like a storm-tossed sea. Every muscle of his body stood ready to pounce. "Never," he growled. "Never say that whore's name in this house again. Friend or not, you can find another position away from here."

"Forbidding all to speak her name will not make her and what she did to you go away." When Edwin grabbed for the nightgown, Henry held it a second longer. "I knew what she was before we left Normandy. The king knew it well. Why do you think Morghan was set beside you at the feast? The moment your eyes locked in Westminster, it was decided she would be your wife.

"Secrets do nothing but hurt. The king forbid me that night at the feast from telling you Morghan was already promised as your wife. Both secrets have caused nothing but pain. Now you would keep what happened in Normandy a secret from your wife? Can you not see that telling the truth from the start should have been the best way to proceed?

"If you were honest and truthful with the woman, you would not have wasted the first three days of your marriage in an angry drunken haze."

Edwin tried not to listen as he dressed his fevered wife. He was such a fool to allow this to happen. Instead of dreaming of Morghan, he should have let go of his hate and anger and taken a good look at who was actually given into his care.

Guilt gripped his guts like an iron band. Honor was not much better. It was honor that made him return to Normandy to keep a promise made in the heat of passion. It was bruised pride that refused to accept what they did to him. It was about time he allowed his heart to rule his life, not his emotions.

Before he could form a reasonable response, Robert entered the chamber. "I was told Lady Morghan needed…" His words trailed off when his eyes settled on the still woman in the bed.

"I need you to help me save her." Edwin's words were begging, his eyes making a plea for the young man's help.

"Is she ill? I know nothing about illness." Pointing to the woman on the bed, he added, "That is your lady wife's place."

"Morghan is ill only because a cut became infected." Holding up her hand, Edwin showed his squire the wound. "You know about wounds. This is a wound." Now he sounded as if he was speaking to a dense child. "Tend it."

"I know about stitching and binding battlefield wounds such as a sword cut or even that from an ax. That does not look to be made by either."

Edwin ran his fingers through his hair trying desperately to calm his raging temper. Why was everyone just standing here watching his wife die? Henry stood back glaring at him. Robert was actually arguing with him. "I care not what kind of wound it is, I want you to tend it. *Now!*"

Robert paled slightly beneath his normal slightly tanned complexion. Since the day the king gave his services over to this man, not once was Edwin anything but kind and gentle with him. Even while deep into his cups, the man never struck him or yelled obscenities like other.

"I will need hot water, some clean rags, and of course the ointment Lady Morghan said she would be making today." Though his voice shook slightly, Robert stared directly at his lord when he made the request.

Between Oleta and Henry, all the items were gathered. Twenty minutes later, the squire announced he could do no more to help. If her fever went any higher, Edwin was to bathe his wife in cool water until it broke.

Since he could do no more, Robert left, Henry fast on his heels.

While Morghan lay there unconscious, Edwin took a good look about. Just as in his hall, his private chambers had undergone subtle changes. The first was the intricate coffer Henry pulled his wife's gown from. It was made from solid oak, the metal bands holding the slats together, a polished steel. Intricate rose designs were scattered about, created with tiny fragments of bone.

In comparison, his was a plain pine, nailed together instead of banded. They looked to hold an equal amount, yet Morghan's held the scent of lavender, the scent he was quickly consigning to her.

There were other more subtle changes. The table beside the bed held a neat row of small glass bottles. Each was a different color. The blue one smelled of lavender, a scent he was quickly coming to like. The pink one held a rose scent. The green smelled of spring. There were two others he could not quite name.

He loved her lavender scent, but wondered what the others would smell like on her skin. Perhaps one day he would earn the right to know. That was if he could get this woman to care for him.

He was ten kinds of a fool to allow someone who deserved nothing from him to rule his life. If only he had listened to what the king tried to tell him instead of acting the fool, he would be holding Morghan in loving arms right now, not watching her through frightened eyes.

His perusal of the chamber continued on to the walls. Beautiful tapestries lined every square inch of exposed whitewash. His mother never possessed the skill of sewing. A straight line escaped her most days. These were so lifelike they made him actually believe he could smell the delicate flowers, feel the breeze, or see the mountains.

Though they were all magnificent, it was the one over his bed that drew closer inspection. It was a ship. A very familiar ship. It was… his ship. To his knowledge, Morghan had never been aboard his ship. He did remember her asking if the tall ship docked in London was his, but that was as far as it went. She must have done a great study of it before she left.

Taking several steps closer, Edwin stared at the tiny figure standing on the deck. His breath caught when he realized it was him. "You have such talent Morghan, it fairly takes my breath away."

Guilt raced through him, drawing his attention back to the still form. Henry was right. If only he opened his eyes and seen who had been given to him, none of this would have happened. This entire situation was his fault, and somehow he needed to find a way to make it up to her.

"My lord?" Oleta stood at the chamber door, a bowl of stew and a chunk of bread in her hand. "I brought you something to eat." It was kind of her, but at the moment even the thought of eating made his stomach turn. "Lady Morghan has quite a talent, does she not?"

"She made all of these?" Edwin asked despite the fact he already knew the answer.

"Aye. Told me herself she enjoyed weaving and dyeing her own wool. Perhaps when she is feeling better, you could allow her the store of wool sitting in the weaver's hut rotting."

"When my wife is feeling better, she can have anything her heart desires." There was a slight catch in his voice. A quick look at Oleta said she also heard it.

A soft moan sounded from the bed. Turning his attention on his wife, Edwin saw her flushed face. Before his eyes, Morghan started the shake violently. "We must bring her fever down. I will get some cold water, you change her damp gown."

There were a few men injured or sick on his ship, though none this badly. Bathing in cool water did seem like the perfect way to break a fever. He had so much to make up for, and Edwin barely knew where to start.

Bathing her arms and face in cool water helped slightly. As dusk descended, Morghan became very still, her breathing shallow. A strange hush fell over everyone in the keep. In fact, no one spoke at the evening meal.

Even Gunther was abnormally subdued. Normally, he wandered about the men, eating what dropped onto the floor. A slight smile tugged at the corners of Edwin's mouth. There was no doubt many of his men purposely allowed bits to drop for the hound.

Tonight he lay at the foot of the bed and refused to move. Twice Edwin tripped over the beast, but other than a look passing between them, the beast would not be moved.

In the deep hours of the night, Morghan began moaning and shaking violently. Without hesitation, Edwin stripped and climbed into bed, gathering her into his arms. Whispered words and a soothing touch eventually brought her a measure of peace.

How odd. Edwin so often dreamed of holding Morghan in his arms. Here he was, finally holding her, feeling her skin against his, and yet he could not do all he wanted to her. Even ill, his body craved an intimacy between them. As soon as her fever passed, he intended to make love to his wife, this time making certain they were both cognizant of the fact.

Dawn brought more of the same. When Morghan's fever was up, he would hold her tight and ride out the chills. Every few hours, he coaxed some broth into her. Since it always arrived hot, Edwin figured Oleta was keeping vigil over the cooking pot.

He was getting tired. He'd spared little time for sleep during the past two nights. Only snatches could be attained between Morghan's chills. How much more of this could he withstand?

When the first visitor arrived, Edwin was stunned. He knew word of his wife's illness would travel quickly through the keep, but he never expected this.

It was the carpenter. In his arms, the man carried the most intricately carved cross he had ever seen. "I brought this for Lady Morghan."

Setting it on the bedside table, the man stood, hat in hand, staring down at the still figure. "It's beautiful."

"When your wife wakes, tell her I have chosen the sight for the chapel, and it will be completed long before winter sets in."

"A chapel? I never thought to have one here. What made you decide we needed one?"

"Your lady wife asked for it as payment for the safe delivery of my son. As you know, my Anna delivered two dead babies in the past three years. This one would have died too if it were not for Lady Morghan's skills. Building a chapel for her is a very small price to pay. If she had asked for another keep as payment, I would build one to rival Ironwood."

There was word Morghan had delivered a son on the morning

following their marriage. He had no interest in whose wife had been delivered. "I will tell Lady Morghan what you said when she awakes."

A quick bow, and the carpenter was gone. No sooner was the carpenter out the door when a young woman came in carrying a bouquet of flowers. "These are for Lady Morghan." The maid handed over the flowers and stood a moment staring at the still form.

"Lady Morghan came to my cottage yesterday. I do not know how she found out about my grandmother, but she gave her the greatest of gifts."

"And that would be?"

"My grandmother fell nearly two months ago and has clung to life for weeks. The pain has been excruciating. Lady Morghan eased her pain so her last moments on earth were not filled with agony. My grandmother passed during the night in her sleep quite peacefully."

Morghan arrived here only a few short days ago. How could she have touched so many lives already? Did not one need to be in a place for a long while before his people accepted her?

Edwin looked from person to person. Several more stood waiting their turn to present him a gift of thanks on Morghan's behalf. One man-at-arms stated simply his wife had smiled at him and spoke kindly to him before presenting an ointment for the scar on his face. He had taken it only to placate her, but found it actually eased the skin about the sword cut.

Each story found Edwin questioning his motives toward the woman he had wedded. He knew Morghan possessed a beauty of face and body. Now his eyes were opened to what lay deep inside her. Morghan's heart was as big as her smile.

An aching began in his chest. Oh, how he longed to see her smiling face turned on him. If he had not been such a fool, he would already know what a treasure he has been given.

The last person to enter his room was the last person Edwin expected to see. The Duke of Wessex stood at the foot of the bed, the scowl on his face frightening enough to quell even the most feared enemy.

"Sire, what are you doing here? I thought you rode out to defend

Ashford against renegade Saxons." Edwin nearly stumbled over his words because of his shock at seeing the high-ranking lord. If anyone would begrudge him his marriage to Morghan, it would be this man. After all, Lady Olivia had been offered and rejected.

"I did." Drawing close, he reached out to feel what he could already see was fevered skin. A curse passed his lips; the look he turned on Edwin could bring a lesser man to his knees. "How long has she burned like this?"

"Two days." Seeing a bowl of water and a cloth beside the bed, Wessex tested the temperature. "I use cold water to bathe her face and arms." Edwin quickly answered the unspoken question. "But it turns warm before long. I get her cooled down, and a few minutes later, the fever rises again."

"What have you given her to drink?" Looking about, Wessex took in all the flowers and the elegant cross. He stood in the hall watching all the people coming from this chamber while Henry gave him a report on what was happening.

Morghan had done exactly as the king thought she would—befriended and charmed the people of Ironwood.

"Broth Oleta made. Ale did not stay down." Following Wessex's gaze, he quickly added, "These are gifts from the people of Ironwood."

"That shows your people have more sense than their lord does. I will assume you have finally opened your eyes to the gift you were given."

Did every man in the kingdom know what kind of fool he was?

"Yes, sire, I have." Edwin felt like a little boy being scolded by his father. Well, he deserved it. If not for him acting like a spoiled child who was not given his own way, this never would have happened.

"If you had opened your eyes sooner, this could have been avoided." Taking Morghan's wounded hand in his, Wessex unwrapped the bandage. The cut was healing but still drained puss on one end. No one needed to tell him what caused it.

"Where is her bag of herbs? I know she possesses a skill in healing. It must be around here somewhere."

"Henry said he escorted Morghan to search for herbs the day she took ill." Opening her coffer, Edwin searched for anything that could be a medicine bag. Nothing. He looked under the bed next. Beside a small wooden cask containing her sewing, he found a leather pouch. The smell that wafted out was strong, making his eyes water.

Handing over the pouch, Wessex easily found what he sought. "Boil some of this in fresh water and bring it back to me." Turning his back on Edwin, he effectively dismissed his vassal.

Henry followed Edwin into the chamber when he returned. The hot brew was slowly spoon-fed to Morghan while Edwin held her in his arms. Since the moment he entered the chamber and took one look at her fevered face, Wessex prayed he was not too late. Doubt over his limited knowledge of healing could end Morghan's life as easily as could save it.

He thought Edwin would come to his senses before anything like this happened. Rage boiled inside him. How could one man be so self-absorbed as to not see the gift he was given?

If Morghan lived through this, he would petition the king on her behalf. She should be allowed the choice of staying or returning to Ireland and having this farce of a marriage dissolved.

"Henry, I have decided to stay for a while. I need to get a message to my men at Ashford."

"I can have a messenger ready in ten minutes, Your Grace."

"Fine. Once that is done, I want another to be sent after a priest."

Edwin sucked in his breath so fast, he nearly choked. No. The man could not actually mean what he was saying. "Morghan is not that ill, is she?"

Wessex turned an angry stare on him. Only once before had Edwin seen such a look of pure rage. During the battle against Harold, his men mistakenly thought him felled in the battle and began fleeing the battlefield. It was no less quelling now.

Leaning his elbows on his knees, Wessex drew a deep breath. "She is nearer death than I first thought. I try to hold out hope, but there may be none. It is almost as if she has lost the will to live. Morghan sacrificed her life to save your honor." Edwin knew in that moment the duke puzzled out what had actually happened on his wedding night.

"I never asked it of her."

"No, but she gave it all the same. Have you once looked at the true woman who was given to you? Did you even try to understand how different she is from what you thought you wanted?"

Turning, Edwin stared at the pallet stacked in the corner. He could still feel Morghan's fingers and lips on his body. He had already begun to understand just how different this woman was. His mind was already made up to accept her no matter what his heart felt. He refused to believe it could be too late.

"I am hungry." Wessex announced. "Tend your wife while I eat and prepare my messages."

Crawling in beside his wife, Edwin drew her into his arms, holding her fevered body close. For the first time in years, he actually prayed.

Deep in the night, Morghan's fever broke, drenching them both in sweat. Edwin quickly washed the sweat from her body and dressed his wife in a clean dry gown.

Dawn brought Morghan fully awake. Someone held her in warm strong arms. One arm was tossed over her hip, the hand splayed against her belly. A feeling of rightness and warmth settled deep inside her. Morghan knew she must fight it.

There was no telling exactly what happened in the last few days, but her reluctant husband needed to be taught he could not toy with her emotions and expect her to forgive and forget.

That was a thing of the past. There was once hope Edwin would come to his senses and turn to her. The days of fighting the fever had shown her it was a useless endeavor.

She risked all for a man who would not even share his secrets. While she battled for her life, what did he do? Finally decide that his own bed was more comfortable than the floor?

Enough was enough. There would be no more battling fate. He could have his freedom.

Turning slightly, she tried not to rouse her husband. Edwin's features were relaxed in sleep, and she could almost believe he cared. Heavily muscled legs spooned against hers. Only a thin pair of braies covered his private area and the top of his long legs.

The sight of his half-naked body brought back memories better left tucked away in the dark places of her mind. A marriage could not be made by one person alone. No matter how much she wanted to reach out and touch the smooth planes of his chest and stomach, Morghan knew it would be wasted.

Was it getting hot in here again? No, she needed to get a better grip on her hormones before she gave her husband her decision. Drawing a deep breath to gain control, she knew it did not help.

Edwin's salty masculine scent tickled her senses, surging a need through her that nearly consumed her. She had to be strong if she was going to make it through what she needed to do.

"Edwin?" Her voice choked out from dryness.

He was instantly awake. Only hours ago his wife's fever broke, and something changed. He couldn't tell what it was but feared it would soon be forthcoming.

"I'm here, Morghan." The bright smile he gave her only made her fever-frazzled mind swim and her resolve slip. Lord, but he was a handsome man when he smiled that way. When he scrambled from the bed, crossing to her side, he dropped to the floor on his knees and took her wounded hand in his; Morghan knew she needed to say her peace before her resolve faded.

His touch was already burning through the bandages. A few minutes more and she would be lost. "You know who I am?" Her raspy whisper prompted a cool cup of water to be pressed against her lips. Slowly, it trickled down her parched throat, soothing it.

"Of course I know who you are. You are my wife." Out of the corner of her eye, Morghan saw someone move at the foot of the bed. She ignored him. What she needed to say could not be delayed any longer.

"I want to go home." There, it was done.

"Morghan, dear, you are home." Placing fingers against her face,

Edwin checked for fever. There was none. Many things were said during her delirium, much of which were in a language he couldn't understand. He thought the language she spoke must have been Irish Celt. Could her odd statement be from the fevers still clouding her mind? "You are home. You are in Ironwood."

"You do not understand." Oh, why was he not getting this? Tears stung at the backs of her eyes, but she refused to let them fall. Why was he making this so difficult on her? Why would the words get stuck? "I want to go home to Ireland."

Morghan's words hit him like a fist to the chest. She wanted to leave him? After so many months of dreaming of the woman, he finally had her in his arms and his bed. Now she wanted to leave?

What had been the point of all the touching she so patiently performed in the middle of the night? Before he even knew his wife was the only woman he longed for, he made the decision to accept her. Now she was changing her mind?

No! his mind screamed. He could never allow her to go. If he refused to take her, what choice did she have? There was no way to travel back to Ireland except on his ship.

The instant that thought came, it was followed by another. Her brother would be arriving in three weeks to bring the remainder of her things. Would she be able to convince him to take her back to Ireland? Connor had been very angry with him before leaving.

So that gave him three weeks to change her mind. "I am afraid leaving here is out of the question. You are my wife now, and I intend to keep you." Standing, Edwin headed for the door. "I will see something is brought in to break your fast."

"Edwin, if I choose to leave, you cannot keep me here."

"That, my dear, is where you are wrong." Stopping at the door, his hand on the latch, Edwin turned back. "You spoke vows to me before God, Father Matthew, and my king. Your own father was witness to the vows we made. He alone placed your hand in mine. You are my *wife*. You can go nowhere unless I give you leave to." God, that sounded barbaric even to his own ears.

He had not meant to be so cruel, but her words cut him deeply. Without looking back, he slammed out of the chamber.

A single tear rolled down her cheek as Morghan turned toward the only other person in the room.

18

It took two days before Morghan left her bed.

Most hours of the day found her sleeping, trying to recover, but several times Edwin paused outside their chamber door listening to his wife softly crying. Every tear that fell down her cheeks tore at his heart, pounding at the wall he so carefully built about it like a battering ram.

He went away that first day, intending to drink himself into oblivion. Sitting in the stables, a skin in hand, he just could not do it. Every foul curse he ever heard passed his lips while he poured the ale onto the ground. Drowning in drink was what created this situation in the first place.

In fact, it had cost him dearly. If he was sober, he would have seen who stood beside him before Father Matthew and not wasted so much precious time. That was a mistake he planned never to make again.

He crawled from bed before dawn and stood on the battlements watching the night sky brighten into the soft pink and orange rays of dawn. Morghan's protested attempts to keep him from their bed fell on deaf ears. At one point, she wanted him to touch her, and he did not.

When he thought her to be deeply asleep, in the wee hours before dawn, Edwin would softly caress his wife. If she could do it to him, he certainly had the right to do it to her. Soft moans and closely snuggled body were his reward.

Even now, the memories made him smile.

As he watched his people going about their daily routine, he could not get his mind off the hurt he saw in Morghan's eyes when she said she wanted to leave him.

When Morghan walked out into the midmorning sun accompanied by Robert, Edwin found himself unable to look in any direction but at his wife. "Do you intend to let her go?" Henry's words made him jump. He was so focused on Morghan, he had not heard his friend's approach.

Following Edwin's gaze, Henry watched the slow progress Morghan made on the squire's arm. Just outside the kitchen door, she sat on a bench turning her face toward the bright sun. Her left hand was still heavily bandaged and held close to her chest.

"None here want to see her go. You are the only one who can make her stay." Edwin made no reply; he simply continued to stare at his wife. "Find a way to reach past her anger." Yes, he already started that. "I beg you not to let what one woman did to you influence your marriage any longer."

"It is not just what she did that bothers at me, and you know it." Despite his resolve not to bring up that subject again, this friend seemed determined to keep poking at the wound.

"Aye, I can see where the other three would wound you more. Let me ask you one thing. Would you ever treat your child the way they did you?"

Edwin stared at his master-at-arms, unable to believe he heard such tripe could come from the man's mouth. "If ever God in heaven was to bless me with children, I would never—no matter what they did—turn my back on them or betray them." Anger seeped from Edwin's every pore. Shaking his head at Henry, a smile tugged at the corners of his mouth. "Your point is well taken, my friend. I must leave the past in the past and create the future I want."

"Will I see you on the practice field this day?" Henry asked.

"I have one thing to arrange for my wife. Then I shall join you."

"Good." A slap on the back emphasized the word. "You can use all the sword practice you can get. A wonderful sailor you might be, put a sword in your hand and you become only a moderately accomplished fighter."

A soft laugh was Edwin's only reply. There was much to do to get ready for this evening, and the sooner he begun, the sooner he would finish.

"Lord Edwin watches you."

Morghan did not need to be told her husband watched her; she felt his eyes on her the moment they stepped from the kitchen.

It felt good to sit here in the sun, soaking up its warmth. Self-pity kept her in her chamber for the last two days. She wanted no one about her, not even the boy who stood beside her now.

This morning, she felt Edwin leave their bed. Why the man insisted on joining her there when she did want him to was beyond her. The moment he slid beneath the sheets, Morghan turned her back on him and moved as far to the other side as possible.

Never once did Edwin try to touch her or get close. He was giving her what she wanted. Or was he? Did she truly want him to stay away and never touch her? No, her heart cried out. She wanted nothing more but for her husband to take her in his arms and kiss her until she no longer remembered why she was angry.

A cold settled over her after Edwin's leaving of their bed that only the warmth of the sun could banish. Why were her emotions in such turmoil? She made up her mind to go back to Ireland and accept the fate her father deemed to be her future.

Edwin's words, the morning she became ill, stung at her pride. But were they that bad, or had her fever turned them into more? Two days of lying abed allowed her plenty of time to think on what she really wanted for her life. The answer surprised her.

"Do you feel up to a walk?" Robert stood over her like an overprotective father.

"Not just yet." Her father was definitely not going to be happy with this turn of events. She heartily agreed to the contract, and at the first sign of trouble, she cried she would run away from England and everything here. Was that why Wessex stayed so long? Did the king fear her father would somehow change the terms since she failed to fulfill her part?

Yet she had done as her father asked. She spoke her vows to a man she longed to be near. "None here at Ironwood need worry. My father will not withhold his support because of my actions. The men and supplies will be delivered to the king as promised."

"That message was not filled with his sorrows, my lady." Robert hurried to assure her. "He simply thought Lord Edwin a very different man."

"How so?"

"There was not much support for his claim to the English throne among the people of Normandy. True, the noblemen of France accepted it, but the common people saw only the cost of war on their lives. When Lord Edwin joined him, the king was impressed. I remember my father speaking of it."

"You know what happened in Normandy to change him."

Robert turned away from his mistress, scratching Gunther behind the ears. "I do. But before you ask, I cannot tell you. It is for the best that Lord Edwin explains it to you. He refused to listen to one word of advice any man gave him."

"He is not the only one that can be stubborn." Morghan's mutter brought a soft laugh from the boy.

Morghan allowed her eyes to scan the wall walk, seeking her husband. His eyes never moved from her. Was there a way to get her to stay? Her heart still cried out for Edwin, but her rational mind could not dismiss his hurtful words.

Never before could anyone consider her a quitter. If there was something she wanted, she always found a way to obtain it. Was she now ready to give up on the progress she made through touching Edwin? Could she turn her back on the man she already loved?

"Though it is not your place to insinuate yourself in the lives of your lord and lady, it is not your fault Edwin no longer cares for me."

"That, my dear lady, is where you are wrong. Do you remember much from when the fever was upon you?"

"No. Nothing."

"Here are a few facts you should consider, my lady. Edwin never left your side. He bathed you in cool water when your fever raged. You would only swallow broth, if he fed it to you. For hours on end, he sat there talking to you. I heard him tell stories from his childhood when he thought no one was listening.

"He may have even told you what happened in Normandy, you just cannot remember it." Robert followed her line of sight. A smile tugged at his lips when he saw Morghan stare directly at her husband. She was not as apathetic as she proclaimed.

"How convenient to tell such to an unconscious woman," Morghan answered sarcastically. Edwin was so handsome standing in the bright sunlight. It showed through his golden hair setting it into a blaze of color. Could he have told her that which she desperately wanted to know, and she did not remember it?

"The point is, my lady, Lord Edwin realized what you did for him and how you could lose your life for the decision to save his honor. It frightened him to his very soul. One day, he will wake up and realize you were the better choice all along. My parents have been wed for many years. I came late to them.

"Do you believe they loved each other the day they spoke their wedding vows?"

"My father spoke very highly of yours."

Robert smiled and looked out over the bailey. "You are very much like my mother. Your heart is strong as hers is."

Hands gripped the wooden railing until his knuckled turned white. Squire or not, boy or not, Robert had no right to smile at his wife like he was. Anger flared hot in the pit of his stomach. He was just going to have to…

"Hold, Edwin." Henry grabbed his friend when he made to pass. "First you claim you do not want a wife, now you act the jealous husband when another pays her court. Which is it to be?"

Jealous? Him?

Never before could he remember being jealous of another living being. Ever so slowly, the anger seeped away. Henry was right. Robert was just a boy tending to his mistress. What could it hurt?

It did hurt! It hurt all the way down to his very soul.

"No need to answer that, my friend, the truth is written on your face." Henry released his hold and took a step back. "If you want Morghan so much, why not tell her? Beg her forgiveness for whatever you said to upset her and tell her it will never happen again."

What had he said to upset her? Hell, what had not he said? He could not remember many kind words coming out of his mouth toward her or about her. "It's too late. How can Morghan ever forgive me?"

"You would be surprised what a woman can forgive if you speak the truth to her. Tell her about Normandy. Explain to her how you felt when you faced your parents. Begin your life together in total honesty, and you can build a foundation to last a lifetime."

"I cannot do that, and you know why."

"You need to take a good long look at what you want out of life, my friend. Do you want to stand here watching your wife? If Morghan is what you want, tell her. If standing here wallowing in self-pity is what you prefer, then pack Morghan up right now and sail her back to Ireland. A convent life is all that awaits her there. I only ask you decide right now how you want your life to be. Alone and bitter, or held in the loving arms of a beautiful woman."

With his peace said, Henry walked away.

Could it be as simple as making the decision he wanted Morghan and going after her? Was there a way to make up for all the hurt he had caused her? An idea took root in his mind, refusing to let go. He knew what he wanted and just how he intended to get it.

At the evening meal, Edwin waited patiently for his wife to arrive to begin eating. Morghan never showed. So his wife turned cowardly, did she? Well, he was not about to allow her to hide in their chamber and ignore him. Grabbing two goblets, wine, the trencher of food, and a small loaf of bread, Edwin headed out to find his bride. His plan would not work if Morghan refused to cooperate.

He found her standing at the window looking out at a fast-approaching storm. She never even turned when he entered. Placing the items on the bedside table, he drew close but did not touch her. "I never thought you a coward, Morghan." A soft growl met his words.

"Hush, Gunther!" Morghan snapped at the dog. "What are you talking about?"

"Why are you hiding here instead of sitting beside me at the evening meal?"

"I am not very hungry." Her stomach grumbled, giving testimony to the lie.

"Come, my dear, you can do better than that." Holding out a silver goblet to her, Edwin waited for her to take it. When Morghan refused, he drew a loud heavy sigh. "I suppose I should be the one to tell the king that you do not like his wedding gift. Both the wine and the goblets were William's gift to us."

Snatching the goblet from his hand, Morghan spilled some on her bandaged hand. Gunther growled a bit louder this time. "Oh, for heaven's sake." Moving to the door, Morghan opened it with a snap. "Out." She ordered. The huge hound looked to Edwin. "That's right, I am talking to you." Head hanging low, Gunther slowly walked out.

"No doubt Robert has a treat for the beast. My squire spoils him."

"The lad has become very attached to Gunther. Or perhaps it is the other way around."

"You do not mind?"

"Gunther was a gift. I got him when he was a small pup. Though he technically belongs to me, anyone who drops a scrap of meat or pets him gains his loyalty."

Sipping the dark red wine, Morghan watched her husband over the rim. This was not like Edwin at all. Exactly what was he up to? Not once since they were wed had Edwin bothered to eat a meal in her presence. Why was he starting this now?

Could it be he sat the head table awaiting her tonight, and she disappointed him by not showing? If that was the case, she no longer cared what he expected of her. Why all of a sudden would he change himself so drastically?

"Come, dearest, let me feed you before it gets cold." Seeing Edwin was not going away and leaving her in peace, she sat on the bed. An instant later, she jumped up again. Perhaps the bed was not the best choice. She took the only chair instead.

"Why are you doing this?" Morghan asked around bites of beef.

"Is it so unheard of for a husband to want to spend a meal in the company of his wife?"

"It is for us." Morghan washed the bit of beef down with a sip of wine. "I can count at least a dozen meals since we were wed, and not one did you care to attend." A chunk of boiled turnip was fed next.

"You need not point out to me my shortcomings, my dear. Henry and Robert have done that chore for you. Their sharp tongues alone have filleted me quite nicely." Another piece of beef. "I hope to make up for my lack of attention from here on out."

"What about my wish to return to Ireland?" A long drink washed down the suddenly tough beef. A drop of juice stayed on her lips, and before Morghan could lick it, Edwin's tongue was there. The soft brush of his lips turned into a soft kiss.

"I have given it much thought," Edwin said, sitting back. I have a title and land now. An heir is needed to pass on both." Morghan choked on the next bite of beef, the implication of his words sinking in. "Know this, I will never touch you as a husband does a wife, if you say no. After you provide me with an heir if you still wish to be sent to a convent, I shall find one here in England to accommodate you." A piece of cabbage was fed before any objection could pass her lips.

"Though if our first child is a daughter, I would ask you remain in my bed until a son is produced." A blush rose to stain her cheeks. "You may think yourself only a pawn in a contract between two kings, but I consider you my wife."

Images of the dream they shared on their wedding night flooded back to her mind. Would making love to Edwin be as good as it felt in the dream, or would it be better? Every nerve in her body ached to find out. When the time came, would she be able to tell him no?

"Would you tell me what happened in Normandy?" She would start testing his words right now. If Edwin truly wanted this to work, she would know by his answer.

It was a bad sign when the eating dagger fell from his hand to clang against the rush-covered stone floor. Edwin's face lost all color. The look of pure horror in his eyes tore at her heart.

This was it, the moment of truth. Though he knew Morghan deserved to know all, the words would not come out. Heart pounding, his throat closed. She would ask the one question he was not certain he could ever answer. Panic gripped him so tight, Edwin thought he would stop breathing.

"What happened there has nothing to do with the way I intend spending the rest of our lives." Retrieving the dagger, he gathered the meal remnants in trembling hands. "I have other matters to tend." A swift exit left Morghan wondering if she would ever get an answer to that question.

19

MORGHAN CLOSED HER eyes and leaned back against the rim of the tub.

Never in all her life was she privy to anything like the monstrosity Edwin's men carried into her chamber an hour past. A fire blazed in the hearth, and a small parade of servants and men carried buckets of steaming water, dumping their contents into the huge copper tub.

When Oleta entered, Morghan took her aside and demanded to know what was happening. In response, she received a soft smile and the words "Lord Edwin thought you might like privacy for your bath." When she was done, the men would return and remove the tub, taking it back to the bathing cottage.

From one of the men, Morghan learned her husband commissioned the thing constructed to his own standards last Yuletide while in London. Just as his Viking ancestors believed, Edwin believed bathing was beneficial to the body and soul. He ordered a community bathhouse open to all at Ironwood, setting aside specific hours when the women could use it undisturbed.

The hot, steamy water was easing the fever-induced aches from her body, relaxing every muscle until Morghan thought she would doze off. This was so much better than the small wooden tub back home she used to squeeze into. It would be missed if she went away.

A sadness settled deep in her chest when she thought of leaving here. It was not as if she actually wanted to return home to Ireland; it's just that Edwin's words hurt her very deeply. All during her long hours of fighting the fever, they kept coming back to haunt her.

As badly as they hurt, just the thought of spending the rest of her days in a convent made her ill. She was not cut out for a life spent in silence and prayer.

Morghan never envisioned her life being one of pious worship. Each time her father threatened to send her off to a convent, she knew it as an empty threat. Though deep in her heart she knew he never meant it, she was not so certain about Edwin.

There must be some hope for them. It had not been her imagination that Edwin stared at her in the abbey six months ago, or that he stood the wall walk today watching her every move. Edwin's harsh words resounded through her mind. He said she would not be allowed to leave until she bore him an heir. At the rate they were going, that gave her a year or more to break through to him.

If only she could get someone, anyone here to open up about what happened in Normandy, she would have a fighting chance. She never was very good at fighting ghosts. Flesh and blood she understood. Matters of the spirit were something entirely different.

Her mother often pointed out she was not a very patient person. Her rash actions lately proved that point to perfection.

Perhaps now would be a good time to begin cultivating that patience. Despite their resolve to keep hidden the events in Normandy, someone would let something slip one day, and she would figure it out. By then, she hoped to have Edwin so in love with her, he would not mind that she knew.

The chamber door opened and closed so softly, Morghan was not sure she heard it at all. Oleta said she would return when it was time for the men to take the tub away. Daydreaming of Edwin must have cost her time to enjoy the soothing waters of the bath.

Dipping her hand in, Morghan found the water was still plenty hot. Yet if not the cook, then who? There was only one way to answer that. "How can my time be up so soon, Oleta?"

"I do not believe that it is."

Shocked, Morghan sucked in her breath so quickly, she choked. This man was the last person she expected to enter while she took a bath. "Edwin! What are you doing here?" Sinking low in the tub to hide her nakedness, water splashed over the rim.

Her reaction was what he expected. Morghan wanted her privacy, not having anyone bothering to enter until she finished, and that was exactly what he counted on. Her blush was enchanting, and he could not think of a better way to begin seducing her. "Last time I looked, this was still my chamber as well as yours." Discreetly looking about, he quickly added, "Though I never thought it could look this comfortable. Thank you."

Morghan was aware of nothing about her but the man sanding a few feet away. Just his presence made her heart quicken. True, Edwin had spent the last two nights in this chamber, but he often left in the small hours of the morning. Still recovering from the fever, she was too tired to get up and beg him to stay.

Remembering the way his naked flesh and taut muscles felt beneath her fingers made her hot even now. Oh, how she missed touching all his beautiful body. Well, not exactly all. There was still one part that escaped her touch.

Edwin smiled to himself. He purposely avoided intimate contact with his wife to give her time to heal. Now her time was up. He had every intention of continuing what he began earlier, before her question caused him to run away.

Why could he not simply open his mouth and tell her what his family had done to him? The wounds were healing, thanks to Morghan. It could only help to tell her, yet every time he tried, the words choked him. Would he ever find a way to speak them?

Tonight, he enlisted Henry's help. His friend was the one to handpick the men to bring in the tub and water. Edwin informed him they were not to be interrupted. Nothing short of a Saxon attack would be tolerated.

If being able to keep Morghan meant seducing his own wife, then so be it. Actually, the thought made him anxious. Not since he was sixteen did he need to persuade a woman to share his bed. By the time he finished his plan, Morghan would not only be pregnant, she would be so in love, there would be no more talk leaving him.

A smile tugged at the corner of his mouth. This could be the most fun he could remember having since he was a boy.

"Can you not see I am at my bath?" There may have been an intent to make her words sharp, but they came out sounding more like a caress. In fact, they almost sounded breathless. The look in Edwin's eyes reminded her of a cat stalking its prey. Perhaps putting Gunther out was not a good idea.

"Of course I can see you are at your bath, my dear. I have perfect vision." The smile Edwin turned on her made her insides flip over. Lord, he could be handsome when he smiled like that.

Gone was the brooding man she came to recognize as her husband. In his place stood the seductive teasing man who led her through the market in London. It would be so easy to give in to this version of Edwin. What she wanted was his whole heart, not just a tiny portion. For that, she would need to play this out to her own end.

She would settle for no less than his heart, body, and soul.

When Edwin removed his belt, folding it and laying it on top her coffer, Morghan held her breath at what he would do next. Oh my, he would not. When Edwin reached for the hem of his tunic, she closed her eyes. Try as she might, there was no forgetting the look of his tight muscled chest and the sprinkling of blond hair.

Too late.

The image came with full force just as the tunic joined the belt on her coffer. Her mind raced at how much time she spent touching that chest. Morghan knew every valley and bulge of muscles. The feel of his nipples hardening beneath her lips snuck into her mind, no matter how hard she tried to keep it out.

A blush stained her cheeks. How in heaven's name was she going to survive this?

"You are most beautiful when you blush, my dear." Edwin's voice was deep and sultry. The whispered words brushed against her ear sending chills along her nerves, ending at her belly.

How easy it would be to reach out and touch him. Her body screamed from want of a single intimate touch. Exactly how she planned to stay strong and resist such temptation eluded her. *Remember the final goal*, she reminded herself over and over. All the sacrifice would be worth it when Edwin finally gave in and allowed her love to bind them.

Her mind on reciting her litany, Morghan was not paying any attention to what her husband was doing. When his hand dipped below the surface of the water, she jumped. "What are you doing?"

"Careful," Edwin's voice was soft, too soft and sensual for her peace of mind. His free hand grasped her wounded one, the thumb slowly caressing her wrist. "We would not want to get this wet now, would we?" Her pulse kicked up a notch.

Unable to tear her eyes away from his delicate thumb, Morghan watched as the soft caresses continued, the motion sending tiny chills up her arm through her body to settle deep in her belly. Heart pounding, she wondered how Edwin was not feeling it beneath his touch.

Surely, he had no idea of what he was doing to her. Could he be touching her on purpose? Could he be using her tactic against her? If that was his plan, he would surely win, for this was setting her blood on fire.

Oh lord, it felt so good. Edwin's simple touch felt like nothing she had ever experienced before. Her eyes felt dreamy and heavy. "I do caution you against falling asleep in this tub, wife." Morghan's eyes snapped open. Had she been about to fall asleep?

A quick check stopped the downward slide into the tub. Water lapped at her chin. It would not do to drown.

She needed to put a stop to this before he made her senses completely scrambled. "I am quite capable of bathing myself, Edwin." Was that breathless voice actually hers? "I have been doing so since I was a wee lass." Oh no, her Irish accent was slipping out. That proved just how much she was allowing him to affect her.

"I am not here to question your abilities, my dear." Morghan wished he would stop calling her "my dear." The way he said it made her insides turn to jelly. "It is just that you have been through so much of late, I thought a bit of pampering in order. About earlier, I'm sorry."

Morghan stared at him wondering exactly what he was apologizing for. Surely, it wasn't for the meal he brought her. There was nothing wrong there. The food was hot and tasted good. Could it have been the near kiss? Surely, if that bothered him, Edwin would not be here right now acting as if he was seducing her.

The only thing left was the way he left. She feared she pushed him too far in asking about Normandy. Surely, by now, she knew men kept their secrets very close. Perhaps she should test the waters and find out just how far she could press him. "If it is the near kiss you regret…"

"Not the kiss." Edwin's hand dipped beneath the water to drag the bathing cloth up one leg ending a mere inch from the place that ached for him. "Never a kiss." The whispered words tickled her ear. This was fast becoming torture.

"Then the meal was not to your liking. Perhaps if you had eaten more yourself, you would be satisfied now."

"No, there was plenty. Besides, I enjoy watching you eat. It reminds me so much of the first meal we shared. Surely, you have not forgotten that night."

Forgotten it? Was he insane? If she lived to be a hundred, she would never forget that meal.

Gentle nipping kisses tugged at her earlobes at the same time Edwin's hand traveled up one thigh, across the apex, and then back down the other. Heart pounding, Morghan knew she needed to decide right now what she wanted from this union. Was she going to allow Edwin to plant his seed and expect her to carry his heir, or would she see through what she had begun a sennight ago?

The choice was an easy one to make.

Threading her fingers through his hair, Morghan drew his mouth down to hers. Instantly, it opened allowing her tongue to dart in and duel with his. The bathing cloth and hand skimmed over the flat plains of her stomach across her ribs to her full breasts.

Slow tight circles caressed her nipples until they became hard aching buds. No one had ever touched her like this before. Other than a few chase kisses, no man had even dared to open his mouth to hers. This kiss made her head spin, her body ache.

Heat rose so quickly in her, Morghan was surprised the bathwater did not boil around her. The sensation of his touch was what she remembered most from the dream. They grew and spread to consume her entire body. If Edwin was to take her to their bed right now, she would gladly become his wife in every way.

Any problems they had could be solved if they both tried hard enough. She was willing, but was Edwin? If only he would confess the deep dark secret he kept sealed inside him.

The longer the kiss lasted, the less her mind functioned. When her hands encircled his neck, a pain shot through her wounded palm. Swallowing the cry, Morghan struggled to get back to where she was a minute ago.

Edwin knew something was wrong the instant Morghan stiffened beneath his touch. Breaking the kiss, he pulled back and looked into pain-filled eyes. What had he done this time to cause her pain? He was trying to be so careful, to touch her only where he could bring pleasure.

"My hand." Those two words were like a dousing of cold water. So engrossed by the kiss and her reaction to it, he forgot all about the wound.

How could he have allowed himself to get so carried away? Since her arrival, his actions hurt her over and over again. First he had given her a wedding from hell, and then turned around and ignored her on their wedding night, forcing her to cut herself to save his honor.

All during the hours he held her while she raged with fever, he swore if God allowed her to live, he would never hurt her again. If he was given another chance, he would find a way to make everything up to her. Now here he was still hurting her. When would his selfishness end?

"I am sorry." Those three words seemed grossly inadequate. He was more than sorry about a lot of things. Taking her wounded hand in his, Edwin hoped his wife would not feel the shake of his. He could see no further damage to the palm. Whatever Morghan put in her ointment, it worked miracles.

Silently vowing there would always be plenty on hand, Edwin raised the still-pink skin to his lips. He smiled when a shiver ran through her. This was definitely progress.

Though Edwin's body screamed at him to pull his wife from the cooling water, carry her to their bed, and consummate this marriage, he knew it would be moving too fast. He wanted Morghan to say yes and had vowed he would not make a move until she agreed. His body hurt from need, but he promised he would wait until she invited him into their bed and into her body.

One thing he would never break, and that was a promise. No matter how hard he became, no matter how much he ached for release, he would never break this promise to her.

A fleeting thought of finding another woman to ease his pain came and went in the same heartbeat. No other woman shared his bed since meeting Morghan in London, and even the thought of holding another woman deflated his need.

There were other ways of dealing, and he had every intention of finding out which one would work now. "I will have the men return in five minutes to empty the tub and return it to the bathing cottage. I fear this threat cannot often be allowed."

Rising, Edwin needed to take a minute to adjust the fit of his hose to accommodate his swollen and demanding member. He did not miss the smile that crossed his wife's lips. He needed to get away from her *now*. "If you like, I can return to brush out your hair before the fire."

Not waiting for her reply, Edwin left.

The men came ten minutes later. Edwin did not return until she was fast asleep.

20

"Ouch," Morghan cursed and stuck her bleeding thumb into her mouth. At this rate, she would not have any blood left in her body in a sennight.

And for what? The seam she just stitched was hopelessly crooked. Tearing it out would give her no satisfaction. It was not as if Edwin was desperate for a new wardrobe. No, his new clothing was completely her own idea.

He was quite happy wearing nothing but drab brown tunics and hose. She was the one who thought a little color would be welcome.

The state of her husband's wardrobe was not what disturbed her now. No, to be honest, it was the fact that Edwin never returned last night to comb her hair before the fire. After all, it was his suggestion. The more time that passed, the heavier her heart became. She obviously moved too fast and scared him off.

Men did not like brazen, forward women.

Right!

None of her five sisters-in-law were either meek or mild. They would not know the first thing about holding back their tempers. And her brothers would not have it any other way.

She would try her best to be what Edwin wanted in a wife, but there would always be a small part of her that needed to be true to herself. Her father raised her to be independent in a time when men believed their wives did not have a mind to think with.

Was it so unusual for a man to think he could not love a woman? Then to turn about and find he actually could, given enough time? How often did they confuse lust with love, and when hurt, ended up losing the very woman who could save them? Edwin was obviously no different. He reminded her so much of her brother Shamus.

As eldest, and the heir, their father chose his wife for alliance only. Marga thought herself beyond being used by her father at the ripe old age of nineteen. Instead, she found herself in the arms of a huge man who wanted her not at all. It was not until she was lying ill and heavy with child two years later that Shamus broke down and admitted his hurt.

Time was what Edwin needed most, that, and a bit of prodding from her. The king's interference didn't hurt any either. It was obvious the king had a soft spot in his heart for the two of them.

Though it was deep in the night when her husband finally joined her in bed, he spooned his naked body against hers and slept the night through in their bed.

Edwin was not unaffected by her kiss. The evidence of his arousal pressed into her backside for hours. So why did he hesitate about taking her and ending his suffering? What was holding him back?

Looking up, Morghan squinted through the bright sunshine at the practice field. Edwin sparred against Henry, the master-at-arms obviously taking it easy on his overlord. Squires and pages alike stood back watching. There was no tearing her eyes from his naked chest and back, glistening sweat in the midday sun.

Just the sight of his half-naked body brought back memories of the feel of his taut muscles beneath her touch. Heat rose deep inside, and the now-familiar ache began in her belly. If Edwin did not make a move soon, she just might have to become *very* brazen and force his hand.

Her breasts tingled remembering the touch of his hands against her flesh during the bath last night. Was it her reaction that scared Edwin off? So many questions and no ready answers.

"Something interesting about the view?"

Morghan jumped at the deep male voice. William smiled brightly sitting beside her on the bench. "How long have you been there, sire?"

William followed the line of her sight. No woman, wed or not, looked on a man the way Morghan did and not have a healthy case of lust for the object of her attention.

The king and a few of his men arrived only an hour ago, needing Edwin to take him to the north. "Answer me this, Lady Morghan. Why do you not simply tell your husband you spoke in haste, and you desire him?"

"What makes you think I desire Edwin?" Sitting back, she continued to stare at the very man they spoke of.

The king's rich laughter rang across the yard. "Lady, you wear the exact same look in your eyes as you did the day you first laid eyes on that man. Need I remind you, I was a witness to the display between you and Lord Edwin?"

"No, sire."

"If you no longer lust after your husband, then I ask you what you would call it."

Frustration built inside her until Morghan thought she would explode. She did not mean for her intentions to be so blatant. If William could see it, who else witnessed her reaction? "Oh, all right. I not only lust after the man, I believe I love him." That stopped the laughter. "For all the good it does me. If Edwin was to come to me right now, I would give over and not think twice."

William looked from one young person to the other. Edwin was too stubborn for his own good, and this woman matched him to perfection. All his interference so far did nothing to get them any closer. Though he was pleased to see Edwin was sleeping in his own chamber and apparently in his own bed, it was not enough.

"Have you told him yet you love him?"

"No, sire." Morghan's gaze shifted away from her husband back to the king. "I would ask that you not tell him just yet."

"May I ask why I should remain silent?"

"Edwin came to our chamber again last night and actually slept in our bed beside me. We have kissed twice." Actually speaking it out loud made it sound quite trivial. A sleeping arrangement and two kisses was not much to base a marriage on. In fact, a small hope was all it showed.

"They are not much, I know," Morghan confessed. "But somehow I cannot help hoping those simple things could lead to something more."

"You have every right to look on those things encouragingly. I must

confess, I was part of the conspiracy to force Edwin to your chamber. Henry and I thought if we got the two of you in the same place, nature would take its natural course. It could just have easily turned about on us."

"How so, sire?"

"Edwin could have chosen to sleep in the cabin of his ship." All the color drained from her face. Not once did she think of that. The ship was huge, and no doubt the captain's cabin contained enough room for a comfortable bunk. "You need to ask yourself why he never considered that possibility."

"Lady Morghan!" Tommy ran straight toward her, shouting at the top of his voice. The boy's frantic look warned her something was seriously wrong. "Sir Henry sent me to find you."

Find her? There was not one man in the bailey that could have missed her sitting here watching her husband. A quick look to the side told her William did not look even the slightest concerned. Across the practice field, a crowd milled about, close ranks about someone on the ground.

Setting her stitching on the bench, Morghan slowly rose. "Tommy, do you remember what my sewing coffer and medical sack look like?"

"Yes, my lady. They are under your bed."

"Good, fetch them while I see to the injured man." A smile saw the boy on his way.

"I swear these squires are the clumsiest lot I have ever met." Muttering under her breath, Morghan made her way to the nearly two dozen men standing about. William tried desperately to hide his smile, trailing behind. Lady Morghan was just what his stubborn vassal needed.

"Make way for Lady Morghan." It was when the men parted under William's command that he saw her steps falter. No matter what she said, this woman did indeed love her husband.

"Henry, do stop blaming yourself for this." Edwin sat on the ground, Sir Henry holding tightly to his upper left arm. Small drops of blood seeped from between his fingers.

"I agree. This was not my doing but yours. True, my blade actually sliced your skin, but your mind has been somewhere else all morning. Sword fighting requires concentration. This day, you have none." Henry received a blank look for his words. It brought a laugh from the master-at-arms.

"Allow me." Dropping to her knees beside her husband, Morghan pried the other's fingers away. "It does not look so bad." Touching the edge of the cut, a new spurt of blood oozed out. "I do not believe it needs stitches."

Robert knelt beside her and handed over her herb pouch. A relieved look passed between them. Holding out a skin of clean water and cotton strips, the squire watched his mistress work.

"All right, ladies." Henry shouted, grabbing each boy by the arm and pulling them away from the scene. "To the stables. I want to see if you ride any better than you fight."

Several soft grumbles mixed with a few curses. She knew Henry worked the men hard, but they needed it. Life was hard, danger lurking near every day.

"This seems to be your blind spot." Morghan whispered running her finger along the scar of the old wound. The two wounds were only a half inch apart.

Edwin could not stop staring at her delicate fingers working to clean and bind his arm. The long dip in the cold sea last night did nothing to ease his demanding desire for her. After an hour, he was still hard and wanting her as badly as before his little dip.

Henry was right. His mind was on the feel of his wife's body pressed against him last night, not his opponent. Every little move she made during the night pressed her delicate bottom against his hard arousal.

He hoped hard work on the practice field could sweat the need from his body. Memories of her bath last night rushed back on him even now. His body demanded an intimacy he was not certain she was ready to accept.

"That should do, my lord." My lord? Why was she being so formal? Could it be for his men's benefit or a way to try to distance herself?

"Are you certain you need not stitch it?"

"You question my healing skills, my lord?" The smile that tugged at her lips turned his insides to mush and tapped at his heart. All the memories of that day six long months ago raced through his mind. Edwin longed to see more of those smiles.

"I would never do such a thing, Morghan." He should kiss her. His body demanded everything his mind strove to keep separate. All he needed to do was lean close and take what was his by right. Would Morghan push him away or cling close?

Only one way to find out.

"When I was a little boy," Edwin whispered loud enough for only her to hear. "My mother always kissed the cuts and bruises I was forever getting. She said it was magic for healing them."

Morghan knew by the devilish smile he was trying to hide, it was not his wounded arm he wanted her to kiss. Perhaps she should allow him this game. Leaning close, she gently pressed her lips to the bandage. "Do you hurt any place else? Perhaps Henry found another vulnerable spot?"

Edwin silently pointed to his naked shoulder. Morghan kissed it, smiling when she felt a shiver run through him. Next, he pointed to the base of his neck. Morghan obediently kissed there, receiving a moan as reward.

A tap on his chin came next, but when she leaned in to kiss it, Edwin dipped his head and closed his mouth on hers. It was Morghan's turn to moan.

Hot moist lips parted beneath hers, and Edwin's tongue quickly slid in to duel hers. Hands pressed against his chest, Morghan felt when she was lowered across his lap, but did not care. The evidence she had felt all night pressed into her backside was now hard against her thigh.

He wanted her. There was no longer any doubt in her mind he could take her at any time and make her his wife. Though she was enjoying his kisses and the burning they created inside her, Morghan was beginning to crave more. There was so much more to come after a kiss, and her body demanded it all.

Exactly how much could Edwin withstand before he gave in to the demands of his body and ended the torture for them both? Grinding her hips against his arousal, she intended to find out.

"How much longer do you think Edwin can last?" Henry could not take his eyes off the couple sitting in the middle of the practice yard. People passed by as if seeing their lord and lady kissing was an everyday occurrence and nothing to stare at.

"He is quite stubborn, but I do believe Morghan is close to the end of his endurance," William answered, the smile on his face showing he was very pleased with the way things were progressing. "I would not be surprised if his gift tomorrow would bring this dance of theirs to a happy ending.

"I did not realize it would arrive so soon. I will see the head stable master is prepared." Right on cue, the stable doors opened and horses were led out. As much as Henry wanted to wait and see just how far this kiss was going, he had men to train.

"It was not very difficult to nick Lord Edwin. His mind has been on his wife all morning."

"I know you did not want to hurt him, but you must agree the results are worth it. I needed to make certain Edwin saw what happened in Normandy was not the end of his life, but the beginning of something better. He needs only to reach out to the woman who could never betray him."

"If he has not learned that by now, he is not the man I came to know and love like a brother." The wild scream of a horse pulled Henry's attention away from the still-kissing couple. "Hold there!" he shouted, walking away from his king. These men would be the death of him.

Angry eyes watched the young couple make absolute fools of themselves on the practice field.

Why was no one pointing out just how inappropriate their behavior was? Hell, they were nearly making love before the eyes of all their people. Rowena enjoyed it when he watched her intimate encounters. In fact, it often stimulated them both.

Already, he received word from Normandy of Louis's accident. Though he was not dead yet, how much longer he would live was debatable. Plans were already set in motion for his stupid sister to lose the child she carried.

Once they were eliminated, things would be back to the way he needed them to be. His very life depended on eliminating this marriage and getting Lord Edwin to see the error of ever allowing any woman but Rowena into his life.

Perhaps since the king used Sir Henry, he could also. Yes. A smile spread across features that never felt such action. The perfect plan to get back everything this woman took from him was already forming in his mind.

And no one would suspect what he would do next.

21

"O H, EDWIN, SHE is so beautiful."
Morghan softly stroked down the horse's long powerful neck. Never in her life had she seen anything as spectacular as this animal. Pale brown in color, the mare stood two hands above her head, her long graceful neck arched high in a testament to her breeding. A broad muscular chest and long legs said she was bred for speed.

This was only the latest in a string of gifts Edwin presented her. After their kiss on the practice field yesterday, he gave her a large iron key and led her to a building that looked unused. What lay inside thrilled and delighted her.

Against one wall lay bolts of soft cotton fabric in every color imaginable. The pride in Edwin's voice showed the care he took in purchasing them in a small bazaar in Egypt.

Mind running wild with possible uses for the delicate fabrics, Morghan found his next gift even more to her liking. A spinning wheel and at least a dozen sacks of wool from the spring sheering sat along the back wall. Since no one possessed the skill needed to card and spin the wool, it sat there gathering dust, and a few critters judging by the sounds she heard.

Excited, Morghan threw her arms about her husband's neck and kissed him soundly. A hand on her back, Edwin leaned her back until they fell onto the sacks. Giggling between kisses, eyes sparkling, Edwin laid the length of his wife, his hips grinding his hard erection between her soft thighs.

Just when Morghan thought he would take them all the way, Edwin rose, holding a hand out to help her rise.

Last evening's meal was eaten side by side. If the looks of approval William gave them were any indication, he very much enjoyed seeing them together. Deep in her heart, Morghan wanted to end being a bride and become a wife. But Edwin seemed to possess other plans for her. Honestly, one more night of being held and fondled by her husband, and she just might have to take matters into her own hands.

It wasn't as if she did not understand what happened between a man and his wife in the marriage bed. Her sisters-in-law made sure she knew every intimate detail. Though not exactly certain how a woman forced a man to copulate, she was frustrated enough to try anything.

So far, she tried every suggestion they taught her. The only thing left was to stroke his shaft until he was so blind with lust, he would take her no matter what his mind feared. That she would keep as a last resort.

"I am very pleased you like her." Edwin's soft whisper broke through her musings. "She is all yours."

"I have never seen anything like her. Where did she come from?" Forcing her mind back onto the horse, Morghan tucked away the sensual thoughts for the moment. There would be another time to bring them back.

"She's an Arabian." Edwin's hands stroked the horse's neck a mere half inch from hers. "I sent for her from the Holy Land." Walking around the animal, he checked each hoof. He laid out a small fortune for the animal, and he wanted to be certain she was in good health. The teeth were checked next.

"What is her name?"

"As far as I know, the breeder never gave her one." Smiling, Edwin felt his heart race. God, Morghan was beautiful standing there in the morning sunlight. She would look even better when he laid her among the flowers and did what his body demanded.

"I shall take my time and think of the perfect name for you." Morghan whispered leaning close to the horse's ear. "You deserve a name as beautiful as you are."

Edwin smiled. He knew the mare would please her, he only hoped his wife would approve of the next surprise he planned for her. "I will get our meal while one of the stable boys saddle her. When you are ready, I have a very special place to show you."

Though he did not want a meal of bread and cheese, he needed something in case Morghan was not quite ready for what he planned.

"Going somewhere, my lady?" James hissed out the question.

"I do not believe my comings and goings are any of your concern." Not even bothering to turn toward the man, she missed the loathsome look he threw her. Watching a boy saddle the mare, Morghan dismissed the scribe all together.

The longer he stood there watching her, the higher James's rage boiled. This horse was ordered months ago and should have gone to his sister, not this Irish impostor. "You think very highly of yourself." Grabbing her upper arm, James spun her about to face him.

"Release me." Morghan ordered. His response was to tighten his grip. The crazed look in his eyes was one she witnessed only once before. She had been called to heal a man known to be insane. James's brown eyes held an identical look to the madman her father was forced to condemn to death for murdering another. How could Edwin not seen it?

"You enjoy toying with me, my lady?" Trying not to shy away from his heated words, Morghan saw someone running off toward the kitchens. "I saw the two of you on the practice field yesterday. You think yourself a lady but act a common whore."

Spittle dripped from the corner of his thin-lipped mouth. "Do you spread your legs for any who can pay your price?" The hand on her arm tightened, his other painfully squeezed her breast. "Scream, and I will see it your last breath."

"You have two seconds to release my *wife*, before I allow her dog to rip your throat out." Edwin's threat was emphasized by Gunther's low, loud growl. "One."

James stood, eyes flaring hatred at her. People began milling about. Out of the corner of her eye, she saw Henry and William arrive. Henry held a sword in his hand and had the look of a man ready to use it.

"Two." James let go so quickly, Morghan staggered back a step before gaining her balance. "Morghan, take the mare and wait for me at the back gate. I have something I must say to James."

"Come, my lady," Henry said, sheathing his sword. "I will see you both safely to the gate." With Henry on one side, the stable boy who saddled the mare on the other, Morghan allowed herself to be moved away.

"Care to explain what I just witnessed?" Edwin stood, hands fisted at his sides, trying desperately not to strike his scribe. Anger boiled inside his gut, raising bile into his throat.

"Lady Morghan looked to be ready to fall over." James stammered slightly. "I was merely making certain nothing happened to cause her injury."

"By placing your hand on her breast?" No one missed his shouted question. All heads turned to stare at the scribe and lord.

"That was an accident, Edwin." Yes, he looked *that* stupid. "I came to tell you there is a small problem on the ship and found your wife standing here alone. I only wanted to assure her safety."

"Is the problem on the ship something you are not capable of handling?" He knew the other man was lying but would save punishment for a less public place.

"No, nothing like that. I simply thought you would want a report immediately." James's voice wavered, betraying the fact he knew he was caught in the lie.

"We sail tomorrow. I trust you to take care of everything until the moment we raise sails. If you find yourself incapable of the task, I can find another first officer. Perhaps Sanders would be a better choice."

James paled. He never expected this reaction. It was common knowledge Edwin did not want his wife, and so far, there was no consummation of the marriage. So why was he getting so upset over a little feel of her breast?

The two men stared at each other, neither backing down.

"Lord Edwin, I believe your wife is mounted and waiting your arrival." William's voice cut through his haze of anger. "If anything requires attention, I will tend it." Turning his gaze directly on the scribe, he added, "After all, it is my business this trip is scheduled to handle."

In silence, Edwin turned. A snap of the fingers brought Gunther to his side. Three paces out, the dog turned and growled one more time before following his master. Whatever game James was playing, he would discover it soon enough.

All thoughts of the scribe faded the instant his eyes settled on Morghan.

Edwin reined in at the edge of the meadow and turned in the saddle to watch his wife's reaction. How many nights did he dream of bringing her here, lying her down on the blanket of wildflowers and making love to her?

Just a hint of a breeze rustled the tall grass. The sun was bright in a cloudless sky, reflecting off the glassy smooth surface of the nearby pond. Birds chirped in the surrounding tall trees, giving a natural musical tone to the air. How perfect it seemed for what he planned.

Sliding from the saddle, Edwin rushed to aid Morghan from her horse, lowering her slowly down his length. Instantly, his body was alive and wanting. Morghan felt so good, so natural in his arms.

Whatever possessed him to believe Morghan could fit in the same category as a traitor? Morghan proved her loyalty to him when he had shown her nothing but indifference and hurt. She risked her life to save his honor, something he simply tossed aside while wallowing in self-pity.

And for what? For people he would never see again and no longer cared about? William was right. They were his past, this woman was his future. Morghan and the children they would have together were all he needed.

Children.

Yes, he had every intention of giving her as many children as the Almighty could bless on them.

First, however, he needed to seduce his wife and consummate their marriage. Raising her left hand, Edwin kissed the scar across her palm. It would be there forever as a reminder of what she sacrificed for him. No woman had ever offered her life for his before. It was a debt he planned on spending the rest of his life repaying.

"You could have died from this, and I never said thank you." Morghan was speechless. She only did what she thought was right. She expected no thanks or glory for her actions, simply to save his honor.

When Edwin's vibrant sea-green eyes rose to meet hers, there was something different about them. Gone was the look of sadness in their depths, replaced by a flash of passion. Many times she witnessed that look in her brother's eyes but only once in Edwin's: their wedding night, in the shared dream.

As quickly as it appeared, it was gone. She felt it would not take much to bring it back, of that she was sure. Turning, Edwin hitched the horses to a nearby bush and began pulling items out of a saddle pack. He spread a soft wool blanket on the grass, and then produced a sack of food and a skin of wine.

"Oleta said you prefer wine to ale." His back still turned to her, Edwin pulled a large bone out next.

"Ale makes my head ache. I actually prefer cider in the cold months and wine in the warm."

"There is so much I need to learn about you." Tossing the bone some distance away, Gunther trotted after the treat.

"We have a lifetime for you to know everything there is to know about me." There, she had taken William's advice and told her husband she no longer wanted to leave him.

"You want to stay?" The hesitance in his voice shook Morghan to the core. He actually feared she meant the harsh words spoken when the fevers left. Perhaps now was the time to tell him everything.

"I never really wanted to leave. I was hurt by what you said to James, and the fevers distorted everything in my mind." Looking out over the meadow, Morghan knew exactly what this place would look like in the spring filled with wildflowers.

Edwin brought her to the one place he dreamed of making love to her.

"You heard what James and I discussed?"

"It was not difficult. You stopped directly outside the window of our chamber when you spoke." Morghan knew it was now or never. "I do not care if you believe you can never love me. I have enough love for the both of us. Trust me."

When her hand touched his cheek, Edwin felt the last of his barriers crumble. Even though Morghan believed he would never love her, she wanted to stay beside him until death. No woman ever gave him so much and asked so little in return.

No words would come to express how much he admired her faith in him, so Edwin chose action. Drawing her near, he pressed his lips to hers, his tongue silently asking permission to enter. He was not denied. As the kiss deepened, he felt her arms circle about his neck, holding him tighter against her soft body.

Every muscle strained, wanting her touch. He was alive as never before. All rational thought fled, replaced by an age-old instinct to take his mate and seal their bodies as one. The feel of her full breasts against his chest set fire to his groin. If he didn't stop, he would take her here on the hard ground. Not a fitting thing for a woman's first time.

Breaking the kiss, Edwin stepped back. Morghan was breathing just as hard as he was. Gunther jumped onto him, reminding him they were not alone.

"Gunther, hunt." Morghan's order sent the dog lopping off toward the trees. Turning back, she knew the spell was broken. There would be no more kisses for the time being.

"You trained him well." Edwin was spreading the items from his sack out on the blanket. He could not look at her, or she would be in his arms again. As delightful as that might be, there were things he wanted to know about this woman, and kissing her would only muddle his brain, not provide those answers.

"My mother actually began his training just before she died." A sad faraway look took over her features. It made Edwin want to hold her. Though he had not seen a woman with them in London, he assumed they simply left her at home.

He could imagine it was not easy for a girl to lose her mother. Who was there to look up to and explain things to her? "How old were you when she died?"

"Seven. Raiders attacked our home in the middle of the night. I watched my mother give her life to save mine." Morghan fell silent. Blank eyes stared out over the meadow grass toward the pond. One arm about her, Edwin encouraged her to sit beside him on the blanket.

"I am sorry, Morghan. I only recently lost my parents. I could not imagine losing one at such a young age." His parents were dead? So much for the thought of asking them what happened in Normandy. Then again, that could explain what happened to send him into a drunken binge.

If the pain of losing his parents was fresh, it was possible he still hurt for their loss. Her mother died so long ago, she barely remembered that night any more.

Edwin hated lying to her, but to him his parents made their decision and were as good as dead in his heart. They chose his brother over him, not caring what their decision would do to him. Yet how did he feel now? At this moment, his wife was in his arms and soon in his bed. Did he even miss what he could have possessed?

In that instant, the answer came to him. No. He wanted Morghan from the moment he laid eyes on her at the abbey and had only gone back to Normandy to keep the promise he made. His body and mind only wanted Morghan. All his dreams revolved about her.

As if a great weight was being lifted from his chest, Edwin knew what he wanted now. Morghan was his wife, and he would no longer turn his back on the gift that was given him. His body wanted her, his mind dreamed of her. Here she sat waiting for him to come to his senses and take her.

Could he do it right here in the middle of the place where he so often dreamed of making love to her? He needed to slow himself down before he frightened her.

Her body screamed out for the one thing only Edwin could give her. She wanted to be a wife and felt she waited long enough to become one. But did she have enough skill to seduce her husband? What would he do if she touched him right now? Would Edwin accept her bold invitation, or back away? There was only one way to find out.

Morghan craved this with a desire that burned deep in her heart. She wanted a husband that would love and cherish her. If Edwin was not yet ready to admit he could love her, she would be patient. Love would come in time, she was sure of that. She would wait a lifetime if that's what it took.

Mind made up, Morghan removed her veil, laying it on the blanket between them. Fingers threaded through her long red hair, left unbound beneath the long veil. Eyes locked on Edwin, her hands reached for the ties of her tunic and began unlacing them.

22

Edwin could not tear his eyes away from what her fingers were doing.

He was sitting here trying to find a way to convince Morghan to allow him to take her and make her his wife today. But she was an innocent, and he would die before frightening her so badly she would fear sharing his bed.

Besides, the hard ground was not the place to take a woman for the first time. A virgin deserved a soft bed and clean linens.

"Morghan, you do not know what you are asking of me." Voice strained, mouth dry, Edwin struggled to control the growing need racing through his veins. When the overtunic joined her veil, his heart pounded against his ribs. Here sat his wife, torturing him as surely as if she placed a hand on his groin and stroked him.

Eyes fixed on the delicate fingers that once touched him deep in the night, only a few short days ago, he sat staring at them now unlacing the undertunic and removing the garment.

Now the only thing between them was a sheer chemise, the fabric so thin he could not only see the soft rose of her nipples, but the deep red color of the hair at the apex of her thighs.

There she sat nearly naked before his eyes, and all he could do was stare. Though he already held her naked body and bathed the fever from her, he never took a good look at all the pleasures it offered. He could not stop looking now.

Full breasts pressed against the thin material, rosy areolas large, nipples already hard and inviting. Her waist was trim, hips wide, perfect for childbearing. At this moment, he could see her body swollen with child, and it made him harder. If he did not stop, he would have her on her back, his member buried deep in her warmth.

Long legs spread slightly offering him a perfect view of the nest of red pubic hair. His fingers itched to touch such perfection, to trail up and down the soft ivory skin of her thigh. He could imagine the feel of them wrapped about his body while he stroked her.

When Morghan began pushing the material off her shoulders, Edwin reached out and stopped her. His hand shook so badly, one would think him ill. "Morghan, you have no idea what you are doing."

"That, my dear husband, is where you are wrong. I know perfectly well what I am doing." The material slipped another inch. Edwin stared at the creamy white skin. His hand shook more. "I have done all I could think of to make you notice I desire you. Can you not you see I want to become your wife?"

"But here on the hard ground?" Heart pounding against his ribs, Edwin struggled for control. His groin tightened and hardened beyond anything he could ever remember experiencing. His body ached with a need he never possessed before.

"A woman's first time is painful. There are only a few things a man can do to ease that pain. The ground can only make it worse for you."

"I do not care." The fact was she truly didn't care. Her body craved something she only dreamed of. Whether here or in their bed at night, the pain would be the same. "I am prepared for what comes. All I care is that you take me as your wife. *Now.*" She had come this far and was not about to back down.

The instant the chemise fell from her shoulders to pool about her waist, Edwin knew he was lost. His body screamed to join with hers. There was no denying he wanted her. If he waited any longer, he would disgrace himself.

Reaching for the material, his hand brushed the underside of one breast. From that touch, his resistance was gone. Eyes locked on hers, Edwin cupped one breast, his thumb rubbing against the taut nipple. A soft moan met his ears, bringing a smile to his lips. "You like that, do you?" In the next moment, his mouth replaced his hand.

Tongue swirling about the tight bud, Edwin drew it deep into his mouth and suckled hard. Morghan's hard breathing only brought it deeper. Never before was any woman he'd known been so well-endowed. Large full breasts were definitely better.

Morghan watched fascinated as her husband draw a breast into his mouth. He suckled her like a tiny baby. Before her eyes, Edwin's head disappeared, replaced by an infant's, covered by golden curls. It was a son she would have first.

The idea both pleased and frightened her. Edwin needed his heir, but his words still resounded in her mind. Would he send her away after the child was born? Her heart pounded, and her body felt on fire. She would find a way to remain in his arms for the rest of her life.

It was quickly becoming hard to focus on anything but the man suckling the other breast. The sounds of the meadow faded beneath the hard pounding of her heart, the rush of blood through her veins, the aching between her legs.

Though she thought her sisters-in-law prepared her well, nothing could have readied her for this rush of sensations racing along every nerve in her body.

She was ready to explode from this simple touch.

While he suckled, a hand inched up the hem of her chemise. Now her legs were exposed, the sun warming the naked skin. Ever so slowly, she was laid back against the soft blanket. Edwin knelt between her open legs, staring up the length of her body.

"I have dreamed so long of making love to you here in this meadow."

The strain in his voice told her just how hard it was for him to hold back his passions.

"I know. The night we were wed, I shared your dream. I felt everything you did to me in that dream. I woke to the pounding on the door, thinking it was the pounding of my heart."

"There is no way you can know what I dreamed that night. I have never told a living soul what my dreams included."

Morghan looked around at the tall grass and knew she needed to tell her husband everything. Sitting up, she stopped a mere inch from his gloriously naked chest. When had he taken off his tunic? "There is something about me you need to know before we go any farther."

When Edwin simply sat there staring at her naked breasts and open legs, she knew he was trying to make a decision. The bulge between his legs spoke of his arousal. Would this news bring him comfort or frighten him away? The only way to find out was to say what she needed and live with the consequences.

"When we join as husband and wife for the first time, a bond will form between us. My mother's family was deep into the Druid religion, and from that, this unusual bond developed. I will be able to tell when you are in danger, hurt, or ill. In return, you shall possess the same abilities toward me. Only one thing you will poses that I will not."

"And that would be?"

"If ever I am unfaithful to you, you will know it the moment it happens. Never will there be a time I can lie to you, for one look and you will know the truth." Morghan could not look at him now. Fear of rejection built inside her until she thought she would die from it.

For a long time, Edwin sat there watching his wife breath. He never heard anything like this bond she spoke of. Would it be all bad to have her know when he was hurt, ill, or in trouble? And the benefit for him? He would have a faithful wife, for if she ever strayed, he would instantly know.

"Would we often share dreams as we did on our wedding night?"

"If the bond is strong enough, we may share them often. My father and mother shared them all the time. My brothers are not as strong as I am. Their wives rarely know what they do, though Marga knew when my brother's ship was wrecked in a storm and led my father to him before he became too ill for me to heal."

Silence stretched between them. Morghan looked out at the pond, the grass, the birds as they flew overhead. Anywhere but at the man she feared would reject her. She could feel his confusion and fear, even without a set bond between them.

This was taking too long. No matter how much she wanted Edwin to accept her, Morghan knew the longer it took for him to reply, the more chance his reaction would be negative.

Turning from him, she began restoring her garment about her shoulders. A single tear spilled from her eye. The vision of the baby had been false. She would never bear this man's child.

Head bowed, Morghan reached for her tunic and veil. She had not paid much attention to the direction they rode, but figured if she followed the seabirds circling overhead, she would find the water and follow the coast to Ironwood.

Once there, she would find William and have him arrange for her to leave.

She did this to herself. If she did not feel he needed to be honest and simply allowed Edwin to take her, she would be a wife by now, not a rejected bride. Standing, she found a restraining hand on her wrist. Turning back, the look on his face broke her heart.

"You will never be able to go to another man without my knowing?"

"No, my love, never. If I even have thoughts of another man, you will feel it immediately." Oh god, what happened to him in Normandy?

The answer slammed into her mind in a rush of cold water. The woman he loved betrayed him with another. No wonder he never wanted any other woman in his life, let alone a wife.

"You must trust—whether we share the bond or not—I would never betray you in the arms of another. I took vows before God, my father, and the king. I intend to honor those vows."

Morghan did not need words to know that a betrayal was exactly what had happened to him.

Edwin wanted desperately to believe her. His mind told him she spoke the truth, but his heart feared trusting again. Could he take the chance and seal their fates when he joined their bodies? How would he be able to live if he allowed what Rowena did to him to affect this marriage?

William had given him a gift. Could he now turn his back on that gift and allow Morghan to walk out of his life? He brought her out here with the intention of seducing her. Was he ready to give up that plan?

When a tear rolled down her pale cheek, Edwin made his decision.

23

A HARD TUG ON her arm brought Morghan back down into his arms.

His lips fastened on to hers the instant they were close. Tongue running along her lips, Edwin silently begged for entry. He was not denied. Her mouth opened beneath his, and Edwin thrust his tongue deep into its warmth. A soft moan was his reward.

While his tongue swirled and danced with hers, his hands quickly removed the garment she, only moments before, placed back over her tempting breasts. This time, he would not stop. There would be no barriers between him and what he craved. When Morghan was naked, he laid her back against the blanket, never breaking the kiss.

A trail of soft kisses found his lips tugging on one earlobe. Another soft moan was his reward. But he wanted more. He craved hearing Morghan moan loudly while he gave her the ultimate pleasure. Kissing down her neck, he paid homage to her breasts, while his fingers found her most sensitive area.

She was on fire. Morghan could think of nothing but what Edwin's hands were doing to her. Every inch of her body was alive and throbbing.

All she wanted was her husband deep inside her, pouring himself onto the heat spreading through her.

The wait was near torture. Since the moment she placed her hand into his at Tourney Island Keep, Morghan desired this. She needed to become a wife, to know Edwin desired her.

Trying to grab at him, Morghan found her hands captured in one of his and held over her head. The action pressed her breasts farther into his mouth.

This was such heavenly torture.

Edwin knew when Morghan was ready, and he could wait no longer. His member demanded he end the torture and seal their lives, but he was not quite done seducing every last emotion out of his beautiful wife. All his dreams placed them in this meadow while the flowers bloomed. This was the right place to consummate their marriage.

"Take me, Edwin. Now!"

Freeing himself, Edwin settled between her parted thighs. Poised and ready to make her his wife, but something still held him back. He would trust her word, he would always know if she were unfaithful to him, but…

"Look at me, Morghan." Edwin's voice was commanding. Opening her eyes, she stared into sea-green ones so filled with passion, they reminded her of storm-tossed waves crashing against the hard rocks of Ireland. "Swear to me you will never look at another man as long as you live."

Her mind barely functioned; it was so filled by passion. He wanted a solemn vow from her now? At the moment she had been waiting for, he wanted her to speak words to ease his mind. Would she even be able to form the words he needed to hear?

"Once you join our bodies, you will know the truth of what I speak. My father never betrayed my mother. Even after her death, he has never taken another woman to his bed. Our bond shall be forever."

Edwin stared down into eyes he knew told the truth. He did not deserve a woman like this. He had done everything in his power to shun and reject her. She had done everything possible to lure him to her.

Grabbing her firm butt cheeks, Edwin spread her wide and thrust forward. Never had he possessed a virgin. He was now where no man had ever been before. Until a moment ago, Morghan knew no man and never would know another.

A strange energy flowed into his body where they were joined. In that instant, he knew every word she spoke was the truth. Like a tentative touch, her mind reached out to him. There Edwin felt all her love, hopes, and dreams. The very last restraint on his heart crumbled, and Edwin allowed it to be touched by hers.

Rising up on his elbows, Edwin looked into the face of his wife. No longer a bride, she was his in every way. "Now you believe what I say?"

"I must admit there is a feeling about me I cannot explain. It settled softly on my heart." When had he become a poet? When Morghan raised her hips to grind into him, his moment of fancy fled.

His body demanded he finish what he started. Though he knew a woman's first time brought pain, he also wanted hers to bring pleasure. Moving slowly, he could feel when her passions began to rise. Yes, he could actually feel what she felt. This was a turn he never expected.

Every movement he made brought double sensations to him. Edwin could actually feel his own self thrusting into her tight passage. He accepted this bond so he would always know Morghan was faithful, now he was experiencing so much more. The sensations were nearly overwhelming.

The instant he felt her passions build, Edwin knew his time was at an end. When Morghan stiffened beneath him crying out her release, Edwin gave in to the natural demands of his body. While her soft muscles still pulled at his body, Edwin threw his head back, screamed "mine," and emptied himself into her womb.

Morghan caught her husband as he fell against her, completely spent. The memory of the piercing pain was a distant memory, shoved aside by the pleasure she received. Expecting a bond between them was one thing, what they just shared was not what her father prepared her for.

Even now, his passions spent, she could feel Edwin's heart beating as if it were her own. Slowly, she threaded her fingers through his sweat-soaked hair, pushing it back from his face. Would intercourse always be like this? So filled with sensations it nearly overloaded her?

"Lord, I hope so." Edwin's whispered reply startled her. She never meant to say the words out loud.

Rising up on his elbows, Edwin looked down into her sated features.

What he just experienced was far beyond anything he ever had before. Where his past lovers were taken mostly to satisfy his manly urges, this felt more like a blending of body and soul.

Was this what it was like to be in love? Did he never really care for Rowena, but only thought he needed to wed her because he found himself in her so often? So many questions flowed through his mind, their demands for answers frightening. In this moment of joy, he did not want to dwell on what could have been, but what was here and now in his grasp.

Morghan wiggled beneath him, and his shrinking member slipped free. Never before could he remember feeling so sated, so at peace with himself. It was all Morghan's doing, he was sure of that. A quick look down and the full force of the reality hit him.

He was a husband now. A moment ago, he filled his wife with his seed and even now it could be taking root and forming his first child. The truth was he wanted many children and only Morghan to give them to him. All thoughts of Normandy faded from memory, tucked neatly in the back of his mind. Morghan was his life, his breath, his future.

Grabbing a cloth, Edwin rose to clean the blood and semen from his body. "I will be right back." The water in the pond would be cold, but it did not matter. He needed it to shrink the renewed desire building in him. A few minutes ago, he deflowered his wife. Surely, she was too sore to stand another bout of sex so soon.

Kneeling beside the still surface of the pond, Edwin took a long look at himself. There was no outward difference that he could see, yet deep inside he felt a change he could not explain. Could this feeling be love for the woman who had just given herself to him?

Quickly washing, he soaked the cloth in the cool water preparing to return to his wife and soothe her abraded skin.

Morghan's scream stopped his heart.

He was naked and had no weapon but the wet cloth he squeezed in tight fingers. It mattered not. Morghan was in danger, and he needed to save her.

As stealthily as he could, Edwin crawled through the tall grass. He could see nothing. Morghan was silent. What a fool he had been to bring her here. Selfishness was all it was. He dreamed so many times of making love to her in this meadow. He allowed his mind to dwell on that and not about their safety. Some lord he would make.

Not once did he think to bring his sword or a dagger for protection. Still on Ironwood land, he figured them safe. Yet just this morn, William warned him there were renegade Saxons still attacking Norman strongholds. Such a self-centered bastard he was.

A look to the right showed the horses continued to munch at the tall grass. Surely, if Morghan was under attack, they would raise some sort of alarm. He *had* heard her scream. It was not his imagination. A movement near where he left his wife lying naked on the blanket drew his attention. Someone was definitely out here.

Where was Gunther? The dog should have returned when his mistress screamed. At his size, the beast could be some sort of help. A moan met his ears now. Moving faster, Edwin ran toward his wife.

"Gunther, you stupid beast." Morghan could not believe she screamed when the dog dropped the dead bird on her chest.

Sated and drained, she dozed while Edwin left, waking up the instant the dead fowl touched her skin. It was not as if he never did such things. The beast often dropped dead animals at her feet. After all, she did send him away by telling him to hunt.

When Edwin popped up from the tall grass, gloriously naked holding a dripping cloth in one hand, Morghan could not hold back a laugh. Completely unarmed and naked as the day he was born, he stood ready to fight any foe that threatened her. Eyes darting about, she knew he was searching for the cause of her scream.

"Forgive me, Edwin, for frightening you, but I was not prepared for what Gunther presented me." A wave of her hand drew his attention to the dead bird lying beside the blanket then to the splash of blood across her chest.

Stance easing, Edwin stared hard at the dog. The beast sat on his haunches, tongue lolling to one side, and he could swear a smile of satisfaction on his face. "Good dog. Now see if you can find another. Hunt, Gunther." There was not even a look at his mistress before the huge beast lumbered back into the wood.

Kneeling beside his wife, Edwin tried to stop the shaking of his hand as he reached out to clean the blood from her chest. "I am sorry I frightened you. I was dozing when he dropped the thing on me."

"You have nothing to be sorry for. I, on the other hand, proved just how incompetent a protector I am. I brought you out here in the middle of nowhere, far from the protection of Ironwood, lost myself in making love to you, and did not even have the wherewithal to bring a weapon.

"Gunther could have easily been a group of raiding Saxons or a passing villager. I have failed you as a protector. I have failed as a husband. It is my duty to see you protected at all times."

Morghan could only stare at her husband. There was no danger, and she wanted this business between them to be over. She never thought anything so horrific could befall them. Sitting up, she pushed the cloth aside and laid a hand against his chest over his heart.

"Tell me what you feel. Here, deep inside. Could you not feel I was safe?"

Edwin's heart pounded against her hand, and his body began reacting to her touch. How could he want her again so soon? Yet the more he thought on it, the more he realized there was no sense of fear from her, just a slight anger.

"Will I always know when you are in danger?" Their eyes locked, and he knew the answer.

"Always. Our bond is already strong. If anything should happen to me, you would know it. As for being a good protector, I have never doubted you could defend me should the need arise." Placing her left hand against his cheek, she watched in silence as Edwin turned his head and kissed the scar.

Need, pulsing and hot, ran along every nerve ending in her body. A quick look said Edwin felt it too. Giving in to the urge, Morghan pressed her lips to his. Instantly Edwin's mouth opened beneath hers, his tongue plunging deep into the warmth. There was no stopping himself until he had her back on the ground, his body lying the length of hers.

"No. I cannot take you again so soon, though my body demands it." Rising, he pulled her up behind him, and then into his arms. Heading for the pond, he knew the only thing to quench the need would be to bury himself deep inside her again or a long dip in the cold water.

Twenty minutes later, Edwin carried his wife back to the blanket. It was a struggle to wash the evidence of their loving from her body and not give in to the need pounding hard through his body.

Using the blanket, he quickly dried her off and dressed her. Gunther sat watching their every movement, a satisfied look on his face. When he dipped his head, Edwin saw that three more birds had joined the first on the ground. "Good boy." Dressing quickly, he retrieved the fowl, tying the feet together so they hung from his saddle.

Morghan winced slightly when she gained her saddle. "Are you able to ride, or would you prefer I take you before me on my horse?" A silent look at the huge warhorse and Morghan knew she would rather stay where she was.

"Lord Edwin, you have ten seconds to mount your horse before I win the race home."

"Are you challenging me, Lady Morghan?" A smile tugged the corners of his mouth while he settled the birds. "I assure you I have never been beaten at a race before."

"Never?"

"Never, my lady."

"Then I think it is about time you were." The instant his backside hit the saddle, Morghan dug her heels into the mare, and the beast took off. Her laughter floated back to him on the wind, and Edwin smiled while spurring his mount forward.

Two horses raced through the back gate of Ironwood. All eyes turned to stare at the lord and lady, laughing and pulling to a stop before the stables. Three sets of eyes paid close attention to the couple.

"I do not understand it," Robert muttered, staring at the couple now dismounting.

"What confuses you, young de Montgomery?" William laughed at the antics of the two. They acted as if no one watched. Something changed while they were out, and he was exceedingly pleased.

"Lord Edwin is a superior horseman. He rides it as well as he does the waves of the sea. He never loses a race."

Henry smiled at the naive squire. He too knew something changed between the two and was happy for them. "You have much to learn about women, Robert. Lord Edwin did exactly as he should have."

"You mean he lost on purpose, sire?"

"I would not say he lost a thing." The look William turned on Henry said it all. The kiss Edwin was now giving his wife spoke volumes on what occurred on the outing.

Edwin sailed soon. He wondered if he would see much of them between now and high tide on the tenth.

24

"I will see you at the evening meal, my lord?"

Leaning close, Edwin gave in to the urge to kiss his wife once more. No one seemed to notice. Good. He liked being able to touch and kiss Morghan whenever and wherever he pleased. "Until then, my dear, I will be on my ship. James mentioned some problems, and I need to supervise things for myself."

A pout captured her lips, and it made Edwin laugh. "A wife only a few hours, and already you can turn me with a pout." His whispered words close to her ear brought a shiver. "What needs doing is important and cannot wait, my sweet? Look for me at mealtime." With the brace of birds in hand, Edwin headed for the kitchen whistling a soft tune.

"Such a noxious scene, my lady." James's harsh voice hissed from behind her. "Makes one wonder if a title can be bestowed on any lowly man. The lord and lady should not present themselves as rutting beasts before their people. It makes them want to vomit."

Morghan had no intention of turning around or acknowledging this man in any way. James would not be dissuaded. There was something about him that grated against her nerves.

"What a husband and wife do together is none of your concern." Though her tone was dismissive, the dense man did not seem to be getting the idea.

"Yet twice you have paraded it out in the open for all to see. Do you enjoy having people watching you? If so, I could find my way to your bedchamber later and enjoy watching Edwin mount you."

Just the thought made her stomach turn. James stood in the shadows, and she wondered if anyone could see or hear him. People walked by as if he was invisible. "Your threats are wasted, James. You can do nothing to harm me." Gunther growled, letting her know someone was near and listening.

"There you are wrong, my lady. I spent five long years getting things exactly where I wanted them, and I do not intend to lose everything I worked so hard to obtain just because you finally spread your legs. I want you out of this keep before we return. If not…" James let his voice trail off, leaving her imagination fill in the threat.

"You cannot threaten me. All I need do is tell Edwin and you can be stopped. I assure you, he will not take kindly to my life being put in danger."

"Life is so fragile." His eyes turned heavenward, his face taking on an innocence she knew he never possessed, not even as a child. "Edwin could meet with an accident out at sea, or a bad meal that could prove poisonous, and end his life. I could think of a thousand ways he could meet his end. Accidents happen all the time."

A little voice inside her head warned not to ignore this man's ravings. There was much truth to his words. Still, if she were to warn Edwin of his threats, they would have no power.

"If you think to warn your husband, I would caution against it. I have known the man many years. A simple denial is all I need for him to believe me."

James could be right. Edwin was just beginning to trust her. This man he had known for many years. Who would he believe?

"If something happens to Edwin, the king would take over Ironwood."

"Ah yes. William would give it to another of his favorites. You would then be put out. Or perhaps since William gave you to one of his nobles, he might give you to another. Think how it would feel to have another man between your legs, doing as Edwin did this afternoon. If that thought appeals to you, I could provide the service for you. All you need do is ask."

Just the thought of this man or any other doing what Edwin had made her stomach heave. A few quick swallows did nothing to stop the bile from rising up in her throat.

Morghan barely made it behind the stables before the contents of her stomach emptied onto the dirt. "The thought does not please you?" James whispered into her ear. He was relentless.

Oh god, would the man never leave her alone?

"I would never wed you or any other. Once widowed, no man can force me to wed again." What was she thinking? She had no intention of becoming a widow until well into her eighties.

"Really? Being Lord Edwin's scribe, I can produce any document I want. Did you know Edwin cannot read or write? I do it all for him, and he trusts me to write down what he says. So you see, I will have my way in this no matter what you say. With one stroke of the quill, I can take everything from Edwin and give it to myself."

How Morghan wanted to strike the smug look from his face, but she dare not… not now.

Some way somehow, she needed to get proof of his threats before she could even approach the king. "Think on it, my lady. Do you choose to leave or bring harm to your husband? I give you until we return to decide, so think carefully."

For several minutes after James walked away, Morghan knelt where she had fallen, arms folded about her stomach, mind racing. The beauty of the afternoon was gone. If only someone else was present to witness the threats.

But James was clever and made certain no one witnessed his tormenting words.

On shaky legs, Morghan headed for the kitchen. There was one aspect of his threat she could prevent. A quick talk to Oleta and she would be sure Edwin's meals were safe. She just needed to find a way to safeguard the remainder of their lives.

The moment Lady Morghan passed the stables, Robert took off running. He headed not toward his lord but to the practice field and Sir Henry. The master-at-arms would know what to do to stop the scribe.

Morghan pushed the food about on the trencher. Every few minutes, she looked toward the hall doors and wondered where Edwin was. After all, he did promise to be here for the evening meal.

Already the stew was cold, the wine warm and the bread dried out. She could not take it any longer. Her nerves were on edge, and her stomach never settled after hearing James's threats. Could the man be right? Could he take everything Edwin worked so hard to build in a single stroke of the quill?

Her father never trusted one man enough to allow such power. She and her brothers were taught to read and write, add sums, and even speak three languages. At first, Connor objected to his daughter being taught beside his sons, but she proved persistent and sat outside their classroom, using a stick to draw her letters in a patch of dirt.

Kerwin was the one to correct her spelling and share his lessons. When their father found out, she thought he would forbid her such manly endeavors. Instead, he added a chair to the room and sat beside her each night listening to her read.

There must be a way to stop James. Right now, her mind feared him, so she could think of nothing that would benefit her and not him. She could feel eyes on her, but every time she looked up, everyone in the hall was deep in conversation and paying her no attention. Even William and Henry talked low between them keeping their conversation personal.

All too often, she allowed her imagination to run away with her. Surely, if Edwin was in any danger, she would sense it. After all, their bond was safely in place now. Yet would it carry over a vast distance when he was on his ship and hundreds of leagues away?

"Starving yourself will not help your husband, my lady." Oleta's voice beside her made her jump. "Such a waste of good stew." Sitting in the lord's chair, the cook placed a hand over hers. "I sent Tommy to Lord Edwin carrying his meal. Something aboard ship kept him from coming."

"I can just imagine what James did to delay him." This woman was the only person she confided what James said to her. Though it made her feel better at the time, now she wondered if it was such a good idea to involve another in this problem. There was no way she wanted Oleta or any other in Ironwood to be a target of this madman.

"Actually, it was something the king requested." Morghan looked past the cook toward the man in question. William arrived for the meal on time and said nothing to her about delaying Edwin.

"Do you know what has delayed them?"

"Nay, my lady. I was only told it would keep Lord Edwin and James busy for several hours yet."

Several hours? She hoped to speak to Edwin… Oh, who was she attempting to fool. She wanted to feel Edwin's touch again, have her body come alive beneath his demanding touch. This time the experience would not contain any pain, simply pleasure. And oh, how she longed to feel that pleasure again.

"Come now. Eat this and get yourself off to bed. There are only two days left until Lord Edwin sails, and you do not want to spend them worrying yourself sick. I can think of much more pleasurable things to occupy your time." The twinkle in the cook's eyes made her smile despite her fear.

"What am I to do about James?"

"Nothing right now, my lady. I have found in life that most men speak to hear themselves talk. James is no different. Time alone should prove him false." Though Oleta's words should be reassuring, Morghan found they did little to settle her mind.

But what choice did she have? No one else heard his hate-filled words and threats. Would Edwin even believe her if she confessed just how much James frightened her? Morghan did not want to begin making demands of her husband, just when she was building confidence in their relationship.

From lifelong experience, she knew a man's ship was his mistress. Often, a wife took second place. She saw the patience her sisters-in-law showed with her brothers. Shipping was Edwin's livelihood, and a wife should never try to come between them.

Choking down as much of the stew as she could, Morghan headed to the bathing cottage for a quick wash. She still smelled of their afternoon of sex, and when Edwin came to her tonight, she wanted to smell of lavender, not a quick roll in the meadow.

Finding the bathing cottage deserted, she washed quickly, grabbed her toweling, nightgown, and robe. Before anyone else entered, she was dressed modestly and ready to return to the keep.

Stepping out into the bailey, Morghan felt someone a few steps behind her. It was not James, of that she was certain. He made her skin crawl. God, she needed to get a hold of her imagination before it totally took over her mind and she began fearing everything and everyone about her.

Turning quickly, she saw the shadowy figure of her watcher duck behind the corner of the bathing cottage. He was small and quick, not allowing her a decent look at him.

"Come out now!" she called. Her voice sounded a whole lot braver than she felt. Surely, no one would try to harm her while so many men stood within shouting distance. The patrol strolled the wall walk only ten feet above her head.

Fists on hips, Morghan waited for the stalker to emerge. Moments passed, as did several men-at-arms. It was time to change the guard on the wall walk, giving her twice as many men to call upon if she needed help. "I know you were following me, so come on out before…" Well, at the moment she could think of no threat she could easily follow through on. Having only a towel in hand as a weapon made her ill prepared to fight for her life.

A moment later, Robert stepped out of the shadows. Her husband's squire? Why would the boy want to shadow her? "I never meant to frighten you, my lady." His head down, Robert kicked at a pebble in the grass.

"I would not say you frightened me." That was a lie. "It was more a concern for who was following me." Not waiting for an answer, Morghan turned and slowly began walking back to the keep.

Robert dutifully fell in step behind her, Gunther making them an odd trio. "My duty is not only to Lord Edwin, but to protecting you as well." There was something in his voice that made Morghan stop and turn on him.

"You would not be guarding me if you did not fear something or someone." The boy's blush told her everything. "You heard what James said to me this afternoon, correct?"

"Aye, my lady." He was caught at spying and felt ashamed for only a moment. "I heard every vile thing he said to you. When he left, I ran."

"Surely, you did not tell my husband." Morghan held her breath.

"No. I ran and told the king and Sir Henry. Unless Lord Edwin is off to fight, I am not allowed on his ship. You need not worry, Lady Morghan. King William has begun a way to see James Dupree put in his place."

Oh no. Now the king was involved. A soft moan escaped her parted lips. She never meant for so many to be privy to the man's threats. "I would never allow that man to harm you in any way, my lady." Before her eyes, the young squire puffed up his chest and seemed to grow an inch or two. "I can protect you. With my life if necessary."

The ego of such a young man was fragile. She knew from watching her nephew's struggle toward adulthood just how fragile it was. One wrong move, and she could scar him for the rest of his life. There was no way she would willingly break his spirit. "Very well. Just keep in mind Edwin may not be very happy with either of us for keeping this secret from him. Until I can find a way to tell my husband what James plans, we must keep this between the two of us." Actually, between the five of them now. "I do not want James turning desperate because so many people know what he plans. It could cause him to force his hand early, and that is the last thing I want."

"I will keep the secret for now, Lady Morghan. But if your husband asks me a direct question, I will be honor-bound to tell him everything. I swore an oath to my lord, and I cannot break it, not even for you." Morghan hoped Edwin would be too busy getting ready for the sailing to suspect anything was amiss.

Gaining her chamber without any further distractions, Morghan stripped and climbed into bed. Drawing her knees up to her chest, she wound her arms about them and laid her head down. She would wait Edwin like this. In minutes, she was asleep.

It was in that position Edwin found his wife a few hours later.

Hours ago saw him ready to leave the ship, intending to share their evening meal. But James seemed to have other ideas. He did not want to, but after dismissing the scribe for the night, Edwin went to Sander's cottage to speak to the man.

Enough was enough. James was acting as if he owned de Ballard shipping, not him. This evening's ruse was the last straw. Time after time, the scribe came up with small insignificant things to keep him away from his wife and meal. If James thought to insert himself between Morghan and himself, the man was in for a rude awakening.

Sanders was an older man, in his early forties, and on his crew nearly as long as James. His children were grown and chose to stay in Normandy, so it was just Sanders and his wife Sarah now. The older man eagerly accepted his offer of first officer and swore his loyalty immediately. Edwin would begin training him on this journey.

Tired and ready to join his wife in bed, nonetheless, he stopped first to bathe the sweat from his body. The memory of how Morghan reacted to his touch made his body demand more of her sweet warmth. He feared Morghan would still be sore from their first bout of lovemaking that afternoon but would take his chances. The decision of intimacy would be her choice this night.

Dropping his clothing, Edwin eased back the sheet and slid onto the mattress. Morghan did not stir. A soft brush brought the hair off her shoulder. God, she was beautiful, her features soft in the glow of the night candle. His body ached to be buried deep in hers again.

He needed to go slow, or his passions might frighten her out of his arms. Who was he kidding? This afternoon, Morghan answered his every movement with want and passion of her own.

Just remembering her body slamming against his in the meadow was enough to make him groan. If every time could be like the first, he would never tire of her softness and wild passion.

"Edwin?" Sleepy green eyes turned to look at him. Lord, could she look any more beautiful?

"I would like to think you have not taken a lover so soon after giving yourself to me." Though his words were teasing and he wore a smile, he knew the instant Morghan took them wrong.

A heavy cloud descended over her features, darkening them into anger. "I but tease you, my dear. What has upset you so?"

She needed to think fast. This was not the right time to tell Edwin about her encounter with James. "I thought you would join me for the evening meal." Her words were accompanied by a softening of her features. "I missed you."

"Did you now? Only a few hours a wife and you already miss me?"

Words choked in Morghan's throat, so she decided to show him instead. Rising over him, she placed her hands flat against his chest and pushed him back flat against the mattress. Her next move brought her lips to the huge bulging muscles and taut skin of his chest.

Edwin never knew any woman like his wife. She was actually on her knees beside him, her breasts swaying slightly waiting to be touched, taunting him. When her hot moist lips trailed down to his stomach, he thought he would spill his seed. Surely, she had no idea of what she was doing to him.

All evening his mind was occupied by the feel of her body as he thrust into her. Too many times, he was caught daydreaming about the feel of her beasts in his hands, her lips against his.

He wanted them again.

Now.

Grabbing her by the arms, he slid her body the full length of his, spreading his legs slightly, cradling her there. The pout on Morghan's face made him laugh. "Any lower, my dear, and you would unman me."

"I only want to please you."

"Honestly, Morghan, if you pleased me any more, I would die from it." Flipping her onto her back, he settled himself exactly where he wanted to be. In the next breath, a breast filled his mouth, his tongue teasing her nipple with long, slow, swirling motions. "Your touch has set me on fire," he said, moving to the other breast. "Do you know how difficult it was for me to not let you know I was awake while you touched me those nights?"

Her gasp brought the breast farther into his mouth. "You were awake?" The thought horrified her. Never, if she knew he was awake, would she have been able to do such open brazen behavior.

"For every delicious moment of your exploration." Looking up from the breast, Edwin smiled. "Do not be embarrassed, my dear. I rather liked what you did to me. Though I must admit, I enjoy it more when I can respond to you." His words were emphasized by a caress of her intimate folds. "Perhaps later I can allow your Irish touch to have its wicked way."

Right now, he needed to prepare her quickly before disgracing himself.

They made love hard and fast. The second time came slow and sensual. When dawn turned the sky a bright red, it found them exhausted and entwined in each other's arms.

Edwin indeed allowed his wife to touch him all she wanted and enjoyed every second of it.

25

The evening meal was a boisterous one.

Could it be that everyone sounded happier, or was it simply the happiness and love in her heart making the world reflect her feelings? A man laughed somewhere, his melodious tone filling the entire hall.

Two days a wife and already she was melancholy. Edwin would leave on the morrow and be gone for nearly a fortnight. Her love for him would not change in the time he was gone, but what of his? There were no avowals of love from Edwin, no talk of the future they would share, only now and the pleasure he found in her arms.

A blush rose on her cheeks, remembering the stolen moments they shared in the wool hut this afternoon. She could not get enough of touching and kissing her husband, and Edwin seemed to feel the same toward her. Every time they even passed each other, they found themselves in a heated kiss.

"Careful, my sweet, or my men will have the idea their lady did something no proper lady should." The breath from Edwin's whisper sent tingles down every nerve in her body, settling deep in her most intimate place. How could she want him again so soon? Did a normal wife have such feeling for her husband? "More wine?"

Giggling like a young girl, Morghan turned a smile on the man who held her heart. Edwin's smile showed he was sitting there thinking on their shared afternoon. It was sultry and heated. "Surely, my husband, you should take care of yourself before your own expression betrays you."

"A man often has thoughts about women." When he finished pouring, Edwin set the flagon aside. "I simply find my mind centered on my wife." *Where it should be*, Morghan added to herself.

Henry noticed the gate guard heading across the hall and signaled the man to him. His lord and lady were so involved in their own conversation, neither noticed the man.

"What brings you into the hall at this time of night, Jailyn?" Henry's voice was barely above a whisper. He was pleased by the progress Edwin and Morghan made over the last few days. Ironwood was now a happy place. From the look on the guard's face, that might change tonight.

"A messenger stands at the sea gate. He claims to be carrying a message meant for my lady's eyes only." Jailyn looked at his mistress when he heard her laugh. All here knew it was her doing that changed Ironwood so drastically.

"Is the message from her father?" William demanded. Had there even been enough time for Connor to reach home and send out a messenger? He doubted it.

"Nay, sire." Jailyn quickly shifted position. "The man speaks Norman French, not the Celt I heard from Lord Connor's men."

"Are you certain the man asked for Lady Morghan, not me?"

"Aye, sire."

"Do you think Lady Morghan, or her father, has acquaintances in Normandy?" Henry quickly asked.

"None that I know of." William replied. "Does the man wear any house colors or carry any banner?"

"Nay, sire. In fact, he looks much like one of Lord Edwin's crew." All the color drained from the king's face. A quick look and William knew Henry's look mirrored his own. "Should I send the man away?"

William's own messenger arrived just two days ago, bearing nothing of importance from Edwin's family or the unusual situation he ordered men to observe in the village.

William looked at the happy couple, still oblivious of the guard standing before them. It warmed his heart that the two were so into themselves, they did not see what went on around them in their own hall. After trying so long to get them together, he hated to drive a wedge between them. And William had no doubt whatever the messenger needed to say would do just that.

"Allow the man to deliver his message. See him fed and give a space on the hall floor for the night."

It was on the tip of Henry's tongue to question his king but thought better of it. "Do you believe the message is from Lord Edwin's parents?" Henry softly asked.

"I have no doubt it is." Taking a long drink of ale, William glanced at the couple who was about to have their lives shattered. "It can only be bad news he bears, for anything good would have come to me first."

All conversation stopped the moment the messenger entered the hall. Noting the sudden change, Morghan looked up.

A man crossed toward the head table. His wind-tossed blond hair and weathered clothing reminded her of her husband's ship crew, yet he was not any she could remember seeing about Ironwood.

A quick look beside him, and Morghan saw recognition in her husband's eyes, mixed with anger. Whoever this man was, Edwin did not like his being allowed into the hall.

"What brings you here, Raine?" Not only was Edwin's body stiff, but Morghan winced at the anger in his voice.

"I bring a message from your mother, my lord. I am to deliver it only to your lady wife," the messenger added when Edwin held out his hand to receive the parchment.

How in hell did his mother even know he took a wife? Edwin's icy stare turned on the king. "I sent word of your marriage to your parents. I felt they had a right to know." William's glare dared his vassal to question his motives.

"After what they did, they have no right to be privy to any aspect of my life, sire." Edwin rose but found his steps halted by Morghan's hand on his arm.

Edwin turned to look at the delicate fingers touching him. This could be just what she needed to put everything together and figure out what happened to her husband to change him.

"Take the message back where it came from, Raine." Ever so slowly, he turned his stare on the other man. "The news is not wanted here."

"I cannot do that, my lord. Your mother told me only your lady wife can refuse this." Raine held up the message, reveling in the soft shaking of his fingers and how much Edwin's anger affected him. Turning on Morghan, he asked, "Do you refuse the message, my lady?"

All eyes turned on her. Such a quandary. Her heart told her she needed to know what was so important Edwin's mother sent the message directly to her. Of course, if she sent it to her son, Edwin would never open and read it.

Without even knowing what the missive contained, Morghan knew it would hold all the clues to finish building the puzzle of what happened to Edwin in Normandy to change him so much.

But did she need to know what happened any longer? Edwin made an effort to get past what affected him and accept her as his wife. Should that not be enough? Still, her mind screamed for her to take the message and read it. Turning toward the king, she received two slight nods.

Slowly, her hand snaked out toward Raine. Eyes still on Edwin, she accepted the parchment, drawing it close to her breast.

"I warn you, wife, I care not what it says." His tone was so icy Morghan was surprised the temperature in the hall did not drop ten degrees.

"Raine, a meal awaits you in the kitchen," Henry announced. "When done, seek me out. I will arrange a place for you to sleep this night."

"Sir Henry." A slight bow and Raine left.

Grabbing his goblet, Edwin drank deep. Too deep for her liking.

Since the morning she slipped her husband the herbs to cause him to stop drinking, there was not even one incident of overuse.

"Will you tell me what happened in Normandy to change you so?" Morghan held the unopened message in her hands. This could all end now, if only Edwin would trust her enough to tell her what happened. "I would rather hear the tale from your own lips."

"Does it truly matter anymore?" Reaching for his goblet again, Edwin paused. Getting drunk only caused trouble in the past; he would not repeat the incident again.

"We are man and wife now. I have accepted everything about our marriage. Nothing that happened in that time can touch us any longer."

"Good." Morghan turned a small smile on her husband. "Then nothing in here can harm us." Before Edwin could react, Morghan broke the seal and opened the parchment.

Edwin watched as sadness came over his wife's features. Anger boiled deep in his guts. How dare they cause Morghan even the slightest bit of pain? If anything in the message caused her upset or harm, he would return to Normandy and personally see to it that none of them ever contacted her again. For as long as he lived, he would protect her from their vile accusation. How dare they?

All his thoughts faded, seeing a tear slowly roll down her cheek. Then his anger returned full force, slamming into his gut like a six-foot wave. "If anything my mother said hurts you, I will personally see to it that she—"

Morghan's fingers pressed against his soft lips stilled his angry words.

"You should read this." Her softly spoken words did little to defuse his anger.

"Even if I could read, I would not care one whit what my mother has to say. Her poisonous words need to stay away from me."

"You cannot read?" Why did she find that so surprising? Obviously, the scribe had told her the truth. Many men never learned to read. Still, Edwin was no longer a simple sailor. He possessed a title and land. A decent education could only aid in his running of Ironwood. "Have you ever considered learning? It would be simple for me to teach you."

"Thank you, my dear, but I need not know how. I have James to keep my accounts, both for the shipping and Ironwood. If I need a message sent, he can write it for me or a verbal message sent."

Morghan remembered James's warning the other day. She wanted so badly to warn Edwin of James's threat but knew this moment was not the right time to delve into such a discussion. Now was the time to deal with the message and the news it brought. Right now, she needed him to listen to the news.

There were a hundred ways she could lead into the subject of the message, but perhaps the direct way was the best. "Your brother is dead."

Edwin froze. He should not care one whit about any one of them. So why was there a sadness seeping into his heart? Because Morghan broke down every last barrier he so carefully placed there.

"It was an accident." Edwin heard his wife's voice as if from a great distance. "Something startled his horse when he made to jump over a hedge. Louis lingered near death in agonizing pain for three days." It was on the tip of his tongue to tell Morghan this accident, and pain was simply what Louis deserved for his betrayal. But the harsh words would not come out.

As angry as he was at his parents and brother, no one should linger like that while waiting to die. When his time came, Edwin wanted to be old and held in his wife's loving arms.

Morghan's gasp pulled him from his musings. Tears filled her emerald eyes, making them glisten like highly polished jewels. "What more happened?" Telling himself he did not care could not stop the question from slipping out.

"Louis's wife gave birth early. The child died only a few hours after birth." Morghan found herself unable to tell him the rest. From the moment the babe slipped from her mother's body, they knew it was not her husband's. "They named the child and buried her in her father's arms."

God delivered justice on his behalf. The Almighty saw to it that his honor was avenged. Edwin's gaze turned across the hall to settle on James. The look in the other's eyes told him this news came as no surprise to him.

Though very few words were spoken between them since the argument outside his chamber window, the smug look on the man's face made Edwin glad he chose to replace James after this next voyage. His hands itched to slap the smug look off the other's face.

Slowly turning his gaze on Henry, Edwin found his master-at-arms' warning look. The sooner he got James out of his crew and off Ironwood land, the better.

The entire mood of the hall was changed. Many of the men in Edwin's crew knew both brothers. Many played with both brothers when they were boys. It was only natural they would mourn Louis.

Morghan watched her husband very closely. Now everything made sense. No wonder Edwin never wanted a wife. What if this woman was the one he planned to return to Normandy and wed, simply to find her already wed to his brother and carrying a child? Any man would react badly. There was compassion and pride for her husband. If this happened to one of her brothers, it would have torn the family apart.

After all, these weeks of feeling Edwin's underlying hatred and pain was understandable. In the next moment, she felt it finally seeping away. This news was exactly what he needed to end his sense of betrayal and begin healing.

"Come, my dear." Edwin stood, holding out his hand toward her. "Join me in our chambers." Morghan dropped the message and placed her hand in his.

Could this be the moment Edwin told her everything? Would he completely unburden his soul to her and begin healing? No matter what he did or said, she would allow him whatever helped him heal his heart.

Two steps inside the door, Morghan found herself in her husband's arms, his hot moist mouth devouring hers. Before her mind could grasp what he was doing, she was on their bed, flat on her back, Edwin between her wide-spread legs. In the next breath, he was releasing his member from his hose.

He took her hard and swiftly. Morghan clung to her husband allowing him whatever action he needed to release the monster that gripped him for far too long.

Deep in the night, Edwin made love to her softly, gently. There was something different about his loving this time, and it pleased her.

26

Morghan stretched and reached for her husband. Her hand settled on shaggy fur. "Gunther! You filthy beast!" A shove accompanied her screeched words. "Get out of this bed now."

Sitting up, Morghan looked about. Edwin was gone. Lowering her legs over the side of the bed, she looked to the window. The first red and gold rays of dawn were just brightening the sky. Edwin would be sailing soon.

Last night gave an end to her husband's self-torture. Every minute they spent in each other's arms were magical. The sore muscles of her legs and back proved their passion was equal.

Surely, after everything they shared, Edwin did not intend to leave and not tell her good bye. No man would be that heartless. Quickly dressing in a light blue undertunic and the first tunic she could lay her hands on, Morghan left the veil behind and rushed out through the sea gate to the pier.

The lanterns were lit just outside the gate, their light not quite reaching the ship. Others were lit on deck, their light spilling minimally onto the pier. Two men stood on the end talking. One was Edwin, the other she could not remember seeing before. It was not until she stepped onto the narrow planking that she saw it was Henry. No doubt the two men were going over last-minute instructions.

"Were you going to leave and not say good bye to me?" Henry offered a slight bow and backed away. When he saw her approaching, he did try to warn his friend, but Edwin ignored every one of his hints.

"If you would excuse me, I have… Well, I have something I am sure needs my attention elsewhere in the keep. Safe trip to you, Lord Edwin." One last curt bow, and Henry left them alone.

"You were so tired after last night, I thought to leave you sleeping, my dear." Stepping close, Edwin took her in his arms and kissed her. Instantly, her mouth opened beneath his and her body leaned into him. The moment he pulled back, Edwin got a look at what his wife wore. It was impossible to hold back his laugh.

"Exactly what do you find so amusing about kissing me?" Hands rested on her hips, Morghan scowled up at her husband.

"It was not the kiss I was laughing at, dearest." A chuckle threatened to bubble forth despite his best effort to hold it back. "It is simply that I have never seen my tunic look so fetching before. You wear it well."

Looking down at what she thought was her midnight blue tunic, actually turned out to be the new blue tunic she finished for him yesterday. How had she gotten them so confused? Though it fit decently across the chest, the length came only to her midthigh.

Face burning in embarrassment, a soft moan mingled with Edwin's laugh. "Fear not, Morghan. When we wed, I promised all I possessed was yours. I just never thought it would include my clothing."

Cheeks blazing, Morghan buried her face in his broad chest. A few soft caresses up and down her back and Morghan found herself wanting to doze in his arms.

A loud clearing of a throat came from directly behind Edwin. He tried to ignore it. "Forgive me, Lord Edwin, but the tide is about to turn. If we do not leave soon, we will be forced to wait until evening, missing the appointed time the king set for us to be in Normandy."

Edwin looked down into a smiling face. "Duty calls, my dear." He whispered. "Trust me, I would rather crawl back into our bed than sail at this moment. I did not hurt you last eve, did I?"

"No. I am fine, just a little tired."

"You will have plenty of time to rest while I am gone." Turning toward the ship, Edwin shouted, "Has William boarded yet?"

"Aye, sir. Settled right nicely into your cabin, he has. His horse is in the hold safe and sound. All is ready. We only need our captain to be off."

"Thank you, Sanders. I will be just another minute." Lowering his lips to Morghan's, he kissed her once more, conveying all the loneliness he expected to endure. For the first time in his life as a sailor, Edwin found himself not wanting to leave. But duty called, and he obligated to answer. "Though I would rather stay and take you back to bed, I must go."

"I know." Taking a step back, Morghan held out a small crock, a square of linen covering the top. "I made you something to take along."

"Please tell me this is not your ointment." The face he made brought a laugh to her when she really wanted to cry. "I do not believe I can stand the smell of the stuff."

"No, this is not my ointment, though I did tuck some into that small cabinet in your cabin. It may smell bad, but you have to admit it works well." A kiss on her scarred hand was his only answer. "This is a crock of preserves."

"Preserves? What, may I ask, are those?"

"It is hard to describe if you have never eaten it before. Think of it as thick cooked fruit. Trust me. It will taste so much better on bread than the fish they are bound to feed you."

"You remembered my aversion to fish. Good. This should keep me from starving while out to sea. I am surprised not more of my crew share my dislike for fish." His laugh died on his lips. "I will miss you." One last quick kiss and he climbed the plank to the deck.

"And I you." It had never been this hard to say good bye to her father or brothers. How was she going to survive the next three weeks without him?

Edwin stood the deck watching his wife and home fade into the horizon. Never had he resented leaving as he did at this moment. After making love to Morghan for the second time last night, she fell into a fitful sleep.

There was something bothering her; he could feel it in his gut. Through the bond he was rapidly getting accustomed to, he could feel her emotions, though not very strongly. Perhaps when they were married longer, he could do a better job of figuring exactly how his wife felt and thought. "I will be in my cabin with the king, James." Not waiting for the man's reply, Edwin opened the hatch and descended the steps.

The sight that greeted him made him to stop and stare, his mouth dropping open slightly. The king sat at the small table Edwin ordered bolted to the floor, his back toward the door, staring at the very sight that stunned him. Stacked against the wall between his bunk and sea chest were baskets, nearly a dozen of them all together in varying shapes and sizes. Each was covered with a different-colored cloth.

Stacked one on top of another, someone took the time to lash them to the wall using braided hemp. "What on earth... ?"

"In them, you will find an assortment of food including cheese from cow as well as goat's milk, fresh baked loaves of bread, and a vast assortment of meat—some fresh, some dried. Several skins of wine and ale grace each basket. The only thing I can find lacking is fish."

William turned a smile on his vassal. "Someone does not believe your shipboard cook can feed you properly."

"Morghan." Edwin sighed nearly to himself. A laugh accompanied the closing of the cabin door. "But how could she manage such a thing? After what we did last night, I would not have thought she had the energy to do any of this."

The expression of William's face turned to one of a father when the honor of his daughter was at stake. "Exactly what happened last night after you left the hall? I could see you were in a foul mood. If you took it out on your wife, I feel I must take you to task for it. In the absence of her father, I will defend her."

Edwin leaned back against the closed cabin door and drew a deep breath. Oleta must have been baking since last eve to make so much bread. Yes, that woman would willingly be his wife's coconspirator. "Nothing a proper husband should not do to his wife." A satisfied smile now graced the king's features. "My anger and displeasure with my parents faded by the time we reached the bedchamber."

It was not quite the truth, but to say all that happened last night would only upset the king, and that was the last thing he wanted. Secluded in close quarters with an angry monarch was not his idea of a good voyage. Besides, the only apology needed was the one he gave Morghan.

"The gift I gave you is quite precious to me. I gave my word to her father I would keep a watchful eye on her in his stead. Do you know now why I chose you for Morghan's husband."

It was a statement, not a question. Yes, he knew the answer, but could William know about this *bonding thing* they had? "She can never betray you." Okay, he knew. It did not make it any easier to discuss such matters with one's king.

Crossing the room, Edwin headed for his bunk. He spent most of last night thinking on every turn of events to happen in his life over the last few weeks. So many changes happened so quickly, he barely had time to ponder him.

"Ouch." Something poked him through the bunk coverings. Reaching beneath, Edwin drew out his sword. "What in heaven's name is this doing here?" The freshly sharpened blade gleamed in the lamplight. "Why would I need my sword on this simply crossing?"

"I believe we need have a little talk, Edwin. Come, open a cask of ale and one of those baskets. I have a story to tell you."

By the time William finished, Edwin could only sit and stare at him. Never in all his years had he heard such a tale. Some serious thinking was needed before this voyage ended.

"Come, my lady." Henry placed a light touch against his mistress's shoulder, turning her from the empty view. "You can no longer see the ship. It is time you started your day."

Henry was right. Standing here looking out over the softly rolling waves was getting nothing accomplished. There were accounts to review, menus to plan, men to assign to the hunt; perhaps she should not have given Edwin so much of their provisions. Still, their supplies could be replenished easily enough, his could not.

She had taken to heart the threat James had made to poison her husband's food. By now he should have seen the baskets and wondered why she would go to so much trouble for such a short trip. She confided her fears to the king, and though she never asked for his help, the king promised to do whatever was necessary to aid her.

No words were spoken between them as they made their way back up the hill, through the sea gates, and into the bailey. Men-at-arms beginning their daily activities moved about, running to ready themselves for practice. The great hall was filled with activity as well. Some men stacked the pallets against the wall, while others set the trestle tables in place.

Hurrying to her chamber, Morghan wanted to change into her own clothing before too many people saw what she wore. She placed Edwin's tunic in the dirty clothes basket, his scent filled her every breath. She would miss him terribly. Instead of the basket, she folded it and placed the tunic beneath her pillow.

After breaking her fast, Robert brought the household ledgers as instructed by Edwin. Expecting two, Morghan questioned the third huge tomb.

"Lord Edwin said this is the shipping logs. He wanted you to look at them also, though he did not tell me why." Robert quickly answered, placing each ledger separate from the other.

Morghan knew why. Her words must have begun her husband thinking on every aspect he allowed James to personally care for. There was hope for her husband yet.

The first two books were bound in thick leather, the pages showing little wear. One was for house expenses, food supplies, and wages. How often and how much were neatly listed. The other was for the men-at-arms and things like the blacksmith metal and items for the armory. At first glance, they appeared ordinary columns, a list of supplies purchased on the left, and the amount paid on the right.

It was when one looked further into each entry, going line by line, that the discrepancies became obvious. The book containing the records of Edwin's journeys and a listing of each cargo, destination, and money collected proved even more interesting.

Discounting the entries for the movement of knights under William's command, Edwin got little payment for these, Morghan moved on to the other entries. At first, Morghan skipped most of the shipping records, but as she found more errors in the household accounts, she took a second look at the shipping entries.

It would take days to study all the entries and calculate each line. Then again, what else did she have to do while her husband was gone?

Two hours later, her eyes strained from trying to figure out the strange coded entries James made, Morghan sat back and rubbed her aching neck. The man was clever, she will give him that. If she had not kept records for her father, much of what the scribe was doing would have escaped even her perusal.

"Henry, were you here in the spring?" It began to rain shortly after Edwin sailed, so the master-at-arms canceled the outdoor practice for the day. Men sat about checking equipment, replacing worn leather bindings and sharpening personal weapons as well as swords kept in the armory.

"No, my lady. I came only days before you arrived." The sound of a stone being drawn across the metal edge of his sword accompanied his words.

"I have been here since Lord Edwin laid the first stones." Robert piped up. "Is there a question I could maybe answer, my lady?" The boy was eager, she would give him that.

Morghan was not certain her husband's squire would be the one to answer her question, but what would it hurt to ask? Robert was often silent, listening to others who tended to ignore him. He just might have a piece of information that could help her. "Do you have any idea how many lambs were born this spring?"

"Two dozen that I can remember. Lord Edwin was surprised when he was told the number. He had not counted on so many the first year. The sheep were delivered deep in winter during a particularly bad storm."

"That leaves six lambs unaccounted for." Morghan tapped the tabletop with the feathered end of the quill.

"Could they have been used for food?" Henry quickly asked, setting his sword aside and reaching for another. "You should ask Oleta about the supplies she uses. Perhaps she forgot to tell James, or he forgot to write them down."

With the way James always badgered Oleta for her lists of supplies and usage, Morghan doubted that many lambs would have gone by unnoticed. Though it was possible for the little things to not live long enough to be used as food, a very common occurrence, they still should have been entered in the accounts that way.

"And the wool? Have either of you any idea how much was sheered?"

"I have no idea, my lady. I was never privy to such information," Robert answered. "For that, I could take you to see old Samuel." He quickly volunteered. "He is the sheepherder. Nothing happens in the flock, he does not know about. If a wolf got one lamb during the night, he would know even that. The man treats the beasts as if they were his children."

Yes, he was exactly what she needed to ensure the accurate accounting of what she needed. There was a way to prove everything, she simply needed to find it and document it.

When the rain stopped, Robert saddled two horses, while Henry chose three other men to accompany them. Five minutes after speaking to Old Samuel, Morghan had more questions than answers.

There was no doubt left in her mind James doctored the accounts. But why? And what happened to the lambs? Old Samuel said the tiny creatures simply disappeared overnight. No one heard or saw any signs of a wolf, so he doubted one of those creatures attacked the flock. Still, they were missing.

She had no doubt James took the lambs and assorted other animals from Ironwood and sold them for personal profit. Or perhaps he simply found a way to send them somewhere, possibly even to Normandy to his sister or Edwin's family.

Aiding to feed Edwin's parents would be too noble a cause for the scribe.

And just what else was the scribe hiding in the account records?

Edwin would not be back for nearly three weeks. It just might take her that long to check every entry and find every missing item.

27

Morghan paced one end of the great hall, her slippered feet making no sound against the rush-covered floor.

This was not supposed to happen. Edwin was away and though Henry was making a valiant effort of defending Ironwood, it was not as they hoped. Why did someone choose now to attack? Okay, that was about as dumb a question as any she could have thought up. This was the best time to attack. Without its lord, Ironwood was vulnerable.

The stress was beginning to get to her. Next thing she knew, she would be talking to herself.

Anyone who spent a fraction of time watching Ironwood knew Lord Edwin was gone, the king and all the sailors accompanied him. Their numbers were depleted, leaving the keep weak. Even she was forced to admit their timing was impeccable.

Only this morning, Morghan's heart was filled with joy and happiness. She awakened to Robert's announcement that a ship approached from the west. There were no shipments due that she knew of, and Morghan found herself curious as to who would be visiting. It turned out to be her brother Kerwin and her uncle Mason.

Overjoyed to see them both, Morghan nearly cried. Her brother was on a run to Northern Ireland when she received the message to come to England and be wed. Her uncle, never able to stay in one place very long, was away supervising the rebuilding of a church in Dublin. Until the moment she laid eyes on them, Morghan did not realize exactly how homesick and lonely she was. The moment they jumped from the boat, she was in their arms.

Several crates of household goods and nearly a dozen of her personal property were off-loaded and taken into the great hall. Morghan looked at them now, most still stacked against the far wall. It would be days before she would get to them, if they managed to survive the attack.

The presence of her uncle brought out a bevy of questions. It did not take long to figure out Uncle Mason and her father had had a falling out. Whenever they argued, Mason took off on the next ship her brothers were sailing. No matter where it was going, he was on it.

When Morghan asked how long he planned on staying, his answer frightened and delighted her. It all depended on Edwin.

Now it looked to depend on the attacking Saxons and whether or not Henry and her brother could adequately defend Ironwood, and there was anything left for Edwin to come back to.

Only minutes after the noon meal was complete, a shout came from the guards at the back gate. A contingent of men, their swords drawn, arrows flying, were riding full out for the gate. Henry ordered it closed immediately, and soon the men-at-arms were rushing about preparing to defend the keep.

The armory was opened; and as they were trained, the men donned their armor, weapons, and took their positions on the curtain wall, watching the advancement of the enemy.

Another scream from the bailey shattered her thoughts. She was the mistress here and deserved to be out there discussing strategy, not held in the hall like a weak woman.

"Morghan, do stop that pacing," Mason pleaded. "Ye make these old eyes burn to watch you." Putting aside a quiver filled with arrows, he reached for an empty one brought in by a squire and began selecting arrows to fill it.

"I cannot and will not be able to stop until I know what they are doing out there." Turning, Morghan studied the hall full of women and children, her uncle sitting in Edwin's chair at the lord's table, selecting arrows. At fifty-two, he still had hints of red hair heavily mixed with gray. His green eyes matched her own and at that moment showed no sign of concern.

The door opened, and another man-at-arms was carried in, an arrow protruding from his right thigh. "Place him here." Morghan quickly gathered her sewing kit and herbs and headed toward the table reserved for treatment of the wounded.

Robert hurried over, carrying the pot of hot water she had insisted be kept heated over the fire. "Remove his mail and hose," she ordered. While two men stripped the third man, Morghan washed her hands and grabbed the clean towel Robert offered. "Hold him still while I extract the arrow."

The two men who carried the wounded man in held fast, while Morghan grabbed the arrow shaft and pulled. Blood spurted from the wound, striking the front of her, soaking the apron she wore over her kirtle. Pressure was quickly applied, and five minutes later, the wound was sewn shut and bound. After placing their friend on a pallet at the other end of the hall, they headed back out.

"I need to know what is happening out there." Tossing the bloody rag onto the floor, Morghan headed for the door. There were shouts in the bailey, men running back and forth carrying weapons, pitch and needed supplies.

Three steps away from the entrance, Morghan found her way barred by two very determined men. Robert and Uncle Mason stood, their arms crossed over their chests, backs leaning on the door. How in the name of God did her uncle make it across the hall so quickly? For an old man, he certainly moved as stealthily as a cat.

"I cannot allow that, mistress." Robert suddenly looked older than his fourteen years. "If anything were to happen to you, Lord Edwin would have my head." Leaning close, he added the word, "literally."

"Morghan, lass, you know a woman has no place in the thick of battle."

"You would have me stand here and wait like… like…" Her hand waved out to encompass the softly crying women and children behind her.

"Like a woman." Mason finished for her. "Aye, I agree with the lad. Your husband would not approve of your going out there and getting hurt or killed. Sir Henry knows what he is about. Allow the man to do the job your husband gave him.

"Half what makes a good leader is knowing when to allow one's people to do as their position demands. Did Sir Henry not fight beside your king? I believe he knows what is needed to win this battle."

When the door opened again, Morghan got a good look at what was happening. Her brother and Sir Henry stood on the wall walk, torches lighting the entire bailey. Men moved about, carrying boiled pitch, its acrid scent fouling the air. Others knelt, crossbows in hand, sending volleys of arrows over the wall.

"Tell me one thing, Robert," Morghan said, watching all the activity out in the bailey, "how skilled is Sir Henry in the crossbow?"

"His skill is the best in Ironwood. Actually, he is the best I know among King William's men. Why?"

"What of the longbow? What level of skill has he achieved in the use of that weapon?"

"The longbow, mistress? I believe there is one in the armory, but no one here has the knowledge to use it. The men prefer the crossbow. The accuracy is better." As they watched, Henry stood up and fired. Kneeling quickly, he reloaded and waited.

Her nerves at an end, Morghan resumed her pacing. When they were made to close the door, Morghan threatened to do bodily harm to the squire if he so much as touched the wooden panel. After receiving a nod from Mason, it was left open.

The solitary figure dressed all in black, sat *his* horse at the tree line, twenty yards out, watching the men about him.

The message delivered just days ago claimed all the men of importance would sail three days ago. The taking back of this land should have been simple. A few well-placed shots, a swift attack, and it would be all over. Nothing was going the way *he* was promised it would.

Someone was giving orders, and that someone was good. The moon was full, giving them all the light needed for the attack. The way the bailey was lit should have put the men of Ironwood at a disadvantage. So why did it not work to his advantage?

The powerful black stallion beneath *him* pranced restlessly. A horse bred for war did not like to sitting idly by and waiting for action. They preferred to be in the thick of battle. One angry hoof pawed at the ground, its snorts filling the cool air, letting everyone in the area know he was not happy being commanded to stand in place.

"I thought you said de Ballard was gone." The deep, angry voice filled the momentary silence of the wood.

"The message I received said he and many others would sail three days ago. I saw the man's ship in London last Yuletide. Let me assure you, his ship is gone, my lord."

"Yet a ship still bobs on the waves. Who captains that one?"

The black-clad figure on the ground fell silent for a moment. He spoke to the villagers concerning the smaller ship that arrived that very morning. No one knew much about it. "It is only a small coastal runner. It looks to be of Irish design. Perhaps one of the lady's relatives is visiting."

"A sailor would not know much about defending a keep now, would he? I believe we have found their weakness. Now we need to capitalize on it." Through the silence, an arrow sailed directly at *him*. It embedded in the ground not ten feet before the horse. The beast shifted about. It took little to still him.

"Prepare the men to attack." The order was ground between gritted teeth. "I grow tired of this game. Begin with the archers, and then send in the ladders. By dawn, Ironwood land shall be back in the hands of the

Saxons. From here, we regain the remainder of our land. Since William so conveniently left for Normandy, we have time to secure what is rightfully ours. No one can stop us."

Robert stood beside his mistress now, listening to the sounds of battle. Men lay wounded or dead, passed over by the men still living and able to fight. His heart wanted to be out there fighting beside the men of Ironwood, but Sir Henry had given him the job of protecting Lady Morghan, and that was exactly what he would do.

Hand gripping the hilt of his sword, Robert watched. Screams and cries of the wounded came from both sides of the wall. The men of Ironwood were fighting well and would not give up until every last one of them was dead.

In silence, Morghan watched Sir Henry reload, stand, and fire over the wall. Though she had faith in her brother, Kerwin was a sailor, not a knight seasoned and hardened in battle. Her prayers intensified threefold.

"He remains just beyond the range of my crossbow, Lord Kerwin." Henry breathed deeply and set another arrow. "Whoever he is, the man he uses is a Welsh bowman, highly skilled in the use of a longbow. I can never match him in distance with what we have. Their leader has planned well and knows our limitations."

A quick look at the man beside him was all Henry allowed himself. Though he had tried valiantly to aid in the defense of Ironwood, Lord Kerwin was a sailor and no more skilled at war than Lord Edwin.

When the first shouts of attack had come, Lady Morghan's brother had stepped into action beside him. The gates were closed and barred, all women and children were taken to the great hall, and Robert was set to guard his mistress. That was the extent of the Irishman's abilities. Since then, all his orders were defensive moves. They held their own but made no progress.

It was not as if Lord Kerwin was a coward. No, the man sat here beside him in the thick of battle, a borrowed mail shirt his only protection. Courage was one thing, skill was another.

Henry doubted the man could even use the sword he now held. There was a look to the man's eyes, Henry knew all too well. If Lord Kerwin had ever seen battle before, it was a long time ago, his skills mostly unused.

"Have you had much trouble from the raiders before now?" Kerwin asked, peeking over the battlements at the enemy.

"Not much," Henry replied, pulling the string back and setting another arrow flying over the defensive wall. Though he doubted it would do any good, it was all he could think of at the moment to do. Unless an epiphany happened, he was not being given enough time to consider other measures.

"Why are you being so stubborn?" Henry never heard Mason join them. He turned to the old man now. "I know what the two of you are trying to do. Kerwin, you know that shot would be child's play for her."

Henry listened to the two Irishmen arguing. Her? The only "her" he could think of was Lady Morghan. But surely they could not mean his mistress. Kerwin's reply gave him a cold chill.

"Can you imagine, Uncle, what Lord Edwin would say if his wife was injured defending his keep? If not him, think of father's reaction. He would have my head on a pike if I so much as allowed her to scratch a finger climbing a ladder. No! I prefer my head exactly where it is, thank you."

"Lady Morghan? Are you telling me my mistress has skill in the use of a bow?" Henry turned on the old man. Surely, he heard wrong.

"My niece has skill in longbow that far outshines any in Ireland, or Britain for that matter." Mason added quickly. "Your father was a warrior long before he took my sister as wife and beget you boys. He would agree taking out the leader is the only way of ending this. Your sister has the skill to do just that. Why not use every resource the good Lord provided for you?"

"Taking out their leader is precisely what we are trying to do, Uncle.

The leader sits his horse some two hundred paces out. One good shot and he will fall. When they see their leader dead, the battle will end. Simple."

Kerwin turned his attention back to Henry, and for the first time the master-at-arms saw raw determination in the sailor's eyes. When he stood to take his next shot, Henry saw the arrow headed straight for his heart.

Morghan's scream filled the great hall. In horror, she stood watching Henry's body slide to the wall walk, an arrow protruding from his left shoulder. It was impossible to tell, from this distance, just how close it had come to the man's heart. With Henry down, their chance of defeating the enemy was gone. *She* was the only chance left. There was no way she would stand back and watch her home taken over by disgruntled barbarians.

In one swift motion, Morghan reached beneath her tunic and pulled out an ivory-handled dagger. Since James's recent threats, she made certain it was always within reach. Before Robert could react, she laid the gleaming blade against his throat and backed him into the wall.

"I have tried my best to honor my brother's wishes, but whoever is out there plans on taking my home and killing all who dwell in it." Morghan leaned very close to the squire, her words a harsh whisper. "I do not plan on standing here watching while my home is taken by bastards. Not when I have the skill to do something about it. Sir Henry just took an arrow and is even now fighting for his life. Do you intend to let him die while you stand here watching, or do you help me save our home?"

"I will give you three seconds to decide to help me or get out of my way. The choice is yours. One way or another, I am going to get the longbow and go out there. I am the only hope left to the people of Ironwood."

Closing her eyes, Morghan fought the images she suffered for nearly ten years. That time she had been too young to do anything but hide and watch. Now she was a full-grown woman, and the choices were very different.

There was something in her eyes that frightened Robert. She was scared, but there was a determination there that surprised him. He watched in horror as Sir Henry went down and just barely restrained the urge to run out to join the battle.

His mistress was right; things were different now. The master-at-arms was lost, and if another solution was not found soon, every person at Ironwood would suffer. Decision made, Robert prayed he was making the right one.

When Lord Edwin returned, he would find a way to explain why he allowed his mistress into the thick of the fighting.

That was if they had a home left by the time Lord Edwin returned. "Come, my lady." Reaching for the hand Morghan twisted in his tunic, Robert waited for the blade to be removed from his throat.

Winding their way through the dead and wounded, Morghan had to resist the urge to stop and tend each and every suffering soul. They reached out to her heart in their suffering cries.

The armory was a long narrow structure built directly into the back curtain wall. Once inside, Robert quickly found the longbow, handing it to his mistress to string. Stepping through, Morghan strung it in a trice. They could find only five arrows made for the bow. "Sorry, mistress, that is all we have."

"No problem, Robert, I have the feeling I will need only one." Morghan doubted the attackers would allow her more than one shot anyway. Grabbing the arrows, Morghan chose the best one to use first. Her skill with the longbow was good, but if the arrows were inferior, it would be useless. "I am ready."

"Not so fast, my lady." The command in his voice and the grip on her arm momentarily stayed her.

"What now?" Morghan's impatience sounded in every word. "We have time for this." From a peg beside the door, Robert retrieved a mail shirt. "This is your husband's." Quickly feeding it over her head, he tugged it into place. "The fit is poor." You could say that was an understatement. It hung near to her knees and was so heavy Morghan wondered if she would be able to maneuver in it should the need to flee arise.

In the first few steps, she gained a new respect for the men. The mail weighed her down, making her every step awkward. If it restricted her movements too much, removal of the thing would be needed. Nothing could interfere in the drawing of the bow.

A volley of arrows flew over the wall, and Robert pinned his mistress against the wooden panels. Several cries were heard from behind. Again, there was no time to tend the wounded. Taking the nearest set of steps, Morghan inched her way toward her brother and the fallen master-at-arms.

"What in the name of all that is holy are you doing here?" Kerwin's voice traveled to the bailey below, and all eyes turned up.

"I have been watching you and think I know what you plan. Where is the leader?" Peeking over the wall, Morghan tried to make out a lone figure, but there were so many shadows that it was difficult to distinguish men from them.

"I cannot believe I am allowing you to do this!" Kerwin snapped. "Father would have my head if he ever found out."

"Then he will never find out. Please do not treat me as some witless female, Kerwin. This is my home, and I have no intention of allowing some barbarian to take it from me. Instead of thinking what Father would say if I should be wounded, think on what you would be telling my husband when he returns and there is no land left for him to set foot on. If that is not enough to sway you, think on William the king. Would you have the man and his knights fight to retake the land they have already secured once? Is that fair?"

Kerwin wanted to forbid her to even try, but the look in his uncle's and sister's eyes begged him to give her a chance. "I do this for my own safety. If I do not return home to Jean, she will be spitting mad. I promised to be back long before the baby was due." Kneeling on the wall walk, Kerwin leaned up far enough to point out their opponent.

"Their leader sits a horse about two hundred paces due west. See that stand of three trees?"

"Yes."

"Wait until the clouds move and can see him clearly." As if on cue, the clouds parted and the full moon shone down on the lone figure. Dressed all in black armor, sitting a black stallion, the man did not seem the least bit worried if he was sighted.

Morghan allowed the heat of the moment to drive her to this point. Now kneeling here, her target within reach, uncertainly began to settle in. Her hands began shaking, and she needed to stop them before the shot went wide.

"I have seen you make such a shot many times, little sister."

"As have I," Uncle Mason chimed in. "Do not think of him as a man, but that old overstuffed target your father set for you."

Taking a deep breath, Morghan nodded, knocked an arrow, and waited for the men to take Henry's body from her path. Once they passed, she knelt, closed her eyes, and sent up a silent prayer for all their lives.

In her mind, she saw the arrow flying through the air striking the target in the heart. Morghan stood drew the string and fired.

He could not believe *his* eyes. "They send a boy to fight me now. If that is all they have left, our battle is soon won." The men around *him* laughed. "Let the boy have his shot, but only one. We would not want to have him thinking we have time for such childish games. The next time he stands, give him a souvenir he can carry the rest of his life. That is if we allow him to live past our taking of the keep."

The Welsh bowman nodded and smiled brightly, his eyes gleaming to know he would be given the chance to please this lord.

No one heard the arrow slice through the man's throat and embedded in the tree behind *him*. Stunned eyes glazed over as precious life's blood pumped from the double wound in his neck. Each beat of the heart pushed more of it from his body.

Eyes still staring at the fortress before him, *he* steadily fell from the horse, landing with a dead thud on the cold ground.

28

Morghan slowly sank to the wall walk.

She could barely breathe.

Her nerves made her hands shake so badly, Morghan feared they would throw off her aim. The shot was not what she wanted, but at least the end result was acceptable.

Memories of another time she had taken a life flooded her mind, and Morghan began to shake. *Please, God*, she silently begged. *Not now.* Morghan was not sure whose arms wound about her shoulders holding her tight, she was only grateful for the warmth and security they provided.

Sir Henry's soft moan jerked her back to the present. The master-at-arms and so many others needed her now. Later, alone in her chamber, she would give in to the fear and allow the tears to flow. Choking back all her emotions, Morghan inspected the wound.

Tearing a strip from her undertunic, she pressed it against the wounded shoulder. "Hold him down." Time was of the essence. It would be better to remove the arrow before Henry awoke fully. One swift tug and it came free.

"I knew you could do it." Kerwin's smile beamed in the light of a torch someone held above them.

"That makes one of us." Holding pressure on the wound, Morghan found her hand covered by a bloody one.

"You will be sure to use your ointment on me." Henry's soft voice brought a smile to her lips.

"I just made a fresh batch yesterday. Edwin wants there to always be a steady supply on hand in case of emergency. There are many who can benefit from it this time." When the wound slowed, Morghan signaled for two men to take the wounded master-at-arms down and into the hall where she could properly tend the wound.

Leaning against the wall, Morghan watched her brother and Robert supervising Henry's move. Thinking she was alone, Morghan gave into a moment of weakness. A silent tear ran down her cheek.

"You must stay strong for the people now." Uncle Mason was right. This was no time to allow herself to fall apart.

Morghan looked to the western sky. The last rays of the setting sun streaked the horizon in an array of red, orange, and gold. Men rode out and captured two prisoners and brought in the body of the man she killed. She recognized none of them. Not even Sir Henry knew who they were.

The prisoners were chained by the blacksmith to the wall and a guard set to watch them. Edwin would decide their fate when he returned.

She argued against sending a messenger to Edwin and William. Though an estimated twelve men had gotten away, she could not think they would be back to cause any problems once their leader was dead. Overruled by her brother and uncle, a man was chosen who had no family.

Father Matthew was not due back for another month, and even if Morghan knew the circuit he rode, she could not spare a man to find him. So she stood over the graves of the three dead men, spoke words of peace, and sang an old Gaelic song to speed their souls to heaven. When finished, Morghan had silent tears running down her cheeks. The last time she sang that song she was seven, and she stood beside her mother's grave.

"Come, child." Mason wound his arm about his niece's shoulders. "You need to rest." There was no protest when he steered her toward the keep.

On wooden legs, Morghan walked between her uncle and brother. She was tired, more tired than she could ever remember being in her life.

Robert stood beside Kerwin and Mason at his mistress's bedside. Morghan was thrashing about tangling herself in the sheeting. The three had been seeing about the wounded when they heard her screams.

"Should we wake her?" Robert whispered. The sight of his pale mistress shook him to his core.

"No." Kerwin watched the nightmare play out in Morghan's mind. "She has not suffered this in so many years, I thought it was well and gone. It is best to allow her to work the dream to the end."

Pulling up a chair beside the bed, Kerwin lit a candle and waited. This brought back too many memories. "What is it she dreams of that is so frightening?" Robert asked, watching his mistress crying in her sleep. Huge sobs racked her body, tears streaming down both cheeks.

"She dreams of the night our mother was killed." Telling the story, Kerwin relived his own guilt at leaving his mother and sister alone to face their deaths. If only he had not taken himself off and hidden but stayed with them, perhaps he could have saved their mother's life that night and his sister from years of guilt and nightmares.

By the time Kerwin finished his story, Morghan broke into a cold sweat and stilled. "She should be fine for the rest of the night. Do not be surprised if she acts a bit odd for the next few days. She needs to work through what she did to save our lives, and the guilt of not being able to save our mother. When does her husband return?"

"Not for another eight or nine days." Robert quickly replied.

"I wanted to leave on the morning tide, but Father would never forgive me if I left her in this state."

"Connor will understand." Mason reassured his nephew. "You have your own problems at home that need your attention. Besides, I am staying and able to see her through this episode. Do not forget it was I who stopped it the last time."

"All of you need to stay close until Lord Edwin returns. It is not as if she could hurt herself, but Morghan simply needs to be shown love and security. It's the easiest way to combat this nightmare."

"I understand." Henry and Robert said simultaneously. When Kerwin looked into their eyes, he could imagine the boy did understand.

Edwin wound his way through the maze of men sleeping on the floor of his great hall.

What in heaven's name had happened here? It seemed as if every man, woman, and child from his property was asleep on his floor. Was that a woman? Holding his candle higher, Edwin could have sworn he saw several women and some children.

Was that a wounded man? The guards at the sea gate said nothing about problems while he was gone. Surely, if something serious happened while he was away, the men would have said something.

For the past sennight, an urgent need to return plagued him day and night. It was almost as if Ironwood itself needed him to come home. At one point, it was so bad, he actually woke from a nightmare he could not remember, drenched in sweat. William gave him another squire after that and made certain he was never left alone.

The sense of urgency became so strong, it manifested itself into a test of wills. Every waking moment, he pushed his men and the king's to work harder, move faster, and get finished quicker so he could return home.

William simply laughed and reminded all that he was a newly wedded man and most anxious to return to his new wife. But deep down, the king could see the stress in every line of his face and his every move.

It was still a struggle, but Edwin managed to return two days early, not even anchoring out to sea and waiting for the morning tide to bring the ship in. He needed to see Morghan and assure himself his wife and home were safe. Not even when he stepped onto Ironwood land did the odd feeling stop. Seeing these people filling his hall only made it worse.

Nearing his chamber, Edwin heard a growl. "Hush, Gunther." The soft command was met by a very wet nose nuzzled into his palm. Kneeling down, he briskly rubbed the hound's rough fur. That earned him a huge wet kiss.

His next step tripped him over a body lying across the chamber door. Kneeling, he stared into the sleeping face of his squire. The boy could sleep through anything. Not the best quality if one thought to become a fighting man, but the boy did try.

Stepping over Robert, he slowly pushed open the wooden panel and stepped into his chamber.

Morghan laid in the center of their bed, her back to him. The night candle added minimal light to the room. No fire was set, as the night was a warm one. He thought he saw a movement in the shadows at the far end but dismissed it. No one would dare step into his chamber while his wife slept.

The sight of Morghan's deep red hair splayed out over the pristine sheets brought fire to his body. This was what he longed for. Not to see his home again, but to see and feel his wife. A fierce tightening in his loins brought home the knowledge he had not made love to a woman since he left.

Not that there were not any offers. Several of William's maids had remembered him and offered to warm his bed. None had vivid green eyes that darkened with passion, nor the red hair that shone like fire in the sunlight. Simply put, he wanted only the woman he left behind. Edwin wanted his wife.

Quickly stripping, he climbed onto the bed and reached for the very woman he longed to love.

A knife at his throat stopped him cold.

"Who are you, and why have you invaded my chamber?" Morghan's voice sounded odd. Had she been crying?

"Put the blade down, Morghan." His words were met by a tighter press of the knife to his throat. "Do you not recognize your own husband? It is I, Edwin." He did not dare move. Morghan pressed the tip close to his pulse point. One wrong move and his blood would spurt out over the entire bed.

"Not possible. Edwin is not due back for another three days." Why was this happening to him in his own keep? Morghan sounded in the middle of a nightmare or something. The odd urgency he felt for so many days washed over him like the ocean wave sucking him down.

"Morghan, listen to me." Trying not to move, Edwin kept his voice level and calm. Whatever was happening here changed his loving wife from a levelheaded woman to this panicked, irrational female.

"Listen carefully, Morghan. You know the sound of my voice. I felt something was wrong and pressed my men to finish faster. I returned home early."

It certainly sounded like Edwin, but so did that man who snuck up behind her in the bailey three days ago. He had frightened her so badly Morghan thought never to trust another man as long as she lived.

Henry dealt with the intruder, and she never saw him again. Her heart pounding, she asked one last question to verify his identity. Her heart told her this man was Edwin, but her fear would not allow her to accept it so easily.

"Tell me something only my husband would know." Not a heartbeat passed before his reply.

"On the night we were wed, I was too drunk and angry to take you as my wife. Instead, you cut your hand and placed the blood on the sheets to placate your father and the king."

"Many people know of that now. It is no secret about Ironwood. Try again."

"I took your innocence in a meadow about ten minutes' ride north. You told me we would always have a connection between us. You could never betray me with another man, and I would know when you were in trouble. Trust in that bond now to tell you I am your husband."

He was right. Morghan felt a familiar sensation wash through her.

This was Edwin. Her heart screamed the knowledge her husband knelt on the bed beside her, and she held a knife to his throat.

In the next breath, the knife was removed and thrown against the far wall where it vibrated slightly before stilling. In the next beat of his heart, Edwin found his arms filled with a weeping, bawling wife. Her lips kissed his face, his neck, and began lower.

Caught up in the need Morghan was building in him, Edwin forgot about the figure he saw in the shadows until flint was struck and more candles lit. "Explain yourself, Henry." Edwin's demand stopped his wife's advancement. "Why are you in my chamber?"

A silent look passed between Morghan and the master-at-arms. This was not the time or place to discuss what happened while Edwin was gone. "In the morning, my lord." Silently, Henry left.

Torches lit the outer wall, making the bailey look like midday. He saw the sight when they were still several miles out to sea. They drew him like a beacon home.

Sitting back, Edwin studied his wife. She looked tired and drawn. Dark circles creased the delicate skin beneath her eyes. At the moment, silent tears rolled down her cheeks. They nearly shattered his heart. What in heaven's name happened around here? And if he was thinking right, was Henry's arm in a sling? Something was wrong, and he needed to find out what it was.

When he made to quit the bed, Edwin found his wife's delicate hand clutching his arm in a grip so strong, it amazed him. Though it trembled ever so slightly, it conveyed a silent plea no man could miss.

"Love me. Please." Morghan's simple plea shattered any resistance he had left. After all, he was not made of stone.

An explanation for what occurred here could wait until morning. Right now, his wife needed him, and the way her hands stroked his skin was quickly bringing a fire to his groin that could not easily be denied.

"I want to feel you deep inside me." Words quietly spoken between kisses on his skin sent any notion of resistance fleeing.

He would make love to her now and find out later what transpired while he was away. Besides, except for a few people, everyone was asleep. Who would he even ask?

It took little to prepare Morghan for joining, and when he moved her beneath him, she met his demanding thrusts with equal enthusiasm. Spent, Edwin rolled to his side of the bed, drawing his wife close. Morghan was already asleep but clung to him as if he was life itself.

She clung so tightly to him, Edwin was not able to even get up and extinguish the candles. In the morning, several people would be answering for their actions.

Edwin did not like the thought of his wife being in any danger in her own home. It ate at his guts like a cancer. Tomorrow would be judgment day for more than one person in Ironwood.

29

Edwin stretched and reached for his wife's warm body.

Last night had been wretched. First a knife to his throat, and then he was privy to the worst nightmare he could imagine.

Connor he recognized, though the man appeared several years younger than he did now. His first thought was that the woman in the dream was his wife, but she was at least twenty years Morghan's senior. The deep green of her eyes and red highlights in her hair bespoke his sweet wife's mother. If Morghan looked like that when she aged, she would become only more beautiful with the passing years.

It was not until he saw the man's attack that he realized it was Morghan's dream, and he was looking through a child's eyes. If he remembered correctly, she once told him her mother was killed by raiders when she was seven. He never dreamed she was a witness to the murder. It made the loss of his parents pale in comparison.

Edwin felt a lightness he never knew existed. He wanted Morghan and trusted her implicitly. No other woman ever brought such peace to his soul.

His arm stopped midreach. When did his heart stop aching for something he was better off without? When did he open to Morghan and begun living in the present and not the painful past?

The night one delicate Irish hand reached out to touch his stubborn self in the night. That was when.

Morghan's touch put a crack in the wall he built about his heart. She never backed away but pushed forward and kept at him until the entire structure crumbled at her dainty feet. This he knew was love, and he could not wait to tell the world.

Yet what if he declared his love and Morghan did not return it? He was not proud of some of horrid things done to her in the beginning. Could she ever find love in her heart for him? He certainly did not give her reason to love him. Her body responded to his, but now he knew lust and love were two very different emotions. Beginning today, he would find a way to gain her trust and her love.

A soft knock sounded at the door, and Edwin cursed. This was not how he wanted to begin the morning. No, he thought to wake his wife with tender kisses and make love slowly and tenderly for half the morning. Obviously life had other plans.

"Lord Edwin, are you awake?" It was Robert, and his words were urgent. "My lord, you must come now. The king's men approach."

William? He was not supposed to be here for another sennight. He had left the king in Dover only three days ago. To be here already, the man had to have ridden out soon after he set sail and pushed his men hard. Much too hard for his thinking.

Robert did not wait until the door was opened; he opened it himself and rushed into the chamber. Edwin was only given a second's warning to toss a sheet over his wife's naked body. "Robert, how dare you enter while my wife is still abed?" The squire stopped dead in his tracks.

"Ironwood is no longer a bachelor's keep. When my wife is inside, you must never enter unless I gave you permission." The squire silently looked from his lord to his lady and back again. Morghan tried to hide her smile at the boy's stunned expression.

"I beg pardon, my lord, but the king's army approaches. Two columns of them stretching as far as the eye can see. Sir Henry sent me to wake you and ask that you come quickly." Face stained red, Robert turned away from them. "I meant no disrespect, Lady Morghan." His apology said, the boy ran from the chamber.

"You did not need to be so harsh with him." There was no bite to her words. "He meant well."

"I know that. It's just… well, he needs to respect your privacy. You are my wife, and what we do together in this chamber should not be witnessed by anyone, especially a boy about to meet his manhood." Edwin spoke as he dressed, keeping his back toward her.

If at all possible, Edwin's tanned skin turned a deeper bronze while he was away. She sat, the sheet drawn about her naked breasts, watching the ripple and play of his back muscles when he moved. She could still remember the feel of those muscles when she lightly scraped her nails over them last night.

"Keep that look upon your face, my dear," Edwin whispered, "and I just might make the king wait while I crawl back into our bed." Edwin smiled when his wife shivered.

Pausing beside the door, he stared at the dagger that still protruded from the wooden panel. The look he gave her over his shoulder said he would demand all the answers before the day was out.

Robert waited just outside the chamber, a piece of fresh bread and a cup of ale in hand. Edwin downed both while they walked toward the back gate. Henry stood watching the army near. To say it was an army was not an exaggeration. Fifty mounted knights rode behind the king's banner, while nearly twice that many footmen marched behind the knights.

It was an impressive sight, but Edwin wondered exactly where he was going to put all of them. The knights would fit in his hall and in a tented bailey. The footmen he would need to be billeted somewhere. "Food. How am I to feed all those men?"

"There are stores aplenty, my friend." Edwin turned a questioning eye on Henry. "While you were gone, Lady Morghan sent the hunters out daily. She had Oleta began salting the meat and preserving it for the winter months."

"I went fishing." Robert boasted, his eyes bright, his smile beaming at them.

"Morghan is nothing if not thorough." Snapping around, Edwin stared into an old man's face. His voice held the same lilt as Connor and Morghan's, though he did not look much like either one.

"Who… ?"

"You have not spoken to your wife yet this morn?" the old man asked.

"Morghan and I did not do much talking when I arrived last night." Edwin swiftly looked at Henry.

"That is how it should be." The old man sounded as if he was in his own home. It only made Edwin more curious as to who he was. "By the way, did you set the foundation on the keep?"

"I did." Looking toward his handiwork, Edwin felt the same pride he always did when surveying his home.

"My name is Mason Curran. I am uncle to your wife. My sister was her mother." That explained why he looked nothing like Connor. "I have come to stay and help you build a home to last a thousand years."

Anything Edwin would have replied was cut short by the arrival of William's outriders. A knife to the throat, his master-at-arms in his chamber, that odd dream, and now an uncle Morghan had never mentioned. Plus the king's arrival when he had just left the man three days ago in Dover. His life was quickly falling out of his control.

Too many questions holding no immediate answers. Just as soon as he got William settled, he would demand those answers, no matter who he had to badger to get them.

William stopped his horse before Edwin, dismounted, and tossed the reins to Robert. "I had not thought to see you again so soon, sire."

William looked from one face to the next. "I had not thought I would need to return so soon." Edwin noticed Henry looked anywhere but at his lord or king. William knew something he did not. "Sir Henry's message was urgent, and I felt I needed to arrive in all haste to ensure the raiders did not return."

Raiders? His home had been under attack while he was gone? None had spoken a word of this to him? "Henry, how did you hurt your shoulder?" Edwin finally noticed the bandaging and sling.

"An arrow, Lord Edwin," he replied after a moment's hesitation.

"Sir Walter, have patrols formed and sent out. I want every last man found and brought to me." A tall blond knight nodded and walked away shouting orders.

"We already have two prisoners." Robert boasted.

"Prisoners?" Edwin was startled. "I have prisoners?"

"You may as well tell my husband the entire story, Sir Henry." All five heads turned to watch Morghan approach the little group. "He deserves to know *every* detail."

"I believe the hall would be a better place to discuss this." Edwin agreed. Anywhere was fine just as long as he got answers.

The hall was bustling with activity. Oleta ran about directing women carrying trenchers laden with food. There did seem to be enough to feed an army, though at the moment Edwin wanted answers before sustenance.

Sitting at his place, Morghan quiet by his side, Edwin listened to his master-at-arms rattle on about the arrival of his wife's brother, the seed and personal property he brought, and the uncle who thought Ireland no longer needed him. Near the end of his patience, Henry finally got to the meat of the explanation. The Saxon attack.

"I never should have left." None missed the guilt echoed in Edwin's words.

"Do not be ridiculous," William chimed in. "Do you mean to stay hiding here or fulfill your contracts for shipping? I have much need of your services, as do others who depend on the movement of goods to keep the households and businesses functioning. Services you pledged to me before we even left Normandy."

"I am lord here, sire. You granted me this land, and I pledged to hold it in your name." Edwin sighed and sat back in his chair. "How can I do that if I am not even here?"

"By allowing those you leave behind to do their duty." William looked directly at Henry. There was far more to this than anyone was telling him. He for one wanted to hear the entire story. "Tell us, Sir Henry, how did you end the attack?"

Morghan began to fidget. This was the moment she hoped would never come. What would the king and her husband think when they knew the truth? Her relationship with Edwin was still new, still so fresh she did not know exactly how he would react.

An almost-imperceptible nod from his mistress gave Henry permission to tell all. "A single shot from a longbow killed the leader. Once he was gone, the rest scattered like rats. I sent out every man I could spare, but only two were run to ground."

"Yes, my prisoners," Edwin muttered. "So you finally mastered the longbow, Henry. I am pleased."

"It was not I, my lord. I never got very close using the crossbow. I took an arrow in the shoulder and was useless," Henry said, glancing out the corner of his eye at the mistress. Now they would know the whole truth of what happened.

"Then I owe my brother-in-law a great debt." Edwin's mind jumped to the next logical conclusion. "Who would have known..." Henry silently shook his head. "Then, Robert. You mastered..." Henry and the squire both shook their heads. Edwin turned on the old man. Mason joined the silent head shakers.

"There is no one left. Has one of the men-at-arms suddenly taken up the bow and mastered it? If so, I own the man a knighthood for saving my land and people." Henry continued to shake his head.

"Do stop sitting there shaking like that. I want to know who saved my land, and I want answers *now*." Moving his gaze from one person to the next, he found the only person who would not look him straight in the eye.

"*No!*" Rising up over the table, Edwin grabbed Henry by the tunic, ignoring his wince of pain.

"You allowed my wife on the battlements of this keep during an attack?" His voice rose slightly with each word. "Are you insane?"

"Lady Morghan was well protected." Robert piped up. "I fed your mail on her personally." Edwin turned his stare on the squire, his mouth dropping open. The boy was actually proud of himself.

Stunned emotions battled deep inside him. How could they have allowed such a thing to happen? If he lost Morghan… his heart seized. He would die if he ever lost her. Edwin could barely hear Henry's explanation over the pounding of his heart in his ears.

"The man sat a horse about two hundred paces out. I could not get close enough to him using the crossbow. He sat there as if he knew none could reach him. After I took the arrow, Lord Kerwin reluctantly agreed to allow his sister to try. It took her only one shot. The arrow went straight through the man's throat." Edwin winced at the image those words brought.

"I missed." At first, no one paid much attention to the softly spoken words.

Releasing Henry, Edwin looked to his wife. She was so downhearted it melted much of his anger. What horror she must have faced standing there, arrows and men all about her. Battle was never a pretty sight. His arms ached to reach out and draw her close.

"What do you mean you missed?" William asked. So far, he was content to stand back and listen. He had known Morghan was a strong woman. Edwin needed her to stand beside him in life. No wonder she suffered nightmares. Grown men, trained and hardened for battle, often suffered the same.

Dropping to his knees before his wife, Edwin took her ice-cold hands in his own. "Tell me why you believe you missed. The man is dead. You killed him."

Slowly raising her eyes to meet his, Morghan knew the moment of truth had come. "I was aiming for his heart."

30

Edwin rocked back on his heels, staring at his wife.

He needed to think this new twist through. He backed up even farther when Morghan reached out for him. If he allowed her to touch him at this moment, his mind would focus on how much he really needed that touch and not what he needed to consider here. Morghan took another's life.

She was brave, he could not deny that. Not many men he knew would have done what she had to save so many. But she also put her life in danger, and that was something he could never allow again. A shudder ran through him, just thinking of what his life would be without her. After so much passed between them, how could he live if he lost her now?

Morghan silently looked to the king, her emerald gaze pleading for help. Men wanted their wives to be meek, mild, and sit at home waiting for them to return from the sea. She was not that type of woman, never had been, and doubted no matter how she tried, could be one.

Her father taught his children it was everyone's duty to protect hearth and home. Though she would never stand guard or take up arms against another, neither could she stand back and allow people to be hurt when she could do something to stop it. Edwin would simply need to accept her the way she was.

"I need to see the men are served a proper meal." Standing, Morghan practically ran from the room.

Edwin saw the tears glistening in her eyes, and it tore at his heart. Pride in his wife warred with his love for her and his inbred need to keep her safe. What would his life be like if something happened to Morghan and she was gone forever? He never wanted to find out.

Slowly rising, Edwin faced his master-at-arms. "Never," he growled. "Never again do I want to come home and hear that my wife's life was placed in such danger."

Edwin continued on, hands fisted at his sides, his stare boring into his friend. "Your primary duty here is to keep my wife and family safe. I would give every inch of land I possess before I allow any harm to touch her. Do you understand me?"

"Aye, my lord." Henry quickly replied. He knew this was coming, and in fact hoped Edwin was so in love with his wife that it produced this very reaction. It was almost impossible to keep the smile from tugging at the corners of his mouth.

"Good." Edwin dismissed everyone. He needed to be along to get a hold on his emotions before he said something he truly regretted.

Several deep cleansing breaths helped. Now that fear was not ruling his emotions, pride for his wife swelled inside him. Imagine his delicate wife taking courage and doing such a brave act.

How in heaven could he fault her? His mother would never have done such a thing. She would have stayed in the hall, comforting the frightened women and children, but never would she lift a finger to actually do men's work.

No other woman, with the exception of the king's wife, would have done what Morghan did. From the moment he first met her, Edwin admired Matilda's strength and courage. So what if Morghan possessed the same courage and strength? He could leave Ironwood as often as he needed, knowing it would be in strong hands. That thought brought a peace to his mind and soul.

He would seek out Morghan and apologize for what he said. He would praise her for her courage and skill, as he should have done when she stood before him. Yes, there was much he needed to make up for, and he would start by telling his wife how much he loved her.

"A word please, Lord Edwin." James stepped into his path. Great, at this moment, his scribe was the last person on earth he wanted to speak to.

When Edwin tried to step around the scribe, James grabbed his arm, squeezing tight. Edwin slowly looked from the hand gripping his arm to the man he was rapidly coming to detest. "Now is not a good time. Whatever it is you think needs my immediate attention, deal with it yourself. I need to find my wife."

Anger flared so quickly in James's eyes, Edwin took a step aside. The grip on his arm tightened. Enough was enough. Quickly raising his arms, Edwin broke the hold, sending James back a step.

"Touch me like that again, and I will cut that hand off." James pulled his hand back as if he touched a fire.

"Forgive me, my lord, but I cannot find the household accounts. I asked they be loaded on the ship so that I might perform my duty to you and make some entries. I have searched the entire keep and cannot find them anywhere. It is very important that I have them."

"You cannot find them because I gave them to my wife before we sailed. Is there a reason Lady Morghan should not have full access to them?"

Now panic flared in the scribe's eyes. Yes, Edwin did well to follow his instincts this time. "I have always kept your accounts, both for your shipping business as well as the household. The arrangement has worked for us until now. Why would you change things after so long?"

"My, my, James. You sound almost nervous about my decision." Edwin turned and stepped back toward the hall. "Is there anything in the accounts you do not wish my lady wife to find?"

"No... nothing like that." James's stammer made him curious. His gut told him something was wrong here. It was one of the reasons he left the ship's accounts behind as well. Though her saving of Ironwood took precedence, Edwin would speak to his wife later and ask what she found in the ledgers.

"If you will excuse me, I will begin logging this voyage into the ship's records."

"No need for that." Standing before the head table, Edwin reached for his ale. Out of the corner of his eye, he saw James take a small step before freezing. His still stance said there was something the scribe hid in those accounts as well. If there was anything to find, he was confident Morghan would.

"You should not have done that!" James's voice snapped angry.

"And why not?" As Edwin turned on the man, he could feel hatred seeping out of every pore of James's body. Oh yes. The man tried to hide much from him. Just how long would it take before Morghan uncovered everything?

Four men entered across the hall to begin setting the trestle tables for the morning meal. Someone shouted out in the bailey, though even with the doors opened to allow the fair weather in, Edwin could not make out what was said.

Life in this keep ran smoothly, and for that, he could thank Morghan. Even before he began taking an active part in the day-to-day workings of his holding, Morghan had things well in hand.

"You know that Rowena would never insert herself into your business the way Lady Morghan has."

That was the wrong thing to say. For a while, thinking on his wife's competence, Edwin's temper began cooling. Now it exploded with the force of a thunderbolt. "Never mention that traitorous bitch's name in my presence ever again." Edwin's voice rose with each passing word.

Henry, Robert, and William, having just entered the hall, paused inside the door. Though none heard all that was said, Rowena's name stood out. Knowing James was Rowena's brother and his abhorrence of Morghan, William could just imagine the conversation.

It was about time his vassal stopped hiding behind what he felt was betrayal and faced the ghosts that haunted him.

"Of course *she* would not have done such a thing. I have no doubt your sister would be in my bed, her legs spread for any not defending the keep. *She* would never have thought of others, only her own selfish wants."

"If you ever," Edwin continued stepping close, poking his finger directly at James's chest, "ever mention that woman's name to me again, I will cut out your tongue and shove it down your lying throat until it chokes you."

Morghan heard her husband's raised voice and turned toward Oleta. The cook held sympathy in her brown eyes. Though neither could make out exactly what was being said, simply hearing the tone was enough to concern them.

Morghan thought leaving the two men alone to discuss business would help. Obviously it did not.

It would get worse when she pointed out the discrepancies in the ship's books. Besides those she found in the household accounts, there was a problem with every account entry she looked over. Once she pointed them out to Edwin, how angry would he get then?

Taking a step toward the kitchen door, Morghan was stopped by James's next words. "I realize you are unhappy with what she did. Humiliation by a woman is never easy."

Oh, Lord. Surely, they were not speaking about her and what she did. Yet if not her, then who? Morghan thought she had everything figured out from her mother-by-marriage's message. Obviously, there was still a piece or two of the mystery missing. Would there never be an end to this, or would she be spending the rest of her life battling ghosts?

James could see Morghan standing in the door to the kitchen. Choosing his words very carefully, he attempted to drive one last wedge between Edwin and his wife. With any luck, he could still salvage some of this situation and save his position.

"Could you ever find it in your heart to forgive her?" James's words were loud enough for everyone to hear. Now even the men setting the tables stopped to listen.

"Have you gone mad?" Edwin was so angry he could barely speak. How dare this man continue poking at a wound he thought finally healed? "I can never forgive her for what she did."

Morghan could not stand by and listen to any more. A lump choked in her throat. Swallowing back a sob, she turned on Oleta. There was never a question in her mind that she took the right path. She did what was needed to save Ironwood, and given the choice, she would do the same all over again.

How could any woman stand by while her home was being threatened and do nothing? She was not sorry for her actions and never would be.

Morghan's first thought was to run out the kitchen door, grab the first horse she came to, and ride until Edwin's words no longer stung at her heart. But she was no coward. If her husband did not like her actions, let him tell her face-to-face.

Shoulders squared, she stepped into the hall to confront her husband. His next words stopped her midstep.

"How dare you compare my loving faithful wife to that whore? Rowena may have wed Louis, but the child she bore was not even his." How did Edwin know that? Morghan was careful enough to keep that part to herself.

"Despite my hatred of my family in Normandy, I asked Robert to read me the message my mother sent. Marriage vows meant nothing to your sister. She was unfaithful to my brother and would have been to me."

James's bright eyes settled on Morghan. He was not ready to give up on his plan, not when he could still taste victory. "Are you so certain your wife is faithful? I heard from some of the men Sir Henry spent several nights alone with Lady Morghan in your own chamber."

Henry found a hand staying him when he took a step forward. Turning, he stared into the king's blue eyes. "Wait. This needed to come for some time. Allow Edwin to finish it."

Anger still flaring in his gut, Henry nodded and stepped back. Every muscle in his body wanted to pound James into the ground for the slurs against his lady and himself. The look Morghan turned on him further stayed his hand. It was almost as if she knew what her husband was going to say.

"I am well aware Sir Henry spent time in my chambers at night. So did Robert and her uncle. In fact, the night we returned, I saw Sir Henry there myself. Robert slept across the threshold. He guarded his lady with a loyalty I would expect from de Montgomery's son. Do you accuse the boy of sleeping with my wife also?" James stammered a nearly silent reply. "Unlike others, my master-at-arms and squire are loyal to me. He would never do anything to harm my wife."

This was it. The moment Morghan had been waiting for. All during Edwin's questioning, she could feel him getting more and more desperate.

Morghan's thoughts scattered when she felt a knife press into the soft flesh just below her left ear. "Stay back, or the lady's throat will pay dearly."

She felt the tip of the knife pierce her skin, a single drop of blood rolling down the length of her neck. A feeling of surprise washed over her from the man holding her. Obviously James had not intended on actually hurting her.

The look of absolute anger she saw in her husband's eyes made her heart beat faster. Now she knew Edwin loved her. Was it wrong to hope this mess would force him to say the words?

Edwin stopped dead in his tracks. Emotions ran wild through him, each vying for dominance. His hands fisted and unfisted at his sides, imagining James's throat in his grasp. Two deep breaths and he had a good hold on his emotions.

"Hurt my wife, and you can count on a long painful death at my hands." His words were emphasized by the deep growl of Gunther. "A word from me and the beast will tear out your heart. I just might allow him to eat his fill."

Though Edwin looked in complete control, Morghan could feel his anger boiling just below the surface. Another sign.

James laughed close to her ear, pulling her tightly against his chest. Slowly, he began backing out of the hall, forcing her along, yet making certain no one could get close enough to tear her from his arms. "I have been wondering, my lady, just how far will your husband allow us to go?"

"Not far. Have you forgotten my husband's men? Or the king's? Look about you. There are far too many men for you to fight in order to achieve your freedom."

"Such brave words from a simple woman." James laughed. "No one would dare touch us for fear the knife might slip, and your lily-white throat would be cut."

The blazing sunlight momentarily blinded them when they stepped outside. Morghan knew she would have ended this right now but knew if her husband did not face his demons now, he might never do so.

So Morghan allowed James to drag her farther out of the bailey toward the pier. How the man thought he would escape on Edwin's ship was beyond her. Out of the corner of her eye, she saw Edwin's crew standing shoulder-to-shoulder along the rail, their arms folded across their chests. Obviously they had no intention of allowing James to escape that way.

God forgive her for what she was about to do, but she meant only the best for her husband. "Perhaps it would be best if I went with James. No one else needs to get hurt."

The hurt Morghan saw in her husband's eyes nearly changed her mind. Unless Edwin admitted to everything and purged his soul, the secrets between them would eat at him for the rest of their marriage. That was something she could not allow. If their life together was going to have a chance to flourish, everything needed to be out in the open now.

"How can you say that?" Edwin's voice shook from emotion, but Morghan did not allow it to affect her. "You are my wife. You belong here at Ironwood." Edwin's anger flashed in his sea-green eyes. It pleased

Morghan deep inside. Her husband was getting closer. Now just one more nudge should do it.

"Do I? You were so drunk on our wedding day, you paid no attention to who you spoke vows to. On our wedding night, you could not say if you took me or not." It was a struggle for Morghan not to allow her hurt at those few days to take over her.

"Everything I tried, everything I said, was meant to force you to look at the woman you married. Still, you hold secrets. Do you remember that day in London when we spent the day at the markets? The message to return home quickly came from one of your men."

Edwin looked about him. Not one of the men beside him showed the slightest awareness of what she spoke. "None of my men would do such a thing. I was going to speak to your father that night, but when I entered the hall, you were gone. No one would tell me why you left."

"We left because news came from home, and we needed to leave immediately. We left so quickly, I was unable to even leave you a message. When we arrived home, we found all was well."

The knife against Morghan's neck jerked in time with James's laughter. "It was very easy to have a stupid squire deliver the message to your father. He did exactly as I wanted. All of you left."

"Why would you do that?" Edwin quickly asked. "I was just getting the courage to ask for Lady Morghan's hand."

"Exactly! Do you think I wanted you to wed this stupid woman? No! You were supposed to return to Normandy and wed my sister. She waited for you. You promised her."

"Rowena did not wait for me as she promised. When I thought Morghan lost to me, I went to wed her and bring her back to Ironwood. But she was already wed to my brother Louis and big with his child."

The look in Edwin's eyes caused tears in her own. Betrayal. Yes, she could see that changing the fun-loving man she met in London. "Why did you not tell me? Did you think I would not understand?" Morghan asked, choking on her tears. She would not give the man behind her a chance to see her weakness.

"The promises I made were made by a boy. I wanted the easiest way to live my life. Rowena was a woman I took to my bed when I needed her. Unfortunately, I found she was also available to many other men in the village. I thought I lost you. I heard rumors about Turney Keep that your father was making an exchange of your hand for aid to King William. No one told me I was the one chosen to be your husband."

"For that, I am sorry," William said, stepping forward. "I thought if you could fall in love naturally, it would make a stronger marriage." Turning toward Morghan, William continued, "Your father and I argued on the subject. I thought Edwin would find a way to you on his own."

"This is so touching, it makes one want to heave my guts." So caught up in their own conversation, Morghan nearly forgot James held a knife to her throat. Looking from side to side, they were now about halfway down the pier.

Everything came crashing in on Edwin all at once. This woman, the woman he loved with all his heart, nearly died not knowing how he felt. Well, no more. There would be total honesty between them from this moment on. "I love you, Morghan. I believe I have loved you since you laughed at my hatred of fish at the feasting."

Morghan laughed at that memory. The face he made when the dish was served was forever etched in her mind. "And you?"

Edwin held his breath. Now was the moment of truth. He had done nothing to endear his own wife to him. In fact, he had done much to push her away and give her a right to hate him.

"For me, it was when I first laid eyes on you in the abbey." As Morghan spoke, she could feel a change in James. He was getting tired of the conversation. Now was the time she needed to make her move.

"I love you." Morghan moved so fast, no one saw it coming, least of all James. Driving the heel of her boot into James's instep, she quickly followed it by an elbow to the solar plexus. The knife fell from her neck.

Edwin reached out, snatching Morghan from her attacker and flung her toward Henry. Gunther rushed him at the same instant Edwin did. Struggling for the knife, the two combatants rolled farther toward the end of the pier. With Gunther getting his nips in, Morghan could only see a mass of arms, legs, and fur.

A scream tore from her throat when the three tumbled off the edge of the pier and disappeared into the cold water.

Gunther was the first to pull himself out of the water, shaking droplets in every direction. Morghan held her breath. Where was Edwin? Surely, he knew how to swim, or he would never have tackled James into the water.

One hand appeared over the top of a rock, and then another. Morghan was off and running. "Oh, Edwin." Pulling at his wet clothing, "Never do that to me again. You frightened the hell out of me."

"I did not do myself so much good either." Breathing heavy, Edwin pulled himself to his feet, taking his wife in his arms. "Are you injured?" Turning her chin, he inspected the tiny cut.

"I am fine." Looking over Edwin's shoulder, she waited to see the next person to climb out of the water. "Where is James?"

"I do not know. After I went in the water, all I can remember is a blur of gray fur, arms, and legs. Somehow, I lost track of him. I am sorry."

"He will show up one day, and I will get him. Never doubt that."

His arms around his wife, Edwin led the way into the hall.

31

Morghan laughed at her husband's teasing remark.

A fortnight passed since the incident at the sea. No sign of his body was ever found. The king's men searched from sunup to sundown three days straight and finding nothing, King William decided it was time to leave. There were other things demanding his attention.

James's possessions were divided among the other men, but an extensive search found nothing of the money and items James stole from them. A reward was offered for any information leading to its recovery, but so far not even that brought the treasure to hand.

Life fell into a routine all found comfortable. Many of Ironwood's people looked forward to the harvest and the festivities autumn brought. Morghan was already planning the Yuletide celebrations.

The first time she mentioned inviting her husband's parents to visit, Edwin said not a word but stormed out of their chamber. The second time, he informed her he needed more time before he could forgive them. The subject was dropped after that. It may take years, but Morghan intended to get him to accept his parents again. One could always find a new home, but a person only had one family. Lose them and you lose your touch with the past.

"How long will you be gone this time?" Morghan asked, accepting her husband's offer to refill her goblet with wine.

"Just long enough to bring the queen and her household from Normandy to London."

"I have never met Lady Matilda, but knowing women, I believe she will take her time traveling to ensure nothing of hers is broken or damaged." Morghan smiled over the rim of her goblet when her husband groaned.

"I much prefer transporting the king's men. They own only what they carry on their horse and were trained to move quickly. Women are too picky. They must have everything just right before I can set the sails."

"I hope I am not included in that statement." Morghan tried to be stern, but the laugh that choked in her throat made being angry impossible.

"We shall see. Next month, I make a final trip to Ireland for the remainder of your father's aid. I intend to take you along."

"I promise to pack lightly and move quickly." Her words were punctuated by a soft kiss on the cheek.

What was meant to be a light kiss on the cheek turned into a deep, heated kiss and embrace. The men of Ironwood were so accustomed to their lord and lady acting so in the great hall no one paid them much attention any longer.

So when all conversation stopped, Edwin broke the kiss to find out what disturbed the people.

The carpenter walked in, an odd wooden cask in his arms. It measured about eighteen inches in length, height, and breadth. All eyes turned on the man as he headed straight for the head table.

"My lord," the man said, bowing before Edwin, "I found this while setting the stone floor for your chapel." Setting the cask on the table, the carpenter bowed and took a step back.

"How is your wife and son, master carpenter?" Morghan asked, watching her husband out of the corner of her eye.

"They are well. My son grows stronger each day. I owe his life to your skill and loving hand. The chapel will be finished for the christening of your first child, just as agreed. In fact, I believe it can be used for this year's Yule mass." The man's eyes sparkled when he spoke of his wife and son. There was so much love there that Morghan knew his words were from his heart.

A gasp beside her drew Morghan's attention from the man on the other side of the table. Following her husband's gaze, Morghan was hard-pressed not to gasp herself.

Side to side, bottom to top, the cask was filled with coins. Both gold and silver, they glistened in the candlelight. "Did you open this, master carpenter?" Edwin asked.

"Nay, my lord. If it held the bones of a child laid to rest, I would feel it needed to be reburied on consecrated ground. I myself built two tiny caskets to bury my stillborn babes."

"Well, I would inform you it does not contain the bones of the dead."

"I thought not when I felt its weight." Bowing slightly, the carpenter asked, "May I know what it holds?"

Edwin simply turned the cask about and allowed anyone interested to see the contents. A collective gasp rolled through the hall. "It seems you found a great treasure. For your honesty, you will receive one-tenth of the contents," Edwin announced.

"No, sire. It does not belong to me," the carpenter stammered. "Perhaps it was left by the Saxons who lived here before you." In his heart, Edwin knew he was looking at the treasure James stole from him.

"If you do not wish to keep the coin, use it for windows in the chapel."

"I shall do that, my lord." A quick bow and the carpenter left.

"I knew James stole much from me, but I never thought it would come to this much." Dipping a hand into the coins, Edwin let several slip through his fingers. "So you asked the carpenter to have the chapel ready for the christening of our firstborn?"

The mischievous sparkle in Edwin's eyes warmed her heart. "Yes, I did."

"But the carpenter's son was born the night of our wedding."

Taking a small sip of wine, Morghan replied, "Aye, I was there at the birthing."

"How could you know I would give in and accept you?"

"I had faith, my love. Faith that my touch could get through the wall you built about your heart." Lightly, Morghan ran her fingertips up the front of her husband's tunic, stopping just over his heart. Leaning forward, she kissed the spot. Smiling against his chest, Morghan felt her husband's heart begin to race.

"I think you had more faith than I did." Moving her veil aside, Edwin's lips brushed against the top of her head. "What say you and I retire to our chamber and see about the duty of making that first child?"

"You think of it as a duty, husband?" Morghan turned her face up, her smile twinkling mischievously in her emerald green eyes.

"I consider it my duty and my pleasure to give you everything your heart desires."

"Right now, my heart and body both desire you deep inside me." Grabbing his hand, Morghan began pulling her husband toward their chamber. "Perhaps with the money, we could ask Uncle Mason to add a roof over this chamber."

"Anything you want, my love." Closing the door, Edwin took his wife in his arms and laid her on their bed. "Anything you want."

Edwards Brothers Malloy
Thorofare, NJ USA
May 21, 2012